AWARD-WINNING AUTHOR OF
LEAVING PHOENIX AND *THE OTHER CHEEK*

JAFE DANBURY

www.JefePress.com
Ordering Information
Quantity sales: Special discounts are available on quantity purchases by corporations, associations, and others. For details, you can contact the publisher and author at:
jefepress@yahoo.com
jafe.danbury@yahoo.com

Orders by U.S. trade bookstores and wholesalers:
Please contact Jefe Press or visit www.JafeDanbury.com

ISBN 978-1-7333440-4-3 (print)
ISBN 978-1-7333440-5-0 (e-book)

First Printing, June 2023
Printed in the United States of America
This is a work of fiction. Names, characters, locations, and incidents either are the products of the author's imagination or are used fictitiously. Any resemblance to actual persons, either living or dead, businesses, companies, events, or locales is entirely coincidental.
Cover concept by Jafe Danbury
Cover design and formatting by Damonza.com

ALSO, BY JAFE DANBURY:

LEAVING PHOENIX

GOLD, "Mystery/Thriller" 2023 Reader Views Literary Awards

FINALIST, 2022 IAN Book of the Year Awards

FINALIST, 2022 Readers' Favorite Book Awards

GOLD, 2021 Literary Titan Book Awards

Praise for **LEAVING PHOENIX**

"This novel is likely to earn strong reviews by word of mouth. Now is precisely the time for this novel. It is intense and often gripping to read, but it is also highly satisfying as you put yourself in the shoes of a young woman who must unravel her past and face a dark truth. Jafe Danbury displays a well-crafted treatment of tone and pacing, as well as a well-fleshed-out protagonist that you will truly care about. Danbury kneads the tension slowly, allowing Phoebe to accumulate resilience and intelligence as she gets closer to the truth. A must-read for any lovers of suspense and mystery, *Leaving Phoenix* is a heart-pounding and profoundly suspenseful novel that reaches an enormously satisfying arc."

~ READERS' FAVORITE BOOK REVIEWS

"The author is a skillful writer with a sure-footed knack for keeping the narrative moving. A significant element of this is Danbury's decision to delve in detail into the individual backstories of his characters, ranging from Phoebe's grandfather to the Pirate himself. These extended flashback sequences provide a welcome shading to Phoebe's own tale as it progresses, and they further highlight the author's ability to craft moving, believable characters. Liam's story, in particular, the tale of a good man hitting rock bottom and finding his way back to the world, works as an effective narrative counterpoint to the book's main plot threads. A tense and involving tale of a young woman seeking revenge and finding a family."

~ KIRKUS REVIEWS

"Danbury is a master storyteller. Phoenix's life is nothing short of a miracle, and the intricate plot he lays out for his main character traces her life from conception through her fearless resolve to find her mother's killer at any cost. Phoenix is a phenomenal main character and is a picture of strength and determination. The relationship she is able to form with her grandfather after two decades with her adoptive father is touching and quite amazing. In addition, her willingness to relive the past is truly a testament to her incredible strength of character."

~ LITERARY TITAN

"A well-edited story alive with striking images, sharp dialogue, and the pain and promise of self-discovery. Deep character development and welcome lighthearted moments lead the way in keeping the pages turning. The mystery is believable, and the characters are lovable with well-thought-out character arcs and a relationship to story development. Any mystery fan who loves a mostly fast-paced narrative with a splash of romance will find this is a rewarding addition to to-be-read lists."

~ BOOK LIFE REVIEWS, *PUBLISHERS WEEKLY*

"Wow! What a phenomenal book! I don't have many "favorite books" but this one has been added to my very short list! I had such a hard time putting it down, but I did have to sleep and interact with my family, LOL."

~ TRAVEL THRU BOOKS

"Jafe's writing really knocked me. This book has a very well-constructed story. It captures the readers from the beginning with a storyline that gets better and better as you turn each page! It was interesting and captivating from the start."

~ LAURA, GOODREADS REVIEW

"Both thrilling and captivating, this story checks all the boxes for an addictive, heart-pumping read. Complete with a soundtrack of classic rock road trip songs, *Leaving Phoenix* provides the reader a glance into the complicated journey of a young woman's attempt to find her identity. All of us have faced similar experiences entering adulthood, and this book perfectly captures the feelings of vulnerability, fear, and excitement that mix together to form a beautiful mess of emotions that guide us each on our journeys. Buckle up for an amazing read that you won't want to put down-and wrap your arms around nostalgia and youthful audacity."

~ B. Boone, Goodreads

"What a thrilling ride of a book! This is a new to me author. With a great play list of music of mostly classic rock, and a great story line, it hit all the right notes. Phoebe/Phoenix always knew she was adopted but had no idea of the circumstances until a cryptic letter takes her on a deep dive into a past she had forgotten and her search for answers brings he face to face with a serial killer. Awesome story that just keeps building. Will be so curious to read more stories from this talented author."

~ L. Murray

"Can't wait for the movie! *Leaving Phoenix* is an excellent read that is suspenseful, happy, sad...hard to put down! Jafe is an excellent writer who makes sure the characters, music, time periods, personal experiences, settings...everything fits together! An amazing read! I also recommend his other book *The Other Cheek*."

~ Audrey, Amazon review

Praise for JAFE DANBURY'S debut novel,

THE OTHER CHEEK: Boy Meets Girl. Girl Beats Boy.
Just Your Typical Love Story...

FINALIST, "Best First Novel" category, 2020
Next Generation Indie Book Awards

"An intense, sometimes-brutal novel about acknowledging and escaping an abusive relationship."

~ KIRKUS REVIEWS

"Jafe Danbury is a superb writer, riveting my soul to every turned page... Oprah Winfrey must interview Jafe on her Super Soul Sunday program. Everyone should read this superbly written story."

~ ELAYNE SILVA-REYNA,
AUTHOR OF WOLF DREAMER OF THE LONGEST NIGHT MOON

"Jafe's page-turner is a first-class read I would recommend to everyone fascinated by the extremes of human tolerance and abusive behavior..."

~ R. GOODWIN

"It captured me from page one. The characters are so well defined. Jafe writes with true feeling for his characters. Although a very entertaining read for anyone, I can also see how this book could serve as a beam of hope and a beginning of healing for anyone found in the same situation...."

~ P. MINNICH

"Wow! *The Other Cheek* is a great book! Spousal abuse is a tough subject, and male spousal abuse practically a hidden subject, but the writing is superb, and opens up new understanding and levels of compassion for victims..."

~ J. TEMPLETON

"Danbury is reaching an audience not often addressed in realistic fiction... I absolutely flew through Danbury's work, absorbing one of Rich's emotions after the other and fearing Tami right alongside him. I recommend this book to anyone who has survived abuse, thinks they may be a victim, or knows and loves someone who is dealing with a controlling significant other. Danbury is making important strides with *The Other Cheek*."

~ LITERARY TITAN

"*The Other Cheek* by Jafe Danbury throws light on the existing but ignored aspect of domestic violence... This book challenges us to see the vice of domestic violence from a broader perspective. I loved how realistic this book turned out to be. Its authenticity comes from the fact that nowhere did I find it going overboard. In fact, the story remained true to its intent and shook me. It also strengthened my faith in the belief that not all that appears is true. There could be something more malicious and horrifying beneath the surface." ~ "Top 10 Fiction Read of 2020"

~ K. GAUTAM, *BOOKISH FAME*

"Danbury strikes the nail on the head with this one. I would give a copy of this to the guy in your life about to start dating. Maybe to the guy you suspect is in a similar situation. This is for women, too. For every woman who has a man she loves in her life. This is Danbury's debut novel, and I dare say we will be reading much more from him in future, at least I hope so!"

~ *The Book Dragon*

"Kept me turning pages...beyond that I also gained a better insight to see how this type of abuse starts, grows, and morphs into something beyond the victim's control. Thank you, Jafe Danbury!"

~ N. Bozzo

"Yes, this is a story of domestic abuse but there is also a deeper meaning. It is also a story of hope, a story of making it through to the other side, a story of "The Other Cheek."

I stayed up past my bedtime reading this one... that doesn't happen often. This book definitely comes from the author's heart, and I totally respect him for putting his story 'out there.'"

~ M. Ammons, Goodreads review

For Kathleen...

X*...such a mysterious and powerful letter....*

It's the twenty-fourth letter in the modern English alphabet.

It "marks the spot" on the map, sometimes even denoting buried treasure.

It's the dreaded variable we're tasked to solve for in high school math.

It's the amazing ray that allows medical professionals to see our bodies' inner workings.

It's a label for a whole generation.

It's the unplanned-for factor we try to allow extra driving time for.

It alerts us to pornographic material, sometimes to the third power.

In chromosomes, females have two of these, while males have one. Y?

And, in this case, it's every parent's worst nightmare.

CHAPTER 1

IDAHO PANHANDLE
SOMEWHERE NORTH OF COEUR D'ALENE
WEEK BEFORE CHRISTMAS, 2007
WEDNESDAY

THE SKETCHY BASEMENT space was dark as a cave, save what little light the fifteen-inch computer monitor provided, and outside the window the moon was playing hide-and-seek. It was quiet out here. So quiet you'd swear you could hear the deafening crash of individual snowflakes as they hit the ground.

Wisps of smoke danced from the ignored, unfiltered Lucky Strike Red as it dangled perilously from its perch on the edge of the filthy, heavily populated, glass ashtray. What was left of its remaining embers sputtered briefly before the delicate loaf of ash cleaved off and leapt to its death, joining its many expired brethren.

Chubby fingers stabbed at a keyboard. A few slow, hunt-and-peck keystrokes eventually hit paydirt as the desired clip popped up on the ViewSonic computer monitor. From there the mouse-driven cursor hovered over the triangular PLAY button.

A minute-long, emphysema ward-worthy coughing fit ensued before the unfortunate troll recovered enough to get on with it. Clicking the mouse, the video clip window came to life, beginning with a shaky, handheld panning shot from a home video that had been watched countless times. As always, the troll paused the clip as the shot reached the orange car's license plate, and its information compared against what had been written on the chicken-scratched, lined tablet next to the mousepad. One had to confirm and reconfirm such things as there was no room for error. Satisfied, the troll un-paused the clip until the house number was discernable, at which time the procedures were repeated. The clip resumed, and as it did, the tiny human subject commanded close attention.

This was an extraordinary child, and the client had been exceedingly clear in his request for "the redhead." There were several other interested parties as well but, like any hot commodity, the highest bidder prevailed.

As a broker, this troll was all too happy to fulfill the order. This had been a special request, and special requests justified a higher price. Especially this one. The client didn't want just any redhead; he'd been very specific in that it had to be "*the* redhead." This was a rare gem, plus it was an out-of-state order. Those always cost more. Way more. As a result, their agreement stipulated that any expenses incurred in procuring and delivering "the item" would be added on top of what was to be their $150,000 fee. Half now, half on delivery. The fact that the client had specified this gift to himself be delivered in time for his annual Christmas extravaganza meant an additional $50,000 for expedited handling.

This would be the final delivery this year—a twofer, actually—and a lucrative year it had been. A celebratory Lucky Strike met the end of a lit stick match, its owner taking a deep drag. *Cue cough fest.* The team was in place. It had been, for three days now, studying family patterns, times and locations. The clock was rolling.

"I'm thirsty," a young girl muttered weakly from the darkness.

"Quit whining. There should be water in your bowl. Go back to sleep," the troll barked, aiming a sharp beam of light from the three-cell flashlight. As the light swept across the chain-link and plywood enclosure, the disheveled eight-year-old ducked back into her corner.

The troll glanced out the basement window. The forecasted snow would begin falling soon. Before long it was going to be a shit show out there.

CHAPTER 2

LA JOYA ELEMENTARY
APACHE JUNCTION, ARIZONA
THURSDAY

CURT MARTINSEN—*MR.* MARTINSEN, AS the youngsters in his charge referred to him—wished to God he hadn't forgotten his tall, life-giving, twenty-two-ounce thermal container of French Roast on the kitchen counter in his haste to get out the door. At least that's where he thought he'd left it. It was only 8:20 a.m. and he was pretty sure he'd achieve full flame-out before the clock reached 9:00. *Shoot me now.*

Teaching hadn't been his first career choice, but he'd decided four years ago that he was no longer interested in the sanitation industry. He'd burned that bridge anyway, back in California, with the stunt he'd pulled at the Pirate's house. Seems the management of his employer, Diamond P, didn't appreciate his pumping several thousand gallons of human waste inside the home of a wealthy Pebble Beach resident.

4

Ahem. Never mind the fact that the guy, formerly known to most as the Pirate, and for good reason, was a murderous serial killer who'd nearly snuffed out his and his future bride's lives that fateful night before becoming the human pincushion himself.

Bastard had it coming....

Thus, seeking a new challenge here in the Grand Canyon State, and at the very strong suggestion of his loving wife, Curt had earned his Bachelor's in Education at Arizona State and was a freshly minted graduate of the credential program. This, he'd already decided three months in, was the hardest he'd ever worked in his life, especially trying to teach *anything* in December to youngsters whose only thoughts were of all things Santa Claus.

The giant, thirty-three-year-old, ruggedly handsome man looked down from his lofty, six-foot-four-inches-tall vantage point and surveyed the twenty first graders standing on their appointed playground line-up spot. *Was I ever this tiny?* A quick headcount by twos—a concept he'd been trying to get them to grasp in their math this week—confirmed all were here and nobody was missing a backpack. Or a shoe. Or a smile.

"Good morning, everyone!" he managed, leaning down as he summoned a toothy smile and every bit of energy he had left in his caffeine-challenged tank. "How is everybody doing today?"

"Good morning, Mr. Martinsen," was the reply from the usual few who happened to be his little "morning people." A few answered, "Fine," while a smattering of grunts made up the rest of the chorus. And he couldn't blame them. One bit. He was feeling it too on this Thursday morning, the second to last day before the Christmas break. Er, *Winter break*, as it was universally referred to now. He preferred the original moniker and defiantly stuck with it.

"Santa's coming to my house in a helicopter, and he's bringing me a pony! And a unicorn," Samantha boasted, loud enough to make her classmates envious. Knowing full well her statement was in no way based in reality, given that her family of six lived in a two-bedroom apartment, he wasn't going to burst her bubble.

"A unicorn...wow! Really..." her teacher replied, biting his tongue. A scuffle redirected his attention.

"Stop pushing me!" Trino complained to the boy behind him.

"I didn't push you!" retorted the falsely accused Angel, his scowl evident.

"Did too!"

"Did not!"

"Hey, hey, hey, now, boys. Come on, let's all keep our hands to ourselves," Curt said, addressing the collective scurry of squirrels now. The school bell sounded, indicating it was time for all students to head to class.

"Can I be Line Leader?" Abigail asked, a hopeful smile on her face.

"She was Line Leader yesterday!" Anayah chirped. Her hand shot up in the air, waving frantically, volunteering her services. "Can I be Line Leader, Mr. Martinsen? I haven't been Line Leader in a long time, and you said I could be! Please!"

Curt closed his eyes, counted to five, and opened them again. There were now six more hands up, all claiming inequity in the most coveted of assignments. In the interest of time and preventing further meltdowns, he made an executive decision, selecting the quietest and best-behaved student standing before him. "Dianna, how about you be our Line Leader today. Would you like that?" A broad smile stretched across her typically expressionless face. She seemed to stand a little taller too, as if "Hail to the Chief" had just been cued for her. Curt had his answer and his Line Leader, and now the day could proceed. He hoped.

"Okay, class, follow Dianna and show me your best behavior in line. We've been working on our expectations since the first day of school, so please make me proud." *For once....* "Everybody ready?"

A few weak nods. Curt noted that a dozen other class lines were already well on the way to their destinations, and he didn't want his to always be the last train to leave the station. "Okay, here we go...Dianna, you may start us off, honey."

Dianna was the perfect choice for this plum assignment. With her Minnie Mouse backpack squared between her shoulders, her eyes front, and her game face on, she demonstrated a proper, measured pace as the class began their two-hundred-yard journey toward Room Eight.

Might as well have been two hundred *miles*.

As the crow flies it was no biggie, and other than one forty-five-degree pivot turn at roughly the halfway point, it was a straight shot to the classroom. There were even painted lines on the blacktop for students to follow. Short of installing automated people movers, like the conveyors found at airports, what else could the districts do? Students were still expected to walk normally, bipedally, one foot in front of the other. And they practiced the same routine every day. Several times a day. Five days a week. And they were approaching their fifth month of school. If he'd had the time or the inclination,

Curt could've created a dandy math word problem out of that: *If Trino breakdances his way to the classroom on Tuesdays and Thursdays, how many total steps does he take Monday, Wednesday and Friday…and what time does the train arrive in Wichita?*

Even though practice supposedly makes perfect, for whatever reason getting the little guys from Point A to Point B always seemed to turn into some sort of freeform, hybrid of hopscotch and a spastic version of *Riverdance*. If there was a puddle to be found, it would be deliberately splashed. A poster on the wall? Jump up and smack it with your hand. A bug on the ground? Stomp it.

Curt couldn't help wondering: was it because he was a first-year teacher? All things being relative, it seemed like most of his cohorts had better control of their capuchin monkeys than he. He shuddered to think that, after what would soon be a three-week holiday break, all bets were off as to whether they'd remember *any* of the procedures he'd spent so much time ramming home. Come January, it would be like one big reset. But that would be…*next year.*

"Guys!!" He halted the line, pointed to a few of the usual suspects, and shook his head. "Trino, back of the line!" *Oy.* He gave Dianne the nod to resume. As they reached the classroom, backpacks found their hooks along the outer wall, and the students liberated their homework folders—the ones who'd remembered to bring them, anyway. Teacher/student fist bumps were accompanied with a "Good morning" to and from each as they entered the classroom and began noisily pulling their chairs down from their desks.

As the last of the students crossed the threshold, Mr. Martinsen—that's who he was, he reminded himself—closed and locked the door and made his way over to the Attendance folder sitting atop his desk at the front of the room. He took a deep breath and, against better judgment, chanced a look at the clock, hoping by some miracle that it displayed 2:35 p.m., but it didn't.

It was 8:31. *Gawd, where's my coffee?*

MEANWHILE...
POP'S AUTOMOTIVE
GILBERT, ARIZONA

The pristine, orange 1970 Plymouth Road Runner pulled into its usual end spot behind the shop and furthest from the Dumpster. Even with its windows up, the music was blaring loud enough for the entire world to enjoy, and the diminutive driver was enjoying a raucous singalong to "Out to Get You" by Grand Funk Railroad. The driver's door popped open, and the volume increased exponentially as she contributed to the chorus: "Baby, baby, baby. We're out to get you!!" at which time she ejected the cassette and checked in with the mirror.

This impossible-to-ignore muscle car—one of Detroit's finest moments—was her daily driver, yet it was devoid of any door dings or visible flaws, and the owner endeavored to keep it that way. One last rev of the 426 Hemi engine announced Phoenix's arrival, and, as she climbed out, a quick scan of the cabin revealed a thermos in the cupholder. "Oops...bet he's missing that," she chuckled to herself, not without sympathy, before locking the car.

The casual observer might mistakenly assume that a child had taken her parents' hot rod for a joyride because Phoenix barely clocked in at five feet, and she had a youthful beauty that seemed considerably younger than her thirty-one years. Still, she was a firecracker. More like an M80, and if the need arose, she could be pure dynamite. She fumbled with the keyring as she reached the shop's front door. *It'll be nice to be back to two cars again!*

Phoenix (formerly Phoebe) Martinsen (formerly LaFlamme) was the first one there, as she was most days. After punching in the alarm code, flipping on all the banks of lights, and stashing her fanny pack in the metal filing cabinet, she slipped into a clean set of shop overalls. Phoenix's work duds were kept in a locker separate from the guys' because hers were custom ordered to fit her petite frame. As it was, she still had to roll up the cuffs a little. She gathered her incredible mane of blood orange and red marmalade-like hair into a ponytail and affixed her oil-stained POP'S ballcap. It was going to get messy today.

Phoenix made her way back to the last service bay, rolled up the heavy metal shop door to let in more light, and surveyed the dark chestnut metallic 1998 Ford F-150 sitting before her. She had her work cut out for her with this one: a much-needed tune-up; some intense clutch work; and brakes to replace those clearly a danger to society. It had been her assigned vehicle for three days now, and she couldn't wait to get it back to its owner: her caffeine-challenged husband, Curt. She'd already diagnosed and remedied the vehicle's first problem, a troublesome noise emanating from the dashboard area, simply by removing—and tossing—the Mariah Carey *Merry Christmas* CD.

Really?

When all was said and done, there'd be a family discount on the labor but the total would still cause his teacher's salary to hemorrhage dollars. Phoenix didn't have long before she had to flip around the WE'RE OPEN sign, so she made a fresh pot of coffee for the rest of the guys who'd be trickling in any moment and wished she could somehow transport a cup to her desperate hubby.

The owner of the shop, and her adoptive dad, Pop Pop, wasn't coming in, so Mike, the assistant manager, had the "conn" today and would oversee things. This freed her up to work on Curt's criminally neglected beast. He owed her one.

POP POP'S HOME
GILBERT, A FEW MILES AWAY
WHILE PHOENIX OPENS THE SHOP

Dave LaFlamme had stayed home today to take care of an angel.

He was *not* the musician of It's a Beautiful Day fame, and he'd been asked many times over the years. Though he noodled on the guitar in a garage band occasionally, just for fun, that's where the similarity ended.

He was more commonly known as Pop Pop, because that's what Phoenix, er, Phoebe—before she'd come to be known as Phoenix six years prior—had called him ever since he'd adopted her at the tender age of five. "Pop Pop" had been easier for young Phoebe/Phoenix to say than "Papa," so it stuck. He was fine with it, always had been and still was. Case in point, the chosen name for his shop, though he'd abbreviated it by half because it looked better on the sign.

Pop Pop sat on the edge of the tiny single bed in his guest room/home office and looked down at his strikingly beautiful, six-year-old granddaughter, Rose. He enjoyed having her here on the nights that she stayed over.

Rose and her parents lived in "the cottage," a studio granny unit on the property, located at the end of the driveway, near the garage. The granny unit, previously occupied by Pop Pop's mother until her passing, had been Phoenix's little private hideaway for several years before she'd traveled west on her life-changing "adventure" seven summers before.

After Phoenix and Curt's honeymoon in Hawaii, they'd decided to leave California, and any crazy memories of it, behind, and she'd convinced her new hubby that Arizona might offer the best environment to start a family and to raise the child growing in her womb.

Pop Pop had graciously extended the invitation for the newlyweds to stay there while they got on their feet and could afford a place of their own. With its spartan mini-fridge, hot-plate-on-the-counter "kitchen," and a sleeping area with no door, it had once been an ideal space for a granny, and later, a single girl, but it had long ago begun closing in on the young family of three. And the dogs. And the bird…. Therefore, Rose was allowed to have sleepovers at the main house with Pop Pop on occasion.

Pop Pop closed the Christmastime storybook he'd been reading to her and brushed back a clump of her incredible ginger mane—identical to her mother's, in every way—and felt her forehead. She no longer had a fever, thankfully, and the doctor had cleared her to go back to school tomorrow. She'd missed two days this week and would've been heart-broken if she'd not been allowed to participate in the Winter Program at school on Friday night. She was, after all, the Christmas Angel in the program, and she was so looking forward to singing her solo.

"Is Frosty the Snowman real, Pop Pop?" Rose asked, seriously wanting to know if this book was classified as fiction or non-fiction. He set the tiny book down on the nightstand, next to the snow globe, and considered his answer.

"Hmm…that's a great question, Peanut!" he replied with a grandfatherly smile. "What do you think?"

"I'm not a peanut! I'm a little girl!" Rose chirped with a giggle.

"Oops…sorry…you're right, Peanut!" he said, returning the laugh.

"Hey!" She was sitting up now. A broad smile. This was their little back-and-forth game, and they played it often. The return of her sense of humor indicated she was indeed feeling better.

"Well, let me ask you this, Rose," he continued, priming the pump of deeper thinking. "Have you ever seen a snowman talk?"

"No, Pop Pop…I've never even seen *snow* before!"

"Aha," he said, holding up his index finger as he considered where she was going with this. "You've *never, ever* seen snow before? *Ever???*"

"No, silly! We live in Ama-zona! It doesn't snow here!"

"You mean *Arizona*…."

"That's what I said!"

"Okay…You're right; it doesn't really snow very often here in *Air*-izona…."

"Have *you* ever been to the snow, Pop Pop?" the little one asked, sounding a bit like Cindy Lou Who from the Grinch cartoon. He thought back to his stint in the Navy and the winters spent in Norfolk. That had been his first experience with the white stuff.

"Yes, I have seen snow before, sweetie…a long time ago."

"Was it cold?"

He furrowed his brow and made a face in response to what they both knew to be a silly question. "No…it was…hot!!!" he lied, laughing at the thought.

"Very funny, Pop Pop!" Rose chuckled at the comedian sitting on her bed. "I think snowmen can't talk. Snow is water, it's *frozen*. Snow can't talk, so a snow*man* can't talk either," she added, concluding her hypothesis. "So, I think the book is friction!"

"*Fic*-tion?" he asked, adding subtle correction. "You think?"

"I think!" she replied confidently. Pop Pop gave her button nose a squeeze.

"You…are one very smart little girl. You know what I mean, jellybean?"

"I'm not a jellybean! I'm a little girl!" she declared, flopping back dramatically into her down pillow. Their shared laughter was interrupted by the ringer of his mobile phone. As he stood, he motioned to the little juice glass on the nightstand next to her.

"Finish your orange juice, Rose. Pop Pop needs to answer this, okay?"

"'Kay."

It was Phoenix. "Hey, kiddo!" he said. "Everything okay there?"

"That's what I was going to ask you. How's my princess feeling?"

"I'm no doctor, but I'd say she's at a hundred percent." He shot a glance over to Rose, who was shaking the snow globe and singing to herself. "Maybe even a hundred-ten percent!" he added with a chuckle. "Dogs are sleeping off their breakfast. Everything's good in the hood."

"Yay! Thanks so much, Pop Pop. We're just getting ready to open. Everybody's here, they're having their coffee, shootin' the shit, like usual. I hope to have Curt's ride back to him by Monday. Tuesday, latest—if the rest of the parts come in today. I've got to bounce out of here at two and, after I pick up Curt, we should be home three-ish."

"Great. I can do your grilled veggies for dinner, how 'bout that?"

"Oh, yeah. Dinner…forgot to ask you—and you can totally say *no*…you're already putting in a full day of day-care duties—"

"No worries," he interrupted. "Name it. What's goin' on?"

"Curt and I kind of need to make our last Christmas shopping push tonight. Don't want to brave the weekend crowds, and tomorrow night's the Christmas program at school—plus we thought we might make kind of a dinner date out of it too. We've not had ten minutes to ourselves in months, it seems." Even though she was talking on the phone, she scrunched her face into a "pretty please?" expression. "Would…that…be… okay with you?"

Pop Pop knew what Phoenix said to be true. With the time and intense study involved in Curt's credential study regimen, the pressures associated with taking on a full-time teaching job, lesson planning, and the like, they were stretched more than thin. Add to that Phoenix's workload at the shop, doing more than her fair share of the heavy lifting as a young mom. The sum total had created a subtle but discernable friction between Phoenix and Curt in recent months, so he wanted to do whatever he could to alleviate tensions on the home front.

"Absolutely. More than okay, kiddo. I'll squeeze in a dinner date with the Christmas Angel. We'll get along fine! Don't you worry about a thing. *Capiche?*"

"You're the best, Pop Pop! Thanks!" The roar of some pneumatic tools reminded her she needed to unlock the shop's door and turn the sign around. "Okay, gotta go, Pop Pop! Love you!"

"Love you more, Phoenix!" he replied, clicking the END button. He turned to his tiny dinner date, offering a broad smile, "Now…where were we, Princess?"

"Can we watch my video again, Pop Pop?"

"Again? You mean the same one we've watched ten times this week?" he replied with a chuckle. Anything for his princess. "Sure, but you need to go brush your teeth first. Deal?"

"Deal!" she chirped, hopping up and padding down the hall to the bathroom. Pop Pop fired up the computer, waited a minute for it to warm up, then logged into Phoenix's social media account. It was more like a family social media account, and little Rose, at her tender age, was considerably more computer savvy than he.

He didn't even really understand—or take much interest in—the concept of sharing every conceivable family detail with the entire world. But what did he know? It was the "in" thing, and his granddaughter loved seeing herself in the clips

Phoenix had uploaded there. Still, he was old school in many respects. He preferred a phone call to an email any day.

Rose bounded back into the room and jumped onto Pop Pop's lap as he brought up her favorite clip: The one from six months ago and Rose's first experience on the new Slip 'N' Slide.

"Here we go, Princess. You ready?"

"Ready!" she declared, a huge grin on her face. She'd seen the clip a thousand times, but got the same level of enjoyment with each successive viewing.

Pop Pop hit the play button and adjusted the volume on the family iMac. The scene started with some rather shaky handheld camerawork as Pop Pop had slowly panned the camera across the front of their house. The Road Runner was visible in the driveway, replete with its Arizona tag and the MEAN PEOPLE SUCK bumper sticker.

Though by no means deliberately, the shot also provided the particularly astute viewer, if they were interested—and some were—with both the car's license number and the home address. At the end of the panning shot, Rose could be seen wearing her two-piece Little Mermaid swimsuit, readying to make her first-ever run down the twelve-foot-long, yellow plastic surface, made slick by the attached garden hose. At the far end of the slide was a tiny, two-ring inflatable kiddie pool to assure a soft landing. Her otherworldly-brilliant, long, wavy red mane was down, past her shoulders, and had been freshly styled by her mama. Because that's what young mamas do sometimes. Little Rose looked like a miniature version of a swimsuit contestant in a Miss Arizona pageant. She beamed a smile at the camera and struck a pose.

"Ready, Rose?" Pop Pop's voice can be heard saying from behind the camera.

"Yeah!" Rose declared, a huge grin on her face. And with that, her little legs rocketed her across the small span of lawn like a mini Olga Korbut. As her feet made contact with the slick yellow surface, she maintained perfect balance, like a skateboarder, until the end of the run where she jumped up and absolutely stuck the landing in the kiddie pool, her arms outstretched and head cocked back. An Olympian who'd just scored all tens from the judges. The camera zoomed in on her face and her proud, perfect, gold medal smile. "Ta-da!!" With that, the video clip ended.

"Ta-da!" Pop Pop echoed back to the computer. He always responded in the same manner for Rose's benefit, even this thousandth time.

"Can we watch it again?" she asked excitedly.

"No, Princess. Maybe we can watch *Aladdin* on TV instead," he muttered rather distractedly as he more closely regarded the screen area directly below the video window. "What the…?"

Something he'd not paid attention to before: there were more than ten thousand "likes" and more than a few trouble-some comments from viewers. Amongst them:

Cum to papa.
Gimme some. LOL
Mmm…slippery!
I'd like to pluck that rose.

CHAPTER 3

SAGUARO VILLAGE MALL
SANTAN VILLAGE, ARIZONA
THURSDAY, 7:05 PM

P HOENIX AND CURT had apparently spent their combined months' salaries, judging from the number
of bags they were hefting back to the car. Most of
it was toys and stuffed animals and, most importantly, an
almost-life-sized stuffed German Shepherd, which Curt had
wrangled.

It had been incredibly hard on the entire family when their
beloved Gracie, inherited from Liam, Phoenix's late grandfather
back in California, had to be put down two weeks before. She
was a gentle soul, and considering the fact she'd lived fourteen years, ninety-eight in dog years, she'd had a very full and
happy life. A more loyal dog one could never find, and she'd
rallied back from a particularly nasty bout with vestibular dis-
ease before beginning to refuse her meals.

Phoenix and Curt had both been with Gracie when the

veterinarian announced her prognosis and suggested they have her put her down immediately. She was in a lot of distress, and her quality of life going forward would be severely diminished, he assured them. Still, such news had come out of left field, and there had been zero time to process it. Through many tears and several boxes of Kleenex, they'd helped comfort Gracie as she crossed the "rainbow bridge," and the long drive back home without her had been beyond devastating.

A stuffed German Shepherd could never replace the real thing, by any stretch of the imagination, but they hoped Rose might find some level of comfort in another snuggle companion while she processed her grief. They still had Gracie's offspring, Luke, thankfully. He maintained an abundant supply of his puppy energy, and even though dealing with him could be akin to nailing jello to a tree, he was sixty pounds of unconditional love, and they wouldn't trade him for the world. Same went for Phoenix's longtime Chihuahua sidekick, and favorite road trip companion, (the) Prick. They'd been through a lot together, Prick and she, and he'd long ago assumed his rightful position as the alpha in their pack.

Curt placed the faux furry figure atop the rest of the packages and gently slammed the Road Runner's trunk lid. "Whew, glad we were able to get that all done tonight."

"Me too," Phoenix replied softly. She was lost in thought as she studied the stick-family decal that adorned the bottom-left corner of the Road Runner's rear window. It seemed like an odd choice on such a badass muscle car, but it'd been a gift from Pop Pop the previous Christmas, and Curt had all but refused to put it on his F-150. With smiling family figures, two large hounds, and a tiny dog, the decal represented, from left to right, their young family. That was, until Gracie died. "I miss her so much," she added wistfully.

"I know, honey. We all do…do you think we should consider getting Rose a real puppy again?"

Phoenix shook her head. "You can never replace a pet. Especially a dog like Gracie. We need to wait a while. Rose will get over it. We all will. But now would be too soon. Let's revisit that idea later, maybe, see how we feel. Okay with you?"

"Of course, baby." Curt put his arm around her waist and guided her in the direction of a new-to-them pizza joint a few shops away. "I'm starved. You too?"

"I'm a vegetarian, and I could eat a friggin' *horse*. Yeah."

"C'mon. A teacher friend told me about this place. Supposed to have live music some nights and decent wood-fired pizza."

"Sounds like the best date night ever," she said, punctuating with a hug.

Curt carefully made his way back to his and Phoenix's table. He was carrying a plastic serving tray, upon which were two frosty beer steins, silverware, and one of those plastic, numbered table placards so the server could match your food to your table.

For a Thursday night, the Hungry Coyote was packed. It remained to be seen if it was because of how awesome their woodfired pizzas were or if people just had a jones for live music. They'd find out soon enough. It was just good to be out together.

Curt had placed their order already: a large, slightly customized combo pizza that Phoenix and Pop Pop had turned him on to. They'd dubbed it *the swineapple* and it had become a family favorite with them. Essentially, it started off as a veggie pizza (no onions!), then: hold the black olives on Phoenix's side; swine of choice–either Italian sausage or bacon–on the carnivores'; and pineapple chunks on the entire rig.

Curt set the tray on the table, next to the two impressive salads Phoenix had already constructed at the salad bar. His stein was filled with a Budweiser while Phoenix's was empty. She promptly remedied that by liberating her ever-present bottle of Sunny D from a jacket pocket and pouring it into the frosty vessel.

"Thanks, babe," she said, her voice slightly raised to be heard above the band.

"You're welcome," Curt replied with a smile. He raised his stein. "To a long overdue date night! Cheers!"

"Cheers!" she parroted, smiling as she clinked hers against his.

The five-piece band had been allotted a tiny "stage" area in the corner, opposite the salad bar. It made for an intimate setting, and as the band segued from the Eagles' "Desperado" to one of Phoenix's longtime favorites, the funky signature classic by Average White Band, she gestured to the band with an enthusiastic thumbs-up, accompanied by an appreciative "Woo-hoo!"

This Average White Band selection was particularly noteworthy, perhaps because this band was neither average nor white. Consisting of five young, twenty-something local girls of various ethnicities, this diverse combo was dressed in matching tight, sparkly miniskirts and featured a competent lineup, including a saxophonist, who'd be getting a good workout during this number, no doubt.

For a bar band, and especially being such young musicians, they were tight. The guitar and sax were in lockstep groove with the rhythm section, and it was no longer a mystery as to why there was a full house on this Thursday. Phoenix nodded her approval to her date, and as she took a big pull from her drink, the song's chorus kicked in, with all five of the girls singing and without a clue as to how badly they were butchering this AWB tune: "Pick up da pizza, uh-huh! Pick-up da pizza, uh-huh! Pick-up da pizza, uh-huh! Pick-up da pizza!" The sax solo kicked in and Phoenix's flat palm slapped the table hard, like a wrestling ref signaling a pin, as she unleashed her fruity beverage all over their salads, the table, and her date.

She looked up at Curt, and seeing him completely drenched, she broke into the mother of all belly laughs. He soon joined her in an irrepressible yuck fest, cementing this as arguably the most hilarious date they'd had since "the dart incident" in that Salinas biker bar seven years prior. They'd needed some levity for such a long time, and they enjoyed the welcome laugh.

CHAPTER 4

LA JOYA ELEMENTARY
FRIDAY, DECEMBER 21
7:05 AM

THE ROAD RUNNER pulled into the spot along the curb in front of the school's Office and adjacent to the main gate being unlocked by a custodian. From the passenger side, Curt looked over his left shoulder and addressed the princess, secured in the rear booster seat.

"Have a great day, sweetie, okay? I'll see you after school, and then…*everyone* will see you sing in the winter program *tonight!*"

"Okay, Daddy! Love you!" Rose proclaimed.

"Love you more, Rose!"

"Doubt it!" she replied with a giggle.

"Okay, you two…" Phoenix said, interrupting what could become a long exchange. "Have a great last day, honey. Don't let the monkeys eat you alive. Early day today, you said, so call me later—let me know when to pick you up, okay?"

"Yep, will do. Have a good day, baby. Thanks for the ride, and…for your work on the truck. I owe you."

"You have no idea!" Phoenix said with a laugh.

Curt grabbed his satchel from the floorboard, slung it across his shoulder, and gently closed the door. Phoenix grabbed the thermos from the cupholder and held it out to him.

"Ahem," she said with a chuckle. "Forget something?"

"Oh, my God, dodged a bullet," Curt said as he grabbed it through the open window. "Thanks, honey!"

"Dogs a bullet?" Rose interjected.

"Never mind, Rose. Dad's being silly. Okay, honey, gotta go…see you later," Phoenix said to Curt as she pulled away.

He returned Rose's waves until the Road Runner disappeared at the end of the street, at which time he pivoted and once again became *Mr. Martinsen* as he entered the castle's gates.

Vacation starts tomorrow.

Seconds earlier, and unnoticed by anybody, a non-descript and windowless white van slowly pulled away from a neighboring curb and assumed a trailing spot a hundred yards behind the orange car.

OASIS MARKET
GILBERT, ARIZONA
20 MINUTES LATER

It was a twenty-five-minute drive, but Phoenix had narrowed it to eighteen with a little help from the 426 Hemi. She'd chosen this store because it was smaller and less crowded than the big box supermarkets this time of day. They'd have to make it a quick stop if they were to get Rose to school on time. They might be a few minutes tardy but it wouldn't be the end of the world.

Phoenix had told Rose's teacher, Miss Ballesteros, that she planned to send along enough juice boxes, cupcakes, and fresh fruit for the entire class's last Fun Friday before the Christmas, er, holiday break. *Christmas!*

Phoenix found an empty cart, stood Rose inside it, and took a moment to zip up her daughter's winter hoodie coat before they proceeded inside. It had been a bit brisk all week, by Arizona standards, and she wasn't taking any chances now that Rose was feeling better—and was a featured singer tonight! "Hold on, sweetie. Here we go."

Once inside, and the automatic doors had closed behind them, the white van went into motion, taking a slow, serpentine route until it pulled into a perfect spot, directly beside and quite close to, the orange car. Phoenix had chosen to park at the far end of the lot, like she almost always did, and this was ideal for the purposes of the van's driver.

The driver positioned the van's sliding cargo door accordingly. He slunk down a little in his seat. As he was already on the short side, he didn't have too far to go. After a quick check of his watch, and with a gloved hand, he adjusted his mirror for a better look at the store's exit. The position of their vehicles didn't make for an ideal vantage point, so he'd have to rely on the Creep. He tapped in a text message:

Where are you?

A few moments went by before he got his grammatically challenged reply :

> There here.

He shook his head and took a deep breath before keying in his response:

They're here. They're! They are.

> What? I see them.

The van man immediately regretted starting this whole "Who's on First?" text-a-thon.

Just keep an eye on them. Don't get too close. Let me know when they're coming out.

> ok. Bananas

What the fuck?

Phoenix grabbed a large bunch of bananas from an adjacent endcap bin as she pushed her precious cargo into the bakery department before stopping alongside a large display table of white boxes with clear windows on them. Inside each were various batches of what were supposed to be holiday-themed, overly frosted, sugar bomb cupcakes. She scrunched her face as she inventoried the atrocious color offerings, none of which existed in the real world. It was slim pickings, but Phoenix grabbed a box containing a dozen dayglo-turquoise snowmen ones and another dozen dayglo-pink Christmas unicorn ones. *Unicorns? Really?* She didn't have the luxury of time, so she placed the boxes into the cart. *These should get the little monsters sufficiently jacked up.* She said a silent apology to the teacher, then began wheeling toward the produce section.

"Careful of the cupcakes, Rose. Don't step on them, honey."

"'Kay, Mama."

The Creep was a large man. Like, almost Yeti-large. He had poor posture, appeared outwardly awkward, and was a dim bulb. To the extent possible, he maintained a discreet distance several yards behind them. He didn't need any produce. Hell, he never even ate the stuff. Ever. *Rabbit food, all of it.* Still, he pushed his empty cart past the Roma tomatoes, pausing at the artichoke bin. Keeping his eyes on his mark, over at the apples, he pretended to shop, grabbing a thorny 'choke without looking at it. *"Yowch!!"* he hissed. His thumb was bleeding from the damn thing. He angrily tossed it back into the bin and opted for the decidedly less-threatening cucumbers adjacent to the offending vegetable.

He chanced a glance, looking out from beneath the bill of his tattered ball cap. She hadn't noticed him, nor had the kid. The Creep had yet to shake his lingering bronchitis and tried his best to stifle his sniffles and nagging cough. *Don't call attention to yourself.*

He tore a flimsy clear bag from the overhead roll and fumbled to find an opening. With his enormous hands, he wasn't known for his dexterity. After several frustrating seconds he tried the other end of the bag but failed to breach it. He blew on it, shook it, and quietly cursed it before resorting to a most unsavory tactic: he called up a generous, full-on loogie and spit it into his free hand. *That ought to do it.* It'd been way more than the job required.

This didn't go unnoticed by an older woman nearby who,

utterly horrified, abandoned her search for the perfect honeydew. She clucked as she wheeled away her nearly full cart.

Creep's lubed fingers had successfully found an opening in the ridiculous excuse for a bag, and he thrust three slimy cukes into it. He wiped the extra phlegm onto his ratty bowling shirt, exacting all the manners of the namesake in Jethro Tull's "Aqualung."

The mark was on the move again now, grabbing two round, prepared fruit trays as she made her way to the cookie aisle. Creep was in tow, maintaining a stealthy distance as he watched the kid, who was standing in her mother's cart, singing to herself. His phone vibrated in his jeans' front pocket. Another text from his partner waiting outside:

> *Where are you?*

The mark had stopped mid-aisle, near the Chips Ahoy! display. Creep hung back, staring at his phone. His reply:

cookees – be pashent

The man in the van stared at his phone's display in disbelief. *Cookees? What the hell?*

Creep was close enough to hear the mother-daughter exchange, and unless you were blind, it was impossible not to notice that both mother and daughter had incredible–and identical–manes. Even Creep's inferior processors registered this fact. He didn't mean to stare, yet he couldn't help doing just that from the corner of his eye.

"Which ones should we pick out, baby?" the young mother asked, beaming at her six-year-old mini-me.

"Ginger Stamps, Mama!" she answered enthusiastically, pointing to the packages in front of her.

"Ah, Ginger *Snaps* it is, my little ginger snap!" she replied, grabbing the package.

"Can I have some now, Mommy?"

"May I have some now, you mean?" she gently corrected with a smile.

"Yes, silly!" her daughter laughed. "May I have some, please?"

Phoenix opened a box and handed it to her daughter. "Okay, but I still need to pay for them, Rose. Not too many, okay?"

"'Kay!" All smiles as the first crispy cookie snapped in her mouth. Phoenix placed two additional boxes in the cart, adding to what would be Miss Ballesteros's survival kit.

Creep took a moment to stab in an update:

wear r u. I dunt no how long. she dossint notiss me.

The van man shifted in his seat upon receipt of this particularly insightful status report. Alex Trebek would've had a field day with these Neanderthalic utterances. *Never again... last time...* the driver promised himself. He took his time entering his response, choosing his words carefully so as to not be misunderstood:

Just let me know when she has paid for her things.

I'm in position. Let me know when she is leaving!

Can you handle that? FUCK!

Phoenix grabbed four small cases of fruit punch-flavored juice boxes, then entered her checkout lane as Creep pulled his cart into an adjacent one. He placed his petri bag of cucumbers—and two boxes of the ginger snaps—on the belt. As he grabbed a twenty-dollar bill from his front pocket, his phone vibrated. His eyes darted between the checker, his phone, and his mark in the next lane. Looking at his display now, the corners of his mouth turned ever so slightly downward as he absorbed the text's mean tone.

Phoenix thanked the checker, collected her change, and—
after taking a requisite moment to organize the bills so they all
faced the same way and were filed in order of their monetary
values—stashed her wallet. It was just the way she did things.

"Hold on, kiddo. Here we go," she said softly, smiling as
she pulled away.

"Here we go," Rose parroted, savoring her fourth cookie.

Creep fervently typed his message as instructed.

Outside, the driver's flip phone vibrated. He checked the
display:

> *Their comming – NOWW*

A glance to his rearview mirror confirmed this fact. He
slowly slouched down out of view, listening for the approach
of the cart's hard wheels on the rough pavement.

Phoenix wheeled the cart toward their car at the far end
of the lot. There was a smattering of cars here and there but
the lot was mostly empty. *Save the one jerk who needs to park
his van right friggin' next to me. Really??*

Any other time she might take the time to leave them
a note but she was in a hurry. Still, this jerk had pulled up
so close to her driver's side she'd have to suck it in to climb
inside.

A-hole. She parked the cart, with Rose still inside it, by
the left rear bumper and started to pop the trunk. *Shit! The
gifts are still in there!* She went around to her passenger side,
unlocked the door, and began loading groceries onto the floor
of the front seat.

With all the stealth of a trapdoor spider, the driver opened
the van's sliding cargo door, only about an inch as to remain
unnoticed. That inch provided him with a window to all the
visual information he needed.

"Mommy?"

"Just a second, sweetie. Almost done!" Phoenix answered from the front seat.

The van's engine quietly started on the first turn of the key. With lightning speed, the sliding door opened noiselessly along its track, and the figure emerged, a gloved hand covering the little girl's mouth, preventing any chance of another word—or the scream Rose was now attempting. With an economy of movement, great stealth, and a quick turn of the man's body, Rose was thrust into the cargo area, where she landed on an inflatable mattress and several beanbag chairs.

Phoenix heard what sounded like a sliding door closing and was about to give the inconsiderate driver a piece of her mind when the sound of chirping tires interrupted that idea. As she came back around to the back of her car, she saw the van streaking away. It had to be going sixty as it jetted out of the lot. She turned to her now empty cart, her eyes wide with panic as she spun around in a 360-degree arc, first left, then right, and then back again, searching for any sign of her daughter.

"Rose! Rose!! *ROSE!!!*" Each scream escalated in both volume and desperation. But there was no sign of her. Only a half-eaten package of ginger snaps laying atop the trunk. "PLEASE!!! SOMEBODY!!! HELP ME!!! *MY DAUGHTER'S BEEN TAKEN!!!!*" Phoenix bellowed to the world. To the universe. *"ROSE!!!!"*

Two store personnel rushed out of the store and a few other customers scurried over to aid the distraught woman standing by the orange car at the far end. As they reached Phoenix, the respondents found her desperately wailing but her air had been sucked away, allowing her only silent, primal screams now, her face hideously contorted as she pointed to the stick-figure family unit decal on her back window:

The one with the big, red **X** now scrawled across the stick figure of the little girl.

CHAPTER 5

LA JOYA ELEMENTARY
ROOM 8
SEVERAL MINUTES LATER

MR. MARTINSEN HAD ALREADY taken attendance and was in the process of going over the morning's calendar with his class. It was a morning ritual that involved establishing which day of the week it was, the month and year, the current season, and so forth. He paused as he pointed to the square indicating their current date.

"Okay, very good. Yes, we know the month is December. And we know the day of the week is Friday," he said, his finger pointing to today. "So, who thinks they can tell me, using a complete sentence, what is today's date? You have to *say* all of it! Who can tell me ?"

He looked out into the small sea of children. Several hands shot up. In fact, *every* single hand shot up, and they waved like so many palm trees in a hurricane. This was accompanied by a chorus of children all vying for attention and a chance to demonstrate their knowledge.

"I know!"

"I know!"

"I know!"

He let it go on for nearly a minute. *They knew.*

Their twenty identical utterances went into a perpetual loop and were more than enough for someone to mistake it for a bad needle skipping on a Bill Withers record.

Since every student felt confident presenting, Curt chose the one who almost never participated voluntarily, the one who rarely uttered a word. His expression showed an until now unseen level of certitude, and he'd apparently just had his "aha" moment of understanding.

"Maximillian!" Mr. Martinsen said with a smile of encouragement for the small boy with the big name. "What's today's date, Max?"

Little Max slid his chair out a bit so he could stand and deliver. He stood proudly and glanced at the calendar one more time. Then, with all the gusto of the sergeant-at-arms announcing the arrival of the president at the State of the Union, little Max declared, "Today's date is Friday, December twenty-first, two thousand seven!"

"Yessss!" Mr. Martinsen confirmed. "Verrrry good, Max!"

But Max wasn't done yet. With a huge grin in place, he went for the bonus round as he added, "And when we come back after the break, the year will be two thousand *eight*!"

Buoyed by a round of applause from his peers and kudos from his proud teacher, Maximillian was on top of his little world as he took his seat. Mr. M. gave him a big thumbs up.

Max, you are SO going to be Line Leader for the rest of the day.

The classroom's landline phone rang, and the room went quiet. "Class, please take out your counting-by-twos math worksheet and work quietly. Mr. Martinsen needs to answer the phone."

As the students rummaged in their math folders, Curt went over to the phone, next to the paper tray on the tiny table near the door.

"Good morning. This is Mr. Martinsen," he answered in a quiet tone.

"Mr. Martinsen, this is Kelly in the office...."

Kelly Bozzo, the school's secretary, was one of his favorite people in the world and the absolute best person for the job. A better admin he'd never come across, and he should know; he'd subbed at a hundred schools before taking this assignment. She was the perfect combination of sweet, fun, and efficient. In any situation that might arise, Kelly—and her equally-pleasant office counterpart, Brenda—could be relied upon to handle it. The fact that Kelly had foregone her usual "Good morning" salutation didn't go unnoticed by Curt. He could be reading into it but in that moment he thought he'd noticed something in her voice.

"Hi, Mrs. Bozzo," he replied, maintaining their honorifics—or titles of respect—in the presence of students. "What can I do for you? I already sent the attendance folder if that's—"

"No, we got that, thanks," she said, pausing as she gathered her words. *He's obviously not checked his cellphone.* "Can you please come to the office?"

"Sure, but I have recess duty, so...."

"Not at recess. I mean, can you come to the office... *right now?*"

Curt's brow furrowed slightly as he looked over at the students who were all on-task and working independently. "Is there somebody who can…?"

"Somebody's on their way," she replied, not intending to sound abrupt. Curt noticed a strain in her voice, and she'd never been curt with him previously. Curt. In the briefest of nanoseconds, he wondered if the origin of his own first name meant *curt*, or *rude one*….

"I…*can*…uh, is everything okay?" he whispered. That question, even uttered quietly, didn't go unnoticed by some students, all of whom had much better hearing than he, prompting a few heads to look up.

"Something's come up; I'd rather tell you when you get here," Kelly replied. There seemed to be concern added to the mix. "Please come now."

"Okay…" Mr. Martinsen said, but she'd already hung up.

A knock announced his "somebody" had arrived. As Mr. Martinsen opened the door he was greeted by a young, twenty-something, first-year substitute, Miss Matthews, who'd guest-taught his class on several occasions. She looked to be barely out of high school but her future in the class-room was bright.

"Mr. Martinsen, sorry to interrupt you, but the office asked me to spot you for a little while," Miss Matthews said with a nervous smile. "They didn't say how long or anything."

"Thanks, Miss Matthews," he said, ushering her in. He'd never learned her first name but his students liked her, and she was familiar with his routines. "Um, okay…so, the class is finishing up a couple of math worksheets, and when they're done you can have them work on their Santa calendar activity. They know what to do, and there's a finished sample on my desk. Recess is at 10:10 but I'm sure I'll be right back. You know where everything is, right?"

"Yes."

Mr. Martinsen pivoted to his kids. "Class, I need to go to the office for a few minutes. Miss Matthews will be here with you until I get back, and—"

He was interrupted by a small but enthusiastic chorus of *Yay!!* He held up his hand, cleared his throat, and added, "You'll owe me three minutes at recess for interrupting me." This quieted them immediately, as taking away any recess time got them where they lived. He continued where he'd left off. "*And...*you'll be working on your December calendars after you've finished your worksheets. Got it?"

"Got it!" was the choral response.

"Make me proud, everyone."

He turned back to his sub, nodded, then mouthed "thanks" to her, and exited the room.

It was a two-minute walk to the front office from Room 8, but Mr. Martinsen did it in one. He glanced at his watch, and, with a sigh, entered the school's control center. *Am I getting fired?*

He took two steps into the room and was immediately met with a couple of atypically sober-looking faces. The usual smiles and warm greetings were absent this morning, and a quick scan of the room told him something was off. *Way* off. Kelly's expression was one of abject concern, bordering on horror; he couldn't tell yet.

"Um, you wanted to see me...about something?"

"Have you not checked your phone?" Kelly asked delicately.

Curt's expression told them he hadn't. He always kept it off during class time so as not to have it be an interruption during instruction, or a distraction to himself. He thrust his hand into his front right pocket and retrieved his tiny Samsung SCH-U450. It was still powered down, which explained why he wouldn't have received any calls. Or texts.

As he powered it on and waited for what seemed like an eternity for it to warm up, both Brenda and Kelly walked over and put a comforting hand on his shoulders. The school's principal, Miss Garcia, exited her adjoining office and entered the office lobby area. She was joined by a young police officer. They both had their game faces on.

Curt's screen began to light up, and as he squinted at the small display, it informed him that he'd missed twelve calls. It wasn't even 9:00!

"Mr. Martinsen," Miss Garcia said with measured but genuine concern, "would you please join us in the conference room?"

"Is somebody going to tell me what's going on?" Curt said with building panic. "Was there an accident at the shop? My wife? My father-in-law? Are they okay? Please! What's—?"

Miss Garcia took his elbow and gently guided him toward the open conference room, a stone's throw from the front counter. "Please…"

Curt looked at each face, then surrendered to the suggestion. It was clear they weren't going to tell him anything while they stood in the middle of the lobby.

The conference room was rather small, as it was only really set up as a place for staff interviews, parent-teacher conferences, and the like. The round, wooden table had six chairs, and once Curt took his seat, Miss Garcia, Kelly, and the police officer sat. With a stiff lip, Brenda nodded to Kelly, indicating she'd handle the office before she closed the door behind her.

"Mr. Martinsen, I'd like to—"

"Curt...it's Curt...please!" He hadn't meant to sound so abrupt, but he'd abandoned the *Mr. Martinsen* formalities. He needed to know exactly what was going on, and right now!

"Curt," Miss Garcia conceded. "This is Officer Herrera, and he'd like to ask you a few questions if that's okay with you."

"Fine... Hi." Curt directed his laser-focused attention to the man in uniform now. "Is my family okay? Is anybody hurt? Do...I...do I need...a union rep? A...*lawyer?*" Curt asked, almost laughing at the absurdity of his last question.

"Mr., er, Curt...thank you," Officer Herrera acknowledged. "No. You don't need a lawyer." His eyes met Miss Garcia's and Kelly's before he turned back to Curt. "Sir, the station received an emergency call this morning at approximately—" he paused to confirm with his notepad. "—at approximately 7:45 from the Oasis Market in Gilbert. A woman in acute distress, having a panic attack, shortness of breath in the parking lot area there."

The furrow in Curt's brow was reaching Cro-Magnon proportions as he stared at the officer. He was familiar with the market and the area, as his wife often did small shopping trips there. *She said she was going to pick up treats for Rose's classroom on her way to—*

"Are you familiar with that location, Mr....Curt?"

Curt nodded strongly. "The woman, what happened?" he asked directly. "Is she okay? Is she—?"

"Sir, the woman in question was...your wife, Phoenix Martinsen."

As Curt absorbed this new kernel of information, his

nods became more pronounced, not unlike one of those vintage drinking bird toys. He might get whiplash any minute. "And?"

"And, yes, your wife is okay…physically. She was not harmed in the incident."

"Incident. Incident!" Curt shook his head, "What *incident*?! Please, for the love of God, cut to the chase and tell me what the fuck is going on!!" Curt caught himself and immediately regretted his word choice. "I'm sorry, forgive me, but somebody's got to fill in the blanks here before I completely lose it."

In a gesture of comfort, Miss Garcia placed a hand on Curt's arm.

"My wife is okay. *Physically*…your word. That's good, right? So what happened, and what was the *incident*." His eyes showed his desperation. He was pleading now. Begging.

"An abduction was reported, sir. Officers were dispatched to Oasis Market, and they took reports from your wife and from several witnesses. They are processing the scene right now."

Curt looked up at the ceiling, and his lip began to tremble uncontrollably. He closed his eyes and took a moment to process this information. His mind was racing. There was more, he knew it. He bit his lip to keep it from quaking and looked the officer squarely in the eye. Not cop to teacher, not cop to husband. Man to man. His look said, *Level with me.*

"Mr. Martinsen," the officer began before catching himself. "Sorry. Curt—"

Curt waved off the apology as he couldn't care less how they addressed him at this point. As long as they told him everything. "Either name's fine," he said quietly. "My daughter—"

"Mr. Martinsen, I'm afraid your daughter, Rose, has gone missing, sir," the officer said. He might be wearing a uniform right now, but he knew his level of concern and sympathy was coming from another place. As the father of two seven-year-old twin girls, he was coming from *that* place. Having a child go missing was every parent's worst nightmare. "We've got every resource looking for your daughter, sir, and we—" Curt's sobs stopped the officer in his tracks. The shoulders of the giant lumberjack of a man were heaving uncontrollably as he sobbed…wailed…like a wooly mammoth suffering multiple spears.

Even Brenda, in the adjoining room, could hear the degree of pain emanating from the other side of the door. She wiped away a tear of her own as she concluded her call with another parent. As a mom herself, she sent up a silent prayer.

Please, Lord…bring Rose home safely….

CHAPTER 6

GILBERT POLICE STATION
FRIDAY
SAME TIME

PHOENIX—WHAT WAS LEFT of her emotionally, anyway—was seated at a metal table in the small interview room. She was joined by two new officers, not the responding officers who'd been first on scene at Oasis Market.

As was the case with all missing children's cases, the parents were being questioned separately, so as not to taint each other's individual statements. While they interviewed Mrs. Martinsen, Officer Herrera was at the worksite of the husband conducting his initial interview with Mr. Martinsen, and they needed to conclude their questions here before they could reunite the couple on what had to be the worst day of their lives.

There would likely be follow-up interview sessions in the event the child wasn't recovered soon. The questions were routine, and more than a little bit indelicate, but investigators always had to consider the parents as possible suspects because in many of these cases, it was indeed they who had perpetrated the crime. Nobody could be ruled out as a suspect.

As these two officers were following protocols and needed to be thorough, they also had to choose their moments to insert their questions to Phoenix between her manic outbursts. It wasn't their first rodeo, and they understood that emotions ran high in these situations. Still, time was of the essence when it came to child abductions, as the likelihood of a good outcome diminished with each passing hour.

Phoenix plucked the final tissue from the box and honked her nose. While she finished and wiped away what seemed to be her last remaining tear, the senior officer, Officer Jeffrey Ramage, held up two fingers to his partner, indicating two more boxes were needed. Officer Bethany Moser, thirtyish and blonde, had thus far seemed to be all business, but she managed a warm smile as she ducked out for a moment before quickly returning with her game face and the requested items. She closed the door behind her and returned to her place at the interview table.

Ramage, fortyish, was a former football tight end at Arizona State. His uniform was stretched tight against his muscular barrel of a frame and his flat-top crewcut completed his persona. He cricked his thick neck and seemed to find slight relief in the resultant popping sound. He shrugged his massive shoulders and flashed a supportive smile to Phoenix.

"Mrs. Martinsen, I'd like you to tell me again, please, when was the last time you saw your daughter, Rose?"

Phoenix blinked her swollen eyes in disbelief. "Seriously? You're going to ask me that again? After I've told you guys…

like, three times? And the officers before? I told *them*! I *told you*! I told *all* of you!"

"We know," Moser interjected, projecting her supportive female side now. "It's all routine, Mrs. Martinsen. We just need to make sure we didn't miss anything. We all want Rose back home safely, I assure you. Please, if you'd please tell us again, as you remember it, it would be helpful."

Phoenix took a deep breath and exhaled her pufferfish cheeks. "Okay…like I said earlier, and multiple times, I was putting my groceries in the car. At the Oasis. Rose was standing in our cart, and I couldn't open the trunk because it was filled with unwrapped Christmas gifts I didn't want her seeing." Phoenix paused, her eyes looking from one officer to the other as if to say, *Okay?*

"Please continue. What happened next?" Moser asked.

"Because that van—that asshole—parked so close to my driver's side, I had to go around to the passenger side to load the groceries. I've told you this already. I was putting the stuff I'd bought on the passenger side floor when I heard an engine start, and what sounded like a sliding door shut, and then the screeching tires. It all happened so fast, and I looked over at the cart and…" Phoenix held up a hand as she scrunched her face into the most painful of expressions. She grabbed the new tissue box and pulled out a handful. She honked her nose loudly. Ramage and Moser exchanged quick looks as Phoenix attempted to collect herself.

"…and I looked over at the cart, and…and Rose was gone!" she managed before surrendering to a place of primal pain she'd felt only once before, back when she, herself, was five years old and running for her life.

An unsolicited flashback washed over her in a hot second:

the horror of having witnessed the murder of her mother, and fleeing the arson fire that had just consumed both their home and her dead mother. Running out into the dark night, in her pajamas, on Christmas Eve, and clutching her secondhand doll, her face frozen in a silent scream, like in the Edvard Munch painting.

Like it was again, right now.

Officer Moser placed a comforting hand on Phoenix's wrist for a moment, but Phoenix yanked her arms back, like she'd been touched by a hot poker, and began wildly flogging herself. "You're so stupid!!!!" she screamed, admonishing herself as she pummeled her head with her fists. "You're a horrible fucking mother!!!" she continued, while Officer Moser came around the table to intervene in the self-smackdown.

"Hey…please stop! Phoenix! Stop hitting yourself. You are *not stupid*. Please—it could've happened to anybody!" she professed, as she wrapped her arms around the despondent woman. She stopped short of telling her she was a good mother because they'd just met, and the facts weren't in yet.

There was no more fight left in Phoenix and she all but collapsed in the officer's arms, like an empty potato sack. "It could've happened to anybody," Moser said again, in a hushed tone as she held her. She shot a glance to her partner who nodded, as if to say, *We're done.*

Officer Ramage's phone vibrated, and he read the display. He got up, walked around the table, and whispered in his partner's ear. "They found the van."

X

POP POP'S HOME
AN HOUR LATER

It would take some time for a team to process the van, so Officers Ramage and Moser sat at the kitchen table of the missing child's grandfather, Mr. LaFlamme. Pop Pop had received a frantic call from Phoenix hours before and his mind had continued to race ever since. An AMBER alert had been issued and the incident reported to the FBI's National Crime Information Center.

Pop Pop had been advised of the protocols, including the need to process the family's living spaces, and he didn't question them. He would cooperate fully. He just wanted his granddaughter back. *Today and unharmed.*

He tamped down his emotions as he nervously scurried about the kitchen, fixing coffee for the officers and tried not to think of what the worst-case scenarios could be. He returned to the table with three mugs, a sugar bowl for Ramage, and creamer for Moser. He took his black, and this was his fourth cup this morning.

"Thank you, Mr. LaFlamme," Moser said as she poured in enough dairy product to turn the coffee a very light beige.

"Yes, thank you, sir," Ramage added, shoveling three teaspoons of sugar into his.

Pop Pop nodded. His eyes were red-rimmed and darted around the room as if clues might be found written on cabinet doors, the ceiling, in thin air.

Ramage took a sip before asking, "Now, Mr. LaFlamme, you'd mentioned Rose spent the night here with you last night?"

"That's right. She did and often does. There's a single bed down the hall for her. Like I said, her parents and she live in the guest cottage here. It's small and, well, she does the occasional sleepover here. Gives my daughter, Phoenix—and her husband—some privacy."

Ramage nodded as he scribbled some notes. "And you said she'd been sick?"

"The last few days, yes. She was feeling much better yesterday and was cleared by her doctor to return to school today. That's where—" Pop Pop's throat clenched. The officers shared a quick glance.

"Take your time, Mr. LaFlamme," Moser offered in her best comforting tone. "We know this is difficult."

"We'll be done shortly, sir. Please take the time you need," Ramage added.

A moment went by before Pop Pop collected himself enough to continue. "That's where Rose is supposed to be right now. At school. Phoenix was on her way there with her when, when it happened." His eyes searched those of both officers. "She's supposed to sing in the school's musical program tonight. It was all she could think of."

Ramage nodded, wrote another note, and queried as delicately as he could. "Mr. LaFlamme, how have things been with your daughter and son-in-law lately. Any problems? Money issues? Any history of—?"

Pop Pop raised his hand and cut him off. "No. No. And… no! Please, I know you're just doing your job—I can appreciate that—but I can assure you there are absolutely zero issues with this family. Okay? Job pressures, sure. Who doesn't have those? But anything beyond what's normal with any family, there are no factors that would contribute to their daughter's disappearance. None. A more loving family you'll never find," he added resolutely.

"Thank you for your answers, sir." Moser said.

Pop Pop was replaying some of yesterday's tender grandfather/granddaughter moments in his mind when he suddenly sat upright in his chair. Both officers regarded him closely.

"Anything else you remember, sir?"

"Yes!" he said as he stood up from the table. "Yesterday. Rose was here. I took the day off, as I'd mentioned, and stayed home with her. She asked if we could watch her favorite video, one we've watched many times."

"This video. Was this on TV, a tape, or—?" Ramage probed.

"Home movie. On the computer, actually. It's a video my daughter uploaded to that video sharing platform…MeeTVee or whatever it's called.

Ramage and Moser exchanged glances. "This video clip could be important, Mr. LaFlamme. Would you mind showing it to us?"

"Sure. No problem," he replied. "Computer's in here," he added, motioning for the officers to follow him down the short hall to the office/guest bedroom. "It'll take a minute to warm up," Pop Pop said as he pushed the power button.

Ramage stared at the blank screen as it began to wake from its slumber. Some familiar icons began to populate the screen, including a long-familiar one for MeeTVee. The officers leaned in closer as Pop Pop clicked on it and several thumbnails of available videos were listed. The video in question was at the top of the list as it had been most recently viewed. "This one," Pop Pop said, as he expanded the window for full-screen playback. He checked the volume and hovered the mouse above the triangular play button.

"What are we about to see here?" Moser asked.

"Last summer…June, I think. No, wait…July. I'd bought my granddaughter one of those Slip 'N' Slide lawn toys, the ones where—"

"We're familiar with it, sir. Go on," Ramage interjected, trying his best to remain patient.

"Okay. Well, I'd set it up on our front grass area and I was filming little Rose's first time on it. The day was hotter than hell, so it seemed like a good idea."

"You can go ahead and hit play, if you don't mind, sir," Ramage said.

Pop Pop clicked the mouse, and the video began. "You'll have to excuse my camerawork."

As the image panned left, across the driveway, the officers were glued to the pertinent details as they saw them: the unmistakable orange Plymouth Road Runner they'd seen at Oasis Market earlier today, a readable license plate, the discernable house number.

And then there was young Rose. An otherworldly beautiful child with hair like her mother's. Neither of the officers had ever seen anything like it. Rose presented as an innocent six-year-old, while exuding an impossible-to-ignore charm and charisma well beyond her years. She was six, going on twenty-six, and that was a concern.

The officers were glued to the image of Rose smiling, sprinting, gliding, then sticking the landing in her celebratory Olympics-esque pose, followed by her close-up smile and the end of the clip. Ramage and Moser shared another concerned look with each other.

"As I said, I was watching this with Rose yesterday—for the millionth time, probably—and it wasn't until then that

I happened to look down below, here," he said, taking the video out of full-screen mode and scrolling down to the Comments section. "I'd never paid attention to these before but, as a grandfather, I find these troubling."

Ramage stared at the number of "likes" the clip had received. The tally of thumbs-up responses indicated there were more than ten thousand of them. This was not your typical home video audience.

"May I borrow your mouse for a moment?" Moser asked.

"Sure," Pop Pop replied. He moved away from the screen, freeing up the chair and the mouse for her.

Officer Moser scooted the chair in and guided the cursor as it began a slow scroll of the perv talk commentary. She read the responses, each more troubling than the last, and had to pause after she'd reached the tenth comment. She suddenly felt sick to her stomach.

Ramage rubbed his face. He'd seen a lot of sick stuff in his years on the force but the implications here were beyond troublesome. There were some truly sick bastards out there, and if his intuition was right, this innocent youngster might be in some real trouble. He turned to his partner and her look echoed his.

"You were right to call this to our attention, Mr. LaFlamme. We'll need a copy of this link so we can investigate it further. It might be helpful." Ramage turned to his partner and his subtle nod said, *I think we're done here.* "Thank you for your time, Mr. LaFlamme. If you think of anything else, please don't hesitate to contact either myself or Officer Moser." He handed Pop Pop his card.

"Thank you, Mr. LaFlamme," Officer Moser said as she made note of the MeeTVee clip identifier. She returned her pen to her pocket and looked him in the eye. "We know your family is going through a terrible ordeal right now, sir, but please know we're putting every resource we have on this so we can bring Rose back home safe."

Pop Pop ran his fingers through his hair and nodded. He'd aged ten years today. "Thank you, officers." As they showed themselves out, Pop Pop glanced back to the screen. The cursor was blinking, pointing to where Moser had parked it in the comments. This particular comment's brevity wasn't especially noteworthy but its single-letter content sent a shiver down his spine.

CHAPTER 7

GILBERT POLICE STATION
FRIDAY
12:45 PM

IT WAS LUNCH time, but you'd never know it. The entire staff was making it a working lunch. This applied to the lead investigator too, perhaps more than anybody. There was still a missing child out there and every moment counted in their efforts to find Rose.

It had been five hours since she had gone missing, and that was an eternity in the case of an abducted child. By this time, she could be most anywhere, and if they didn't bring this little girl home safely to her family, this was going to be the most fucked up holiday ever.

Officer Moser approached the lead investigator's office carrying two white bags along with a couple of fountain sodas balanced precariously in a cardboard drink holder. She'd ducked out just long enough to grab some provisions from the drive-thru burger joint down the block. A glance through the open blinds confirmed Officer Ramage was still on the phone. Their eyes met and she started to turn away but he waved her in.

She quietly closed the door behind her as she placed the food items on an adjacent table while Ramage finished his call. Ramage was standing behind his desk, pacing, the phone glued to his ear, as he multitasked with the report he was reading. The forensics team had just finished processing the white van.

"That's all we got? No useable prints in the van at all but traces of what looks like snot on an inside door handle?" He shook his head. "Terrific...some snot and some orange powdery stuff. Run those through tests and report back to me in an hour." He hung up the phone and looked up to his partner. "Not real productive so far."

Moser handed him a bag and one of the sodas. "Diet Coke, and your burger's sans onions."

"Thanks," he replied. Taking time to eat was the furthest thing from his mind but he knew his partner was right. They had to eat something or they'd flame out. He unwrapped his burger and chomped into it. "The guys found some slimy stuff—they think it's snot—and some orange mystery powder, possibly in the cheese snack family," he said with a mouthful. He swallowed and then continued. "Other than that, one of Rose's tennis shoes was found in the cargo area, wedged between a couple of beanbags."

"Don't forget the red grease pencil they found in the glove box. There's that too."

Ramage nodded as he considered this, taking a sip of his soda. "You got anything?"

Moser picked at her French fries and wiped her hand on a napkin. "Got the team working on the pervy comments on the video. If we eliminate the innocent-sounding ones, like from friends, family, and *normal* people, we've still got a lot to run. Some of 'em have already hit dead-ends as they're shadow web stuff and use hard-to-track virtual private networks, but we'll leave no stone unturned. It's a very scummy crowd out there."

She allowed herself a dainty bite of her burger. After a sip from her soda she added, "We're still prioritizing the 'X' comment though because, like you, I don't believe in coincidences."

LAKE POWELL, ARIZONA
FRIDAY AFTERNOON, 1:05

Other than a couple of sketchy-looking kidnapper types in the front row, it was an otherwise nondescript, newer model four-wheel-drive Jeep Commander SUV. Its Stone White Clearcoat, now dirty from the slush, was decidedly less flashy than the other available option the owner could've gone with: Red Rock Crystal Pearl coat, which screamed *Look at me!* The less flashy the better when you're transporting a recently abducted child in the second seat.

They were five hours into what would likely be twenty-two hours, plus. That is, if you drive straight without anything other than fuel stops and pee breaks to delay your arrival time. No, they would have to break up the drive into a couple of long chunks, the man from the van had decided. He was in the driver's seat again now, literally and figuratively on this, because his copilot wasn't the sharpest tool in the shed, and on his best day probably couldn't find his own ass with both hands and a roadmap.

The driver's name was Dieter. It was a strong two-syllable German name; thus, it was pronounced with the long *e* sound. He fricking hated when somebody read his name for the first time and put the em-*pha*-sis on the wrong syl-*la*-ble or, worse, asked if he was committed to dieting.

Dieter was on the short side at five-foot-six and had a bit of a Napoleon complex, especially around his sequoia of a younger brother, the dim bulb with the orange fingers sitting next to him.

The long drive gave Dieter plenty of time to replay their escape in his head. He was confident they hadn't made any mistakes. Their exodus had been easy. He'd dumped the stolen van in an alley behind the Circle K, a couple of blocks from the market, and made the switcheroo to their waiting getaway vehicle, transferring only the precious human cargo, as the beanbags and inflatable mattress had fulfilled their mission in preventing any bruises to the fruit during the abduction. And, aside from when he'd been texting, he'd worn gloves, so prints weren't a concern.

The switch had taken less than a minute. and after scooping up his partner in crime at the corner bus stop, they'd slithered out of town. They had a good head start, as cops would be looking for the van, and he'd parked it behind the Dumpsters.

They wasted no time. Making a slight jog west on 60, it had been a relatively straight shot north from Gilbert via 101, then Interstate 17 before merging onto the I-40, and connecting with US-89 at Flagstaff. This was their current piece of pavement and would be for a while.

They had seen a few very light patches of snow coming into Flagstaff and the weather in this part of the state, combined with the plethora of pines, made it feel more like Virginia than Arizona.

As Dieter put Lake Powell in their rearview mirror, the highway started a pronounced turn west again. They would be crossing into Utah very shortly.

"That was a bigggg lake," his cohort said, interrupting his thought. It was the first utterance the man had made in over two hours.

"What?" Dieter said, a bit annoyed. He glanced over at the hulk next to him. The hulk, whom he privately referred to as Creep, was his younger brother, Wilhelm, or "Willie," as he'd been called as a kid—and still was by their mother. "You say something, Creep?" he asked, serving up his go-to brotherly insult.

Creep stuffed another handful of Flamin' Hot Cheetos into his mouth and chawed with his mouth half open. "The lake," he said, his hand diving back into the large, family-sized bag, now nearly empty. The evidence was all over his right hand and most of his face. "It was biggg!" He smiled at his little big brother. His hand delivered another load of the crispy day-glow snacks to his mouth. Like a horse eating sugar, and with great gusto, he licked the orange Cheetos dust from his severely stained fingers.

"For fuck's sake, Creep!" Dieter yelled, his eyes returning to the road as he negotiated the turn. He looked back at his passenger. The image was equal parts horrific and comical, as Creep now looked like a freakishly big, drunken crack whore who'd hastily reapplied her ill-advised Dollar Tree orange lipstick between tricks. He'd definitely colored outside the lines.

"You'd better not be getting any of that shit on my seats! Dammit!"

A weak, groggy voice called out from the back seat, surprising them both. Dieter's eyes shot to the rearview. *Shit. The sedative's wearing off.* They had another hour-plus before they'd make their planned stop in Kanab, Utah for the night.

"I want my mommy."

THE JEEP COMMANDER
WAHWEAP OVERLOOK
MOMENTS LATER

Dieter had seen the sign advertising the Wahweap Overlook, whatever the hell that was, and taken the exit. There was nothing else out here, and he had to fix a problem before it became a worse one.

Rose, still groggy from the sedative she'd been administered hours before, was helped from the Jeep by the giant man. Rose looked down at her feet. Her favorite tennies weren't there any longer; they'd been replaced by something she'd never worn before: a pair of Uggs. They were soft and felt warm on her feet.

The shoes were just one of many additions to her wardrobe, courtesy of Creep's Walmart spree the day before. He'd had to guess on the sizes, based on the video, and he'd paid cash for the new parka, leggings, socks, and Uggs— plus assorted road snacks. It was all still in bags in the cargo area behind Rose's seat.

From the comfort of the vehicle, Dieter's eyes scanned in

every direction as Creep walked Rose to the rear of the Jeep and zipped up her hoodie.

"Where's my mommy? I want my mommy," she cried, looking up at the biggest man she'd ever seen.

"You'll see her soon," Creep replied. He hated lying. Especially to a little kid.

"I have to go number one."

Creep's expression made it clear that he was unfamiliar with the numbering system assigned to bathroom breaks.

"I have to go pee," she clarified.

"Oh, okay," Creep replied, a bit embarrassed and not sure what to do.

"Don't watch," the little girl insisted.

Creep released her tiny hand and let out several feet of her long leash. He looked the other way until she'd finished her business.

"Okay," Rose said, giving him the green light. The wind was picking up and it brought a chill. "I'm cold! And I'm hungry!"

"Me too," Creep confessed. The cheese snacks had helped some but he still longed for a big hamburger. Or two.

"Hurry up before somebody sees us," Dieter called out as he rolled up his window.

"Here," Creep said, retrieving two gummies from his jacket pocket and handing them to Rose. She accepted the small treat of melatonin-infused, berry-flavored gummies and popped them in her mouth as he helped her into the second row of seats. A bed of sleeping bags, a small pillow, and a plush unicorn were waiting for her.

Walmart, one-stop shopping.

Creep climbed in on his side and could barely close the

door against the wind. With a slam, and the clicking of door locks, the cabin became eerily quiet, as if hermetically sealed against the elements.

"You give 'em to her?" Dieter asked in a hushed tone. Creep nodded in the affirmative, and the Jeep pulled away, rejoining the main road.

Not far to the Utah border, and it couldn't come too soon.

POP POP'S HOME
1:40 PM

Curt sat at the kitchen table and looked up at the ceiling for guidance. After several unsuccessful minutes, he shuffled down the hall to where Phoenix and her dad were: seated at the desk and staring at the iMac as they read more of the video clip's comments.

"Phoenix, how could you be so stupid?!" she said again under her breath. She had done nothing but admonish herself all day, and that cycle would be in a perpetual loop. Maybe until the end of time. "I'm a horrible fucking mother!!!" she screamed.

Curt put his hand on his wife's shoulder but she half-shrugged it away. She had subconsciously decided she didn't want, or deserve, any love or affection. Not anymore. Not after proving herself to be the mother of all boneheaded mothers and losing her baby girl.

Pop Pop looked over his shoulder to his son-in-law. Curt's grave expression matched theirs. "We'll find her," Pop Pop said to them both. His confidence wasn't based on new information or anything tangible other than what he hoped to be answers to his prayers. "We'll get her home."

Curt nodded numbly. He hoped his father-in-law was right but he knew Rose could be most anywhere by now. He rubbed his face as if he could wake from this nightmare.

"I can't do this anymore!" Phoenix said sharply as she stood, switching off the computer. Her thoughts were torturing her as she conjured up a horrific montage of scenarios, each more unsettling than the last. "She's all alone!" she continued as she paced the small space. Curt took a couple of steps back to give her room. "She's alone…she's scared…she wants her mommy, and I wasn't there for her!!" Phoenix cried out, her failed-mother rage building.

Pop Pop stood, and in a gesture of comfort, placed his massive tree branch of an arm on her tiny shoulder. Phoenix slipped out from under it as she continued to pace, lost in thought. Lost in her shame cycle.

"If that motherfucker, or *any* motherfucker, so much as lays one finger on my little girl, I…" Phoenix paused as she summoned the fireball building within her, "…I promise, I will hunt them down, wherever they are—to the ends of the earth—and make them regret the day they were fuckin' born, so help me God!" she declared to the universe.

As Phoenix stormed out of the room, Curt and Pop Pop exchanged a knowing look. They felt it too, and bearing witness to this level of utter pain, and reexperiencing the depths of Phoenix's fury and resolve, they couldn't help but be reminded of the solo journey of despair she'd had to take seven years before. She was coming from that place, they knew, and God help anyone that got in her way. Just ask the Pirate.

A minute later, they heard the unmistakable throaty rev of the Road Runner's 426 Hemi engine as it was backing down the driveway. Phoenix roared away, down the street in search of a big empty parking lot. The high school was her first choice but not practical with school still in session.

A couple of miles away, she found her spot at the recently closed Chuck E. Cheese, or Chunky Jesus, as Rose used to call it when she had her birthday party there. There was no one around and she had some time—and some rubber—to burn.

She revved the Plymouth and listened to the magnificent sound of the Hemi awaiting her command. *Time to work some shit out, Phoenix!* Her foot stomped down on the accelerator as she cranked the wheel hard to the left and commenced spinning the first of what would be many, many smoky and therapeutic donuts.

CHAPTER 8

PRICKLY PEAR ELEMENTARY
GILBERT
FRIDAY, 2:40 PM

MISS BALLESTEROS SAT at her desk in the empty classroom. She replaced the phone in its cradle and wiped her eyes with a tissue. She'd just finished making the last of nineteen phone calls to parents, and they had to be the most difficult nineteen phone calls she'd ever made in her twelve years as a teacher.

After the morning's terrible events, the not-so-Fun Friday going into the winter break had ended on a downer. One of her favorite students was still a missing child. Her heart was breaking for Rose's parents, and it had all but shattered to smithereens several hours ago.

The school's administration had made the difficult decision to postpone the winter musical program scheduled for tonight. The auditorium's stage decorations were left in place, but the PA system was put back into storage, as were the scores of folding chairs for parents. Students, their families, and staff alike were saddened to know of the cancellation, and the reason for it wasn't something that had been widely disseminated or elaborated on. Some parents she'd called had been privy to the developments, having seen the news reports on television.

As she sat there now, looking across the twenty empty desks, their chairs neatly stacked atop them, a cloak of deep sadness wrapped itself around her. This was the last day of school before what would be a three-week break. The boys and girls were excited to be home, to be with family and, perhaps more than anything, looking forward to whatever Santa might bring them.

This was supposed to be the happiest of times. It was the long-awaited vacation carrot that had dangled in front of her for months. She felt none of this joy.

Not now.

Deflated, she rose from her desk, pushed in her chair, and changed out the white board calendar to January in preparation for their return to school.

On her way out, Miss Ballesteros paused as she regarded the samples of student work neatly stapled to the wall. Rose's work in particular, showed promise with its neat penmanship, above-average artwork, and an actual complete sentence. She put her hand on Rose's sweet self-portrait, said a silent prayer, and turned off the lights as she locked the door behind her.

X

CUMMON INN
KANAB, UTAH
2:50 PM

The two-star, two-story, too-sorry looking place seemed a bit sketchy, even by kidnappers' standards. Dieter had picked out this woebegone establishment from the limited competition listed in the auto club directory. There were a half dozen cars in the lot, tops. Which was fine.

"Wait here. Be right back. Don't talk to anybody, understand?" he said, looking directly at his brother. Creep nodded, and Dieter swung his legs out the open door. He stretched, then proceeded to the lobby.

The new Jeep's seats were comfortable enough, but after the long schlep they'd taken today, his sore ass was longing for a break—and a meal. Preferably in a comfortable booth. Somewhere low-key.

"One night…two queen beds, and the hideaway bed. We have your room around the back, sir, on the ground floor, room number 133. Here you are. Just the one key, you said?" the wholesome looking desk clerk asked. She was maybe twenty and she'd pancaked her makeup on in an unsuccessful effort to hide her acne. Her face looked like a relief map.

"Yeah. One key," he replied.

"If you'd just write your vehicle's license number here and sign, please, you'll be all set, Mr. Kirwan," she said. Her goofy smile was freaking him out a little. "Mr. Kirwan" collected his fake driver's license from her. He'd left a $200 cash deposit. He wouldn't be collecting any change in the morning; these expenses would all be reimbursed by the client. *Should've stayed in Vegas.*

He looked around the lobby and gave a quick glance to the Jeep just outside. "Uh, it's a new car...," he said, craning his neck and pretending to read its plate. He turned his attention to the form, wrote down a fake number, scribbled an unintelligible signature and handed it back to her.

"Thank you very much," she replied as she handed him the card key.

"Any place to get waffles around here?"

"This time of day, I don't think so, sir," she replied apologetically. "There's Mexican across the street and a really good hamburger place right down the way, a couple of blocks down," she added, pointing him in the right direction. "Realllly good...no waffles, I'm afraid, but they have *the* best fries. Kabobs, too! So yummy!"

"Mm, thanks," Dieter replied without returning her toothy smile.

"We hope you have a wonderful stay with us here at Cummon Inn, and in case I don't see you before you check out tomorrow, *Merry Christmas!*"

He didn't have a response to that other than a thumbs-up gesture as he exited the lobby.

"Utah," he muttered to himself as he approached his chariot.

CHAPTER 9

BOB'S KANAB KABOB
FRIDAY, 6:35 PM

JAMES "JIMMY" BERRETH was a second-year officer with the Kanab Police Department. It was a small department, staffed by only six full-time officers and a few reserves. With the town's small population of 5,000—give or take—the twelve-square-mile area was adequately staffed. They rarely saw much action in these parts anyway.

As he polished off the last of his fries, his thoughts went to celebrating Christmas with his new family: his former high school sweetheart-turned-wife, Jillian, and their one-year-old baby boy, Jimmy Junior. Jillian and he had been inseparable since the first week of their freshman year speech class, when they'd been randomly assigned to interview each other and deliver a verbal report. Fast friends became faster puppy loves, and by their sophomore year they'd made lifelong pledges to one another. Baby Jimmy was a gift from above.

"May I get you anything else, Officer?" the young server asked as she got to his table.

"Mm, no, thank you. I'm fine, Kim," he replied with a smile. He was only a couple of years her senior, and he knew her from church. "Just the check when you get a moment."

"Sure thing. I'll be right back with that," she said.

He wiped his mouth with his napkin and took a final swig of his chocolate malt. As he did, his eyes went to another group of diners sitting in a booth about twenty feet away. The booth was perpendicular to his. Two men and a little girl. What seemed odd to him, aside from the fact that one of the men looked like a sasquatch, was that neither of the adults seemed to have any parental-type interaction with the child.

Kim returned with the check, and he handed her two twenties in return. "Thanks. Keep the change," he said. She was a little taken aback by his generosity. "Thank you so much," she replied shyly.

"Merry Christmas," he said as she walked away. His eyes went back to the trio at the booth. The big dude was eating the enormous burger with all the grace and table manners of a crocodile eating a whole chicken. The little girl was seated next to him, and she appeared to be picking at a grilled cheese sandwich. A gorgeous child by anyone's standards, yet her expression exuded sadness. She didn't seem to be overly happy with her food or her present company. And maybe even her situation.

Officer Berreth might be a newbie parent, but he'd been around school kids long enough to know how they act, especially ones who were just starting their Christmas breaks. Something didn't pass the smell test.

The two men didn't seem to be aware of his presence,

so he quietly got up and walked in the other direction as he exited to his patrol car. He climbed into his cruiser, which he'd backed into his spot when he arrived. Its position afforded him a good view of the restaurant. The radio traffic had been quiet for the last couple of hours so he figured he could wait just a little longer.

Ten minutes went by before the odd couple emerged. The big one was holding the little girl's hand and it was an almost comical sight. But it wasn't funny. The girl seemed a bit disoriented, even groggy, as she was ushered over to the late model Jeep. The smaller man came out behind them and was putting his wallet in his pocket. He wore wraparound sunglasses. No pleasantries were exchanged, nor eye contact, by anybody.

As the Jeep backed out of its spot, Officer Berreth noticed the paper dealer's plates. As it slowly pulled out of the lot and onto the main drag—the *only* drag, really—he started up the cruiser and assumed a stealthy position about a hundred yards behind them.

Berreth keyed his microphone. "Dispatch, Unit 6, over."

"Unit 6, Dispatch. Go ahead."

"Roger that, Dispatch. Unit 6 is 10-8, just finished my break and am returning to patrol. Now leaving the Kanab Kabob, over."

"Roger that, Unit 6," the Dispatcher replied.

"Dispatch, unless something's more pressing, Unit 6 requesting 10-47, permission to check out an odd-looking couple of men leaving the restaurant with a small child. They're just leaving Kanab Kabob and the kid doesn't seem so thrilled to be with them. Following subjects for a few to further assess, and make sure everything's okay, over."

"Unit 6, Dispatch. That's a Roger on 10-47. Continue observation and please advise, over."

"Dispatch, Unit 6. 10-4. Underway and following now. Thanks. Six, out." Officer Berreth returned the microphone to its cradle. The sky was turning a dark gray from the storm clouds. He wanted to keep eyes on them before darkness fell and he didn't want to lose them in the intersection.

About a block from their motel, Dieter pulled the Jeep to a stop at the intersection. As he waited for the signal to turn green, Dieter's keen eye caught a glimpse at what appeared to be a police car in the rearview. It was a way back, but it warranted his attention. His nervous fingers drummed the top of the steering wheel. His eyes went to the traffic signal. Its solid red taunted him. *C'mon!*

Creep seemed oblivious, but that was a short putt. Rose lay back on the sleeping bag; her left thumb had found her mouth.

The light finally turned green, and instead of taking a left toward their accommodations, Dieter chose to take a right, away from the booming business district. He completed the turn and proceeded along the road, his eyes darting between the stretch ahead and the rearview. After a few moments, he was relieved to see no one tailing them. He let out a private sigh.

"Where're we going?" Creep said, looking around. There was nothing out here but vacant lots.

"Shut up," Dieter said. Another look at the mirror showed the police cruiser had made the same turn and had fallen into a tailing position. It was slowly closing in on them now. *Damn it.*

"I want my mommy," Rose whined behind him.

"Shhh! In a little bit," he hissed. Dieter's eyes darted around nervously. *Fucking Utah!* He maintained a very civil thirty miles per hour as he considered his options, and there weren't many. There weren't even two.

Dieter's paranoia was justified as he noticed the patrol car had pulled to within three car lengths and was holding there, matching his speed. Dieter's right hand slowly left the wheel and touched the cold steel of the .38 revolver wedged between the seat and the console.

A moment later, the cruiser's lightbar lit up like Christmas. Dieter's right hand made an imperceptible move back to the wheel. There were no other vehicles on this road so he couldn't feign ignorance.

"Just keep your mouth shut. Got it?" he said quietly but with a sharp tone.

"It's a policeman, a policeman!" Creep announced. "A policeman...oh, no!"

"Shut. The. Fuck. Up," Dieter said through clenched teeth. It was a loud whisper, but it couldn't have held more menace had he yelled it. Dieter bit his lip and flipped the turn indicator upward, signaling his compliance, as he began pulling to the curb.

As the Jeep came to a stop, a brighter white spotlight lit up, turning the vehicle's interior from dusk to high noon. Creep squinted his eyes.

Officer Berreth pulled his cruiser in closer, maintaining a couple of car lengths as he came to a stop behind the Jeep. Assisted by the brilliant white spotlight, he observed the vehicle's occupants for a few moments, watching for any suspicious activity. Not seeing any, he opened his door and slowly exited the cruiser, adjusting his tactical equipment in the process.

There was zero traffic at the moment on this non-commercial stretch of road. Officer Berreth took care as he approached the driver's side window, signaling for the driver to roll it down.

Dieter stabbed the button and the Jeep's window whirred down to a stop. "Good evening, Officer. Was I speeding?" Dieter asked, hoping to win a Best Actor award.

"May I see your license and registration please, sir?" Officer Berreth replied.

"Yes, sir, but may I ask why you pulled me over?" Dieter asked, annoyed that the cop had answered his question with an instruction. Dieter wasn't really interested in an answer as much as he was in buying time.

"Sir, is this your vehicle?"

"Yes, it is. Two weeks new. Waiting on the plates. Is that why you pulled me over?" Dieter replied. *Why the fuck did you pull me over, asshole?*

Berreth didn't bother with a response as he shifted his weight to his other foot. He didn't feel like playing the question-and-answer game tonight. He momentarily looked past the driver and directed his attention to the wookie on the passenger side. Creep stared back with a look that said he'd just soiled himself. The officer shifted his gaze toward the second row of seats. The child he'd seen in the restaurant was out like a light.

"License and registration, please," he said again. He hated repeating himself, especially to weasels who thought they could flip the charm switch and avoid compliance.

"Sure," Dieter conceded. He started reaching for the glove

compartment, which was partially blocked by Creep's freakish long leg. "Move your damn knee," Dieter said.

"Slowly, sir, and keep your hands where I can see them," the officer directed.

Dieter felt a river of perspiration cascade from his armpits as he pulled the temporary registration from the glovebox. "Yes, sir," he said, carefully liberating his driver's license from his wallet as well. He handed both documents, one real, one fake, to the officer. The mismatch wouldn't go unnoticed, he knew.

Officer Berreth allowed himself a quick peripheral glance to confirm no other cars were approaching as he stood alongside the Jeep. He held the documents side by side, comparing one against the other. His brow furrowed. "Uh, Mr. Kirwan, is it? Did you say this was your vehicle?"

"Yes, well it's co-owned. But yes, it's mine."

"You're not from around here. Mind telling me where y'all are headed tonight?"

"Visiting family. Utah family. It's the most wonderful time of the year," Dieter replied.

A couple of seconds later he realized how much he'd sounded like a smart ass. "Christmas with Grandma. My little girl can't wait. That's where we're heading, Officer." *Just give me back my fucking license and we'll be on our merry way.*

Officer Berreth's eyes swept the cab once again, landing on the little girl. He wasn't buying it. Any of it. "Sir, I'm going to have to ask you to please step out of the vehicle, very slowly, keeping your hands where I can see them. Same goes for you, sir." This was directed to a very frightened looking passenger. Berreth watched every move as the large man slowly undid his shoulder belt and grabbed his door handle. The guy was huge.

Seizing the moment, Dieter's hand found the revolver and, with a blur of movement, swept it across his body, firing two rounds into the rookie's head and neck. Creep screamed and began jumping up and down like a gorilla. "You shot him!"

The two loud booms, coupled with the big man's screams, jarred Rose from her groggy state. She responded with a series of high-pitched screams that could probably shatter glass.

"Shut up!!! Both of you!!!" Dieter barked at them.

The officer lay on his back, groaning and clutching his neck with his left hand. Blood was pooling under his head, the two shots mortal enough to do the job. His eyes wide with surprise, his right hand near the service weapon he'd not completely unholstered. He blinked twice, his final thoughts going to his Jillian and to his little, now-fatherless Jimmy.

Dieter climbed out, quickly surveyed the area and, seeing no one, proceeded to empty four more rounds into the officer. "Get in the fucking car!!! Now!!!" he bellowed to his idiot sibling. He didn't need to repeat himself as Creep jumped inside, clutching his face. Rose's screams morphed into sobs.

Dieter hastily wiped his prints from the now-empty firearm and tossed it into the glovebox, along with his registration. He slammed the shifter into drive and stomped the accelerator hard.

So much for getting a good night's sleep in this town. They'd have to press on.

Fucking.

Utah.

CHAPTER 10

GILBERT POLICE STATION
FRIDAY, 7:15 PM

OFFICERS RAMAGE AND Moser hadn't taken so much as a fifteen-minute break all day. It had been a working lunch, and other than answering the call of nature hours earlier, it had been a nonstop, twelve-hour day of hunting down leads. And it might just become an all-nighter.

These cases got under your skin, perhaps more than any other, especially considering the innocence of the victims, their families, and the rapidly ticking clock.

The officers were hunched over the monitor on Ramage's desk. They had been provided security camera footage of the Oasis Market's parking lot, but it had been less than helpful in providing additional information thus far. They knew what the perp's vehicle looked like, not only from the mother's statement but also the video, plus they had found the vehicle in question in an alley behind the Circle K—and they had the physical vehicle in impound.

No useable prints in or on the van, other than the partial they'd found on the red grease pencil in the glovebox. That and some disgusting phlegmy stuff on a door handle. And the artificial cheese dust.

"We know it's stolen, has no plates, and it looks like one perp. Male. Mid to late thirties, maybe. On the short side. Five-six or so. Not much taller than the mom, Mrs. Martinsen. Sandy blonde hair, from appearances. His sunglasses and ballcap don't help much," Ramage said, rubbing his tired eyes. "Run it one more time."

Officer Moser recued the clip and clicked the mouse. The wide camera angle captured about seventy-five percent of the parking lot. The morning sun's position created some flare, but the image was clear enough to see Phoenix pulling into her spot at the far end of the lot, the front end of the car facing the camera. The timestamp matched the facts she'd given in her statement.

As the clip continued, they watched Phoenix get out with her daughter, place Rose in the cart and adjust her daughter's zipper, before wheeling toward the entrance of the market. About two minutes later, the white van cruises through the lot rather casually before pulling into the spot directly next—and abnormally close—to the orange car. "Okay, pause it right there," Ramage said. "Look at his hands, he's definitely wearing gloves here, but…what's he doing? He's looking down now. Is he looking at a phone? Playing with himself? What's he doing?"

"Might be," Moser said.

"Might be *what?* Playing with himself?"

"Might be using a phone. Maybe communicating with an accomplice. Can't tell from this, though. The store manager didn't have anything useful from inside the store because that system's down. Possible that he had help, though. What do you think?"

"Possible," Ramage said softly. "Okay, go ahead," he added, motioning to the monitor. The scene continued, offering several minutes of nothing while the driver waited for them to come out. "Fast forward a little," he said. Moser shuttled the footage ahead several minutes, at three times the speed, until Ramage signaled for her to stop. "Play it there, normal speed. Please," he added, remembering his manners.

"Sure," Moser responded. "Okay, here she comes," she said as they watched Phoenix wheel Rose and the groceries to her Plymouth.

"The perp, he's just ducked out of sight. Probably in the van's cargo area. Waiting," Ramage said, seething. He wanted this guy, bad. "Bastard."

They watched the rest of the scene play out without further interruption: Phoenix parking the cart at the trunk area, reaching for her keys, pausing, then going around to the passenger side door with her few plastic bags of items. Phoenix bends down and begins loading bags into the car.

A plume of white exhaust now belches from the van, and over the next ten seconds, it's a flurry of activity as the van's slider opens, the perp emerges, and in seemingly one motion, places a gloved hand over Rose's mouth, pivoting to deposit her into the van, and not too gently. Five seconds later, the van roars away as Phoenix comes around to discover her daughter missing.

"God," Moser muttered, her hand to her mouth as she paused the clip. "It doesn't matter how many times I watch this; it makes my blood boil." Moser had a daughter of her own, only four years old, and all her motherly instincts were at Def Con 4. "Please tell me we're going to get this guy."

"We will," her partner said under his breath. Ramage had no kids of his own, which was rather remarkable considering he had three ex-wives, but any crimes involving children lit a fire under him like nothing else could. "Can you cue up the other camera? Maybe there's something we missed."

"Yep." Moser was more technically astute than her partner, thus he'd relinquished the video duties to her. She clicked a few keys, maneuvered the cursor, and switched to another video window of the parking lot, only a different camera angle, aimed more toward the front of the store. It was zoomed in slightly tighter than the other had been and didn't afford a view including the Road Runner or the van. "Ready?"

"Yeah. But cue it to the place right before they come out with the cart. *Please*."

"Sure," she said as she jockeyed the fast-forward button to the appropriate timecode. "Okay, she should be coming out any moment...." A few seconds went by. "There. Here's Rose, in the cart, mom's pushing her outside," she added. "The girl's eating something. Probably one of the cookies we found by the car."

Ramage watched in silence. He was studying all the moving parts. An older woman was exiting the store a few seconds after Phoenix, wheeling her cart in another direction. Phoenix continues walking toward the camera as she approaches her car, before exiting the frame.

A moment later, another customer, a man—a very large man—steps out into the sun. He's carrying a single plastic grocery bag. A phone is in his other hand. He stops a few feet from the store's entrance. He looks up from his phone, out across the lot in the direction Phoenix is walking. He's just standing there.

"Who's this guy? Notice anything strange?"

"Besides being ginormous?"

"He's standing there, with his phone. Not talking on it. Maybe texting."

"That in itself isn't particularly strange, but he is just standing there, looking out at the lot," she said. "What're you thinking?" Moser asked.

"Not sure yet."

The clip continued and even though Phoenix and Rose had now exited the camera frame, both officers knew it was only a matter of moments before things would go south. The officers' eyes remained glued on this human monolith as they waited for the small crowd's reaction.

"There!!" Ramage said sharply, his finger pointing to this new person of interest. In the video, they could clearly see the moment that Phoenix must've screamed because it got the attention of everyone within earshot. Two store employees were racing outside, and a handful of other customers were rushing over to see what the matter was.

"This guy's the only one not reacting," Moser said, her senses heightened. She exchanged a quick glance with her partner. "He's just…he's just walking away, like nothing's happening," she added.

Ramage's hand slapped the desk. "Bingo!" he barked. He met Moser's gaze. They might finally have something to work with. "Work your magic, partner. See what you can do to enhance this and get some useable closeups of this guy. And see if you can find any more cameras that may've captured him. I don't have to tell you that every second counts."

"Got it," she replied, already at work on the keyboard.

"I gotta go take a leak."

"Thanks for sharing," she muttered.

"*Hot damn!*" Ramage exclaimed as he headed out the door with something resembling a half-smile. He'd almost made it to the loo when, halfway down the hall, he was approached by another officer, Sergeant Mike Patterson. "Jeff, got a second?"

"Hey, Mike, what's up?"

"This just came in. Not sure if there's any connection, but I thought you should see it," he said, handing Ramage a printout. Patterson watched the lead investigator's face closely as he scanned the page.

Ramage's smile was short-lived.

CHAPTER 11

POP POP'S HOME
GUEST COTTAGE
FRIDAY, 7:35 PM

P HOENIX WAS TAKING an unscheduled nap in the main house. Spinning a hundred donuts was tiring work. She'd hit the wall an hour before. Curt had hit the wall as well.

Several times in fact.

He rubbed his sore knuckles as he surveyed the four deep holes he'd punched in the drywall. He peeked through the garage window on his way to the main house. The Road Runner was still in there, thankfully. As he entered the kitchen, he saw Pop Pop sipping a Guinness Extra Stout from a proper beer glass and staring into space.

Curt stuffed his red, swollen hands into the pockets of his cargo shorts. "Hey," he said numbly.

Pop nodded to his son-in-law. "Get yourself a glass, join me. There're more where this came from. Behind the eggs."

"Don't mind if I do, thanks," Curt said. He reached into the back of the fridge and returned to the table with two bottles, and a glass of his own. He grabbed the opener from the table, and after carefully opening the top of his, he took the next two minutes doing a slow, deliberate transfer of the dark, chocolate brown stout into the drinking vessel. The tan, frothy head was beautiful. Like a beer commercial. "Phoenix still crashed out?"

"Last I checked," Pop Pop replied softly. "She's been running on adrenaline. Hell, we all have." He raised his glass, and Curt clinked his against it. Atypical to them, there was no expression of good wishes. No celebratory *Cheers!* or *Salud!* or *Prost!* There was nothing to celebrate.

Not until Rose came home safe.

Curt took a long pull of the stout, his upper lip buried in the creamy head. His tastebuds registered the notes of roasted malt, coffee, and dry, bittersweet barley, but he didn't appreciate them as he usually did. He set down his glass and looked at Pop Pop, who seemed to be interested in Curt's hands.

"What happened to you?"

"Me? Nothing," Curt lied. "I, uh, wanted to ask if you might have a little spackle."

Down the hall, atop the tiny guest bed, Phoenix was in a heavy REM sleep, curled into the tightest possible fetal position, just shy of the one she'd once assumed in the cramped quarters of her mother's womb. Her subconscious was revisiting the dreaded rabbit hole, a spot it hadn't gone to in several years.

Her shields were down, and the subconscious was cruelly replaying a memory she could normally only imagine, one made horrific at the thought of her wombmate and would-be sister, writhing and cringing in her clinic-tainted amniotic sac, bathing in the caustic saline solution for the hour it would take to abort her. It had been a fate she herself had been spared only because she'd been an undetected twin.

As the imagery intensified in her mind, Phoenix's eyelids fluttered against her rapid eye movements, barely able to hold them. Images of her aborted twin faded to black, yet the sounds only she could hear—those of a newborn's cry—remained. After a few moments those sounds morphed into another cry for help. It was unknown, and at first distorted, but immediately unsettling. It was a young girl's voice now; it cried out to her from the void, and it was coming from a place of fear:

"MOMMY!!!"

Phoenix hadn't completely emerged yet, but she screamed out her response: *"ROSE!!!! Rose, where are you?!!"* Her eyes flew open, and she bolted upright, drenched in sweat and completely disoriented. Luke and Prick sprang up onto the bed to save her.

"Rose...Rose...Rose..." she was whispering to herself, her eyes closed again, as both Curt and Pop Pop flew into the room. "Rosie...."

Curt sat on the edge of the bed and held her in his arms. "It's me, baby...it's Curt," he said softly as he brushed away a shock of hair the sweat had glued to her face. "You were having a bad dream, sweetie. We're here," he offered, kissing her forehead.

As the clouds began to dissipate, Phoenix looked over to Pop Pop, who all but filled the doorframe. Luke and Prick tried to kiss away her pain, and as her hands found the pooches' faces, she kissed each.

"It was so real…I heard her calling for me," she managed before breaking into deep sobs. Curt continued caressing her as Pop Pop's gaze shifted to the nightstand and the two peachy-white blobs shapeshifting in the lit lava lamp. She hadn't switched that thing on in seven years, he thought to himself. And he fully understood why.

Pop Pop listened to her sobs, and he felt powerless to help. He knew she was conjuring up her primordial past and was stirring the crucible again now, even if she wasn't fully aware she was doing so. It had once been both the source of her pain and the cauldron of fire she had tapped to both find her identity and forge her steel.

She's risen from the ashes before. Twice…

Pop Pop's thoughts vanished into the ether as Phoenix's phone came alive. Seconds later, from the other room, he could hear Curt's ring as well. And his own.

THE I-15 NORTH
NORTH OF KANAB
SOUTH OF SALT LAKE CITY, UTAH
FRIDAY, LATE

Creep was staring out the window, rocking in his seat like a nervous toddler as the Jeep pressed on like a bat out of hell. He'd never seen somebody die before and he was having a devil of a time processing the event.

Dieter's eyes were constantly monitoring the mirrors with

occasional glances to their sleeping guest in the second seat. Not a word had been said since leaving the dead cop behind. He glanced over at his brother and knew he couldn't explain anything to him right now.

This hadn't been part of the plan. At all. Blood had been spilled, and what should've been a relatively simple procurement had escalated into a whole different level of risk. He'd never killed someone before tonight. It wasn't remorse he was feeling. No, it wasn't that, though he would have preferred not having to shoot him.

He shook his head and rubbed his eyes. He was tired as hell, and instead of grabbing some much-needed sleep in Kanab, his hand had been forced and they were motoring north. There was absolutely no way they'd be able to drive another fifteen hours straight to Coeur d'Alene. He knew his tolerances. They'd have to find safe harbor somewhere in between, and that was looking like Provo.

If Creep had ever learned to drive it might be slightly less arduous, as they could switch off, but it was all on Dieter right now, and they had a schedule to keep. Barring any roadblocks or unforeseen circumstances, an eight-hour rest stop in Provo would make the next, and hopefully final, leg of the journey sustainable. He'd prefer Pocatello to Provo, but he'd just have to see what their stamina allowed.

One thing he did know was that driving at night, in silence and being dog-ass tired and saddle-sore, was getting to him. He turned on the stereo in hopes some tunes might provide some stimulation. As the CD cued to its track, he was delighted. He hadn't used the stereo since leaving the dealership two weeks before and forgotten his Radiohead disc was still in the player. The snare drum and simple guitar riff comprised the twenty-second intro that quite serendipitously led into his favorite track, "Creep."

"Hey, brother, they're playing your song," he said with a half-teasing smile.

Creep slowly turned away from the window. "What?"

"Your song. Shh, just listen," Dieter said, burying a private chuckle. The girl was lights-out, he figured, so he boosted the volume.

Creep enjoyed music, more than most people even, so he paid close attention. After all, it was his brother's recommendation, and this sounded like a sweet love song. He stared straight ahead, absorbing the words and the melody. He was enjoying it, up until the grungy shift that came at one minute in, when the chorus began penetrating him like a million lances. It not only called him by name but reminded him that he was indeed a weirdo and that he didn't belong here....

Two and a half minutes later, the song faded away but only after the creepazoid chorus had repeated itself twice more. Dieter switched off the unit and looked over at his sibling. He hadn't expected to see his massive shoulders heaving, or his snot-covered face contorted in such a place of pain.

"Hey, man…it's okay…it's just a song," Dieter said. Mr. Sensitivity he'd never been, and this was as much comfort as he knew how to provide. "Just a friggin' song…sheesh. And don't get any snot on my leather."

He shook his head and refocused his energies on the road. It was going to be a long ass drive....

CHAPTER 12

POP POP'S HOME
FRONT LAWN
SATURDAY, 8:55 AM

OFFICERS RAMAGE AND Moser sipped their coffees and watched yet a sixth news van circle the block looking for a place to park. Five other news teams, each consisting of a correspondent and a videographer, had managed to park their rigs down the block and get their equipment set up.

A portable podium had been positioned halfway up the driveway, and several microphones, each with a local station ID displayed on its plastic mic flag, were mounted to it. Videographers had each already framed their shots in anticipation of the press conference that would be underway shortly.

Neighbors, as well as curious onlookers, stood across the street. They were aware that one of their own had been abducted, and the community's concern was palpable. Things like this happened all the time on the TV news. But never here. This was a nice neighborhood. A safe neighborhood.

Phoenix and Curt, as well as Pop Pop, stood together, several feet off to the side of the podium. Each of their faces displayed their degrees of pain, uncertainty, and sleep deprivation. Other than Phoenix's unscheduled nap the day before, none of them had slept a wink. Phoenix wore her ASU ballcap and had her hair in a ponytail, as she did most days.

"Should we wait for the other crew?" Moser asked.

"Let's give 'em five more minutes," Ramage said with a quick glance at his watch.

Moser nodded in agreement and looked to her left where the family was standing. "I can't imagine being in their shoes," she said very softly. "They can barely stand, they're so tired."

Ramage followed her gaze, stealthily looking over the top his Styrofoam cup. They did indeed look like a strong breeze might topple them. "Yeah. We'll keep things brief. I'll start, and if they're still up to it, we'll let them make a statement."

"Roger that," she said.

A very winded videographer was jogging down the sidewalk toward the house. He was hefting a carbon fiber tripod, a long lens video camera and microphone, and several cables. His reporter walked urgently behind him. She was holding her phone and a notepad.

"Sorry we're late, thanks for waiting," Monica Travers said as she approached the officers. Her blonde, shoulder length hair was fashionably styled and her makeup impeccable. She belonged to the zero body fat club, and Ramage couldn't help but think she could use a hot meal. They all knew each other well; there was always crime to report on in the greater Phoenix area, and officer-reporter familiarity came with that.

"We're live in two minutes. You good to go?" Ramage asked.

Travers looked over at her camera guy, who was stringing

mic cable over to the podium. The camera was already in place amongst the others. He wiped the sweat from his brow and gave her a thumbs up. "Yeah."

As he fell back into the assembled pack, Ramage tossed back the last of his coffee and glanced at his watch once more. "Okay, showtime," he said to himself.

Moser took a position with the family, giving them a look of assurance as Ramage approached the podium. Videographers took this as a cue to roll their cameras and they each stabbed the red record buttons with their right thumbs. Ramage looked out into the crowd and saw that six cameras were indeed rolling. After a quick nod to the family and his partner, he cleared his throat and addressed the assembled crowd.

"Good morning, everyone. Thank you for coming on short notice," he began before directing his eye contact to the cameras, making sure to sweep across each lens as he did. "I'm Officer Jeffrey Ramage, Gilbert Police Department, and I'm the Lead Investigator on this case. I'm joined by my partner, Officer Bethany Moser, and the family of Rose Martinsen. Before they make a statement, and before we take any questions, please allow me to get you up to speed with what we know so far about this case," he said, pausing for a sip from the water bottle he'd stashed there.

"As you know it's been over twenty-four hours since this incident began. Here are the specifics: At approximately 7:45 a.m. Friday, we received a call reporting there had been a child abduction. A child under the age of eighteen, and an abduction by a stranger. The call came from the parking lot of the Oasis Market where the child's mother, Phoenix Martinsen, had been shopping with her daughter, six-year-old Rose Martinsen."

Ramage paused as he lifted an 11x14 color photograph from behind the podium. The photo was mounted on a piece of foam core, and it showed the smiling image of Rose, enlarged from her first-grade school portrait. He rested it on the edge of the podium, off to his right, and held it in position long enough to allow the cameras, and the folks at home, a good look at it.

From her vantage point, standing between Curt and Pop Pop, Phoenix watched as the officer propped up the photo for the press. She wiped away tears as her lip quivered. This was really happening. He was really talking about her baby.

"Rose Martinsen is Caucasian, female, approximately thirty-nine inches tall, weighing approximately forty pounds, with long red hair, as you can see in the photograph. Several eyewitnesses, along with security videos, corroborate statements taken from the family, and we have since located the stolen GMC van used during the abduction." He paused to set the photo down, resting it against the front of the podium. "We have all our resources working on this case, including the FBI, the National Crime Information Center–NCIC, state and local agencies, and we're working on several leads. I'd like to thank those in the neighborhood who have cooperated with officers and given statements. Personnel at both Oasis Market and the Circle K have been very helpful as well. As I've mentioned, this is a stranger abduction involving a young child, and we all are working around the clock to bring Rose home to her family. We'd like to ask the family if—"

"Do we know where the child may have been taken? Do we believe they've left the state or—?" an overzealous male reporter blurted out before Ramage cut him off. His expression telegraphed his displeasure. *Channel 7....*

"Please save any questions until after the family has had a chance to make their statements, and I'll try to answer them to the best of my ability." He looked over to Phoenix, Curt, and Pop Pop, offering them a nod of encouragement. Pop Pop gestured politely, yielding to the parents.

Phoenix and Curt exchanged looks and walked together to the podium. She stood before the bank of microphones, her eyes cast down, trained on the logos of the plastic mic flags. All the networks were there, plus a couple of Spanish stations.

She closed her eyes briefly, taking in the enormity of the moment, then slowly opened them. Her gaze tilted upward to regard the equipment and the crowd, reporters, officers and neighbors alike. Their next-door neighbor bit her lip, nodding slowly in a show of support, then put her hand on her heart. Phoenix nodded back, mouthing a *thanks* to the woman.

A clicking of still cameras filled the silence as Phoenix took a deep breath and zeroed in on the videographers' lenses. She tried to imagine people at home watching from their living rooms, from a computer, perhaps even on a monitor at the airport. She made deliberate eye contact with each of the six lenses trained on her. This was her opportunity. Maybe, just maybe somebody might know something that could help.

"My name is Phoenix...Martinsen," she said in as strong a voice as she could muster. She cleared her throat before continuing. "Yesterday, our whole world fell apart when our six-year-old daughter, my angel, Rose, was...taken...while I was...while I was putting groceries in my car at the local market. We were on our way to school, where she was supposed to be having a fun last day before the winter break. *Christmas* break! The last day before Christmas break. She was supposed to be singing her special song in the school's holiday program. She was supposed to be the Christmas angel..." she managed before pausing to wipe away a tear.

Pop Pop, hearing the pause, looked up from his shoes to make eye contact with her. He too was teary. He nodded to her and mouthed *I love you*. Curt put his hand on her shoulder.

Phoenix took strength from both as she continued. "She was supposed to be the Christmas angel, and she had practiced very hard on her song. Rose should be home with us right now, doing what little girls do, and being with her family as we all look forward to celebrating Christmas together," she said, her voice quaking a little. "But...she isn't."

Phoenix paused to collect herself and Ramage whispered in her ear. "You okay? We can stop now if you'd prefer not to—"

Phoenix looked him in the eye and shook her head, indicating she wanted to continue. Phoenix tapped into what was left of her reserve power source. Her heart and soul were but dry kindling, and she needed to ignite it. Her thoughts went to her scared little girl. The one who'd cried out to her from her nightmare, calling out to her in the dark: "*Mommy!!!*"

With that thought, and every fiber of her being, she felt the flint inside of her produce the spark she needed. Her core had been relit and something new was burning through her veins.

POCATELLO, IDAHO
A 3-STAR HOLIDAY INN
SAME MOMENT

The shower was running. At least the little girl knew how to shower by herself. Creep wasn't at all prepared to help with that.

X

Dieter had gone out to get breakfast sandwiches while his brother watched Rose. Creep was sitting on the bed, glued to the television screen and the lady talking on the news. The one with the red hair, the lady from the store. Yesterday. A long time ago.

She was crying. Creep's mouth hung ajar as he watched, trying to process it all. She was on TV. Talking about Rose. He glanced over in the direction of the bathroom. The water was still running. The lady on TV got his attention again.

Phoenix was staring right down the barrel of the lens now. Her eyes were red, and swollen with tears, yet the ferocity behind them was unmistakable. It burned through the TV and into Creep's room. And into his heart. She had the attention of her target audience.

"All we want is our daughter back. Safe and sound. Please, if you know anything…if you have our little girl…." Her voice broke, and her hand went to her mouth. The man standing next to her was trying to lead her away, but she shrugged off his hand. She wasn't done.

Creep glanced down at the tiny remote in his giant palm as his thumb hovered over the off button. He didn't think he could watch anymore. The lady was crying, was in pain, was talking directly to him, and her emotions were searing his entire being.

Still, he couldn't look away.

His thoughts flashed to the abduction. To the scared little girl who just wanted her mommy. She had done nothing wrong, yet they had taken her away, away from her family. Her parents were scared. She was scared. And right now, he felt more than a little scared as well.

The voice snapped him back.

"Rose! Rose! If you can hear me, honey, Mommy and Daddy are looking for you, sweetheart! Stay strong, baby!" the TV lady said, almost yelling.

Creep pivoted his head to the bathroom. The shower was still going.

"If you have our little girl…" Phoenix said, slowly, deliberately, pausing for effect, "…do the right thing. Return Rose to us. Unharmed. She needs her mommy and daddy and her pop-pop. And her doggies. In a few days it will be Christmas. Please…for the love of God, bring her back to us…" she said before falling into Curt's arms as they walked away from the podium.

A policeman stepped up and was just about to talk when Creep heard the shower turning off. He switched off the set and stood. He began pacing back and forth, along all three sides of his bed.

"I need a towel!" the voice called from the bathroom.

"On the wall," Creep answered through the door, trying not to short-circuit. As he made his third round of pacing, the sound of the card key in the door froze him in his tracks. Dieter entered, carrying two fast food bags. He closed the door behind him and locked it with the security bar. His brother looked like he was going to blow a gasket.

"What the hell's the matter with you?" he hissed, setting the food bags on the small table. "Where's the girl?" Creep pointed to the bathroom. He stopped pacing but his eyes continued.

"She take a shower?"

Creep nodded, his head clearly elsewhere. Dieter took a couple of steps toward the bathroom and barked through the door. "Hurry up in there. Your food's gonna get cold." He reached into one of the bags and tossed a sandwich to Creep. "Eat up, we've gotta hit the road...gotta get back before the storm hits!" he said before burying his face into the greasy, sausage-and-egg monstrosity.

Creep dug into his, stuffing half of it in his mouth with all the gusto of a great white.

"Close your mouth when you're chewing...jeezus!" Dieter said with a mouthful.

CHAPTER 13

GILBERT POLICE STATION
SATURDAY, 10:35 AM

OFFICERS RAMAGE AND Moser were seated at a round table in the corner of Ramage's office. With them were Phoenix and Curt. Moser's laptop was open, but the screen was only visible to her.

"Can we get you a coffee or anything?" Ramage asked the couple.

"Oh, gawd, no, thanks...I've already got the shakes," Phoenix replied. Curt waved off with a gesture indicating *No, thanks.*

"Okay, first off, let me just tell you that you did great this morning. Press events, especially under these circumstances, are hard. Even for us, and we do a ton of 'em. Anyway, you did well," Ramage said, looking at both.

"Thanks," Curt replied softly. He was still emotionally spent. Phoenix nodded weakly.

"Now," Ramage said, making brief eye contact with his

partner. "There have been some new developments." Officer Moser nodded, handing him a thin file folder.

Phoenix and Curt both leaned in a little closer as Ramage produced a photo. "This is an enlargement of a screengrab we obtained from the security cameras outside the Oasis Market on Friday morning. Quality's not the best, but it's not bad. This was taken at the same time you were there, Mrs. Martinsen, and at the same moment you had yelled for help."

Phoenix studied the photo, her brow furrowed. "I saw this guy. Yesterday. While we were shopping. I saw him... he was shopping. Pretty hard to miss someone that big." She momentarily replayed the experience in her mind.

Curt asked for the photo, and as he stared at it his expression began to take on a slow burn of anger. "You think this guy had something to do with it?" he asked. "This fucker?"

Phoenix looked at her husband. He almost never cursed but she knew where he was coming from. "What's his story? Do we know where he is?" she asked.

"We have reason to believe this individual may have been involved, possibly as a scout, in collusion with the other individual in the van," Ramage replied.

"What specifically makes this fucker a person of interest?" Phoenix asked, echoing Curt's sentiments.

"This was taken at the exact same moment you were in distress, Mrs. Martinsen," Moser interjected. "While you were screaming for help and other shoppers—even store personnel—were reacting, assisting you, this...*guy*...is the only one who didn't react. At all. In fact, a moment later, he just walked away," she added, trying not to use their descriptor.

"And he's in custody?" Curt asked hopefully.

"No, I'm afraid he's not, but we have widely disseminated

the photo. Both locally and nationally," Ramage replied, clenching his jaw. "Another camera captured video of the van but didn't produce as clear an image of the driver. Still, it gives a basic idea as to his height—he's on the shorter side. As we'd mentioned, we recovered the GMC van in the alley behind the Circle K. What we've since learned—and this was gleaned from security cameras behind the gas station—is that there was another vehicle there waiting. A getaway vehicle."

He turned to his partner, then back to the couple. "Officer Moser can show you this footage if you'd like to see it but it will be troubling to watch. In it you can see Rose transferred from one vehicle to another, and it happens in a matter of seconds. If you don't feel up to it—"

Phoenix jumped in. "We want to see it, please," she said urgently, looking at Curt, then back to the officers. Curt cautiously nodded his consent.

Moser spun the computer around so that they could all watch together. "When you're ready," she said, a sensitive look at both.

Phoenix nodded. "Ready," she replied softly. She put her hand to her mouth as Moser clicked the mouse and the video clip began. Initially the camera showed a Dumpster and a partial glimpse at another vehicle parked behind it. A moment later, the GMC van roars into the empty spot. "Oh my God…" Phoenix muttered, her emotions a cocktail of fear, uncertainty, and intense anger.

The driver's door opens, and as the driver emerges, he quickly comes around to the cargo door. We now see the man Ramage described. Short, sandy blonde hair visible from beneath his ballcap, dark glasses. "Jeezus…" Phoenix muttered, wanting to jump into the scene and kill him herself.

The man looks around, then slides open the cargo door and grabs their girl. "You bastard!" Phoenix screamed as the clip continued. "Fuck!!!"

He's wiry but strong as he plucks her from the van and carries the youngster over to the other vehicle. Less than ten seconds go by before he backs it out into the alley, providing first looks at the getaway car, a late model Jeep, off-white. No plates. It shifts into drive and speeds away down the alley. The entire event lasted less than a minute.

Phoenix is sobbing now. Curt put his arm around her, and she disappeared into him, a sobbing mess. Moser clicked the stop button and looked down at the table. Ramage rubbed his face, giving them time.

Several moments went by before Phoenix's face re-emerged, but it was another version of it. Her red-rimmed, bloodshot eyes had a renewed intensity, and her features were set, locked in an expression that left no doubt as to her mindset. This was the face of a mama bear who'd just had her favorite cub fucked with. "Do...do we know the where-abouts of this vehicle, Officer Ramage?" she asked with calm, eerie formality.

Moser handed her partner another sheet from the file, a computer printout of an inter-agency report. Ramage re-acquainted himself with the facts before answering. "Mr. and Mrs. Martinsen, we've received a report of a...of a sighting... of the vehicle in question," he began, tapping the paper with his free hand. "This information came from the Kanab Police Department," he said.

"Kanab." Curt said. "Where the hell is that? Kanab, Arizona? Kanab, Mexico? *Afghanistan?* Where the hell is Kanab?" he said before checking himself. "Sorry...where's Kanab?"

"I'm sorry. Kanab is a small town…just north of the Arizona border. Kanab, Utah."

"Okay…" Phoenix said, seething at the idea her child had now been transported across state lines. "Do we have eyes on them? Did you get confirmation our daughter was there? That she's okay? Please…don't bullshit us. Is Rose okay?" she pressed.

Ramage considered his response carefully before proceeding. "A local officer there, an Officer Berreth with the Kanab PD, called in a vehicle stop he was making there. Last night. Around dusk. He'd pulled over the vehicle and had radioed in his initial concerns. He mentioned a young girl, matching Rose's description, in the Jeep with two male subjects whom he'd considered suspicious."

"Oh, gawd," Phoenix whispered.

"During the traffic stop, the officer proceeded to ask for the driver's license and registration, which had been supplied to him," Ramage said, pausing to collect his thoughts.

"And…?" Curt prompted.

"And, during the course of this exchange, the driver of said vehicle pulled a weapon and fired on the officer, hitting him several times," Ramage said through clenched teeth. His intense anger just below the surface.

"Fuck. Fuck. *Fuck!*" Phoenix screamed.

Ramage exhaled a deep breath. "The officer died at the scene," he whispered.

"Dear God!" Phoenix gasped.

"The vehicle. Rose…where were they headed? What new information have they provided?" Curt asked urgently.

"All we know is that they left in a hurry. North, probably. Our guess is they wouldn't be returning to Arizona. Whether or not their final destination is Utah, we don't know. I don't think so, though."

"Why do you say that?" Phoenix probed.

"The officer, Officer Berreth, was found in the street. He was still holding the driver's license in his hand."

"That's good, right?" Curt asked hopefully.

"Ordinarily, yes. But we've been told it was a fake license. Name of Danny Kirwan, at a fake address in Idaho."

"Kirwan..." Curt said.

"Yeah, we're pretty sure this perp wasn't the lead guitarist with Fleetwood Mac," Moser said.

"You mean Lindsey Buckingham," Curt said.

"No, they mean the *original* Fleetwood Mac," Phoenix muttered to herself without taking her eyes off the giant in the photo. It was an automatic correction. This was her *Jeopardy!* category, after all, and she answered aloud without even knowing she had.

"Regardless, the ID was fake, so all we have is a confirmation of the vehicle being a 2007 Jeep Commander, white metallic probably. That and the occupants: two adult males, one female child matching Rose's description. Heading north."

"This was last night," Curt said to himself.

"Around dusk, yes," Ramage said. "Which gives them a head start, as the incident wasn't reported until sometime later."

"What does your gut tell you?" Phoenix asked pointedly.

"My gut tells me they'd want to get out of Utah."

"Which leaves..." Curt's voice trailed off.

SAGE JUNCTION, IDAHO

Being as his copilot was utterly useless as a conversationalist, let alone navigator, Dieter made an executive decision to get off the I-15. He felt exposed out here, and on top of being sleep deprived, his paranoia was going full tilt. It was only a matter of time before they might get the attention of another trooper, so it was time to change things up.

He'd fueled up before leaving Pocatello so at the junction of Highway 33, they jogged west at Sage Junction. Now that blood had been spilled—and that was something that had never happened in all the years they'd been doing this—the scenario had changed. Drastically.

"I need to pee," Rose said groggily from the back seat. Her breakfast sandwich and potato wedges had satisfied her hunger, and the juice boxes she'd consumed necessitated a stop.

Dieter silently cursed, as he hated adding variables to this mission. The only game in town appeared to be found ahead, with the sign advertising the Sage Junction Port of Entry.

The Jeep approached the facility cautiously. There was a smattering of cars in the lot, plus several trucks that looked like they were in the process of being weighed. Not ideal by any means, and a bit busier than Dieter would like to chance. He turned to look over his right shoulder at the tiny passenger. "How bad do you have to go?"

"Bad," Rose replied.

"Look, you'll have to hold it a little longer. The restrooms are closed here," he lied. *Damn it.* The way forward, on the 33, offered a whole lot of nothing. On one hand, a whole lot of nothing might offer them some anonymity, but other than that there seemed to be zero else in the plus column.

"But I—" Rose started to protest.

"But…but…but. Look, hon, you might just have to go in your Pampers. That's what they're there for."

"But I'm not a baby," she whined. Her tears were in the on-deck circle.

"Fuggit," Dieter muttered between clenched teeth as he made a slow and fully compliant U-turn back toward the I-15. It'd be another two hundred miles north before they'd connect with the I-90 west at Butte but options were few out here.

"I thought we were stopping for potty and snacks," Creep said, his disappointment evident.

"You thought…" Dieter muttered, shaking his head. "You just keep thinkin', Einstein. Let me know when you come up with a brilliant plan, okay?" he said, dripping with sarcasm. "Until then, just shut up. *I* need to think."

Does Pampers make a friggin' Harry and the Hendersons size? Fuck me.

CHAPTER 14

PLEASANT HILL, MISSOURI
THE CLIENT'S MANOR
SATURDAY AFTERNOON

WITH APOLOGIES TO the proverb's originators, it could be said that Missouri loves company. Perhaps especially so if you happen to be a well-connected and exceedingly wealthy Missourian with a penchant for very young children. There was much to do to prepare for such company, and the party was only two days away.

By design, the manor itself wasn't particularly ostentatious. Clocking in at a tick more than six thousand square feet, the exterior presented as tastefully elegant but not excessively so. No more so than other properties in the area, anyway. Its six spacious bedrooms each enjoyed an en suite private bathroom and were spread across both floors, three on each, in order to afford maximum privacy and security.

Though this Pleasant Hill manor was indeed pleasant, it was the geographical setting that had attracted the buyer, as it enjoyed a private, four-acre lot in an area of similarly valued properties, all owned by well-to-do types who only spent time there in the warmer spring and summer months. As a result, privacy wouldn't be a concern this Christmas. Privacy and discretion had been promised to his party guests, and this would be his sixth annual Christmas Eve pedo-palooza.

The property's location, and its proximity to the nearby Lees Summit airport made it a convenient, low-profile hub for his intimate gathering of wealthy and equally pervy pals, who'd be flying in on Monday from different corners including Tampa, Dallas, Baltimore, and San Francisco. Missouri loves company.

And they were all particularly interested in meeting the new acquisition: *the redhead.*

The property also boasted three separate garage buildings, each of which could accommodate up to four vehicles—or three, if one happened to be a limousine, which was sometimes the case. An indoor, heated pool was housed in another building off to the rear of the main house, as were two other nondescript buildings. One housed equipment and served as storage, and the other housed young, longer term "guests" when applicable. Up to twelve at a time. Current residency was at ten. It had no windows.

With four plus acres of surrounding area, and the nearest homes being vacant this time of year, the party's music wouldn't present a noise concern. Nor would any screams if those were to happen. Like happened last year. *Damn, that was a great party.*

The Client had three discreet staff employees helping with arrangements. His right-hand gal, whom he addressed only by the nickname of Candy, served primarily in the "procurement" department. This job description entailed finding and grooming young talent, most often girls in the lower teen years, and assuring invited friends were well taken care of.

The younger the better, it seemed, and in recent years the age range of "guests" at the manor had trended downward. Under fourteen was always preferable, and the rare, under-twelve item was considered a delicacy. What had made the previous year's party particularly noteworthy for his well-paying perv pals had been the indulging of fantasies with the fresh faced, blonde, nine-year-old identical twins, who had been plucked from a shopping mall in Minnesota. They both clocked in at about four-foot-ten, and the guys were still chatting up the dark web about them.

Those very twins, MacKenzie and Rebekah Olson, were still on property, though they were now seasoned ten-year-olds and veterans with a lot of mileage on them. It was they who were busy with the cleaning duties, preparing the rooms, and various other tasks on this Saturday before Christmas. Their vacant expressions spoke volumes of their inner demons, and their trauma. This would be their second Christmas away from home, a place they could hardly even remember.

Beginning their second year here in hell.

"The Client" was how he was known to his Idaho broker. His true identity wasn't shared with them, which offered an all-important layer of buffer and anonymity. Outside of Candy, few knew his real name, and he endeavored to keep it that way.

He really had no occasion to mix with his neighbors when they were on site, which wasn't often anyway. If he did have an interaction with any of the locals, at the airport or in town, he'd provided them with an alias: Richard Atkinson, after a particularly deviant grade school chum who'd been a real *Dick*. Seemed fitting. And it was far enough removed from his given name: Sebastian Brewer.

Sebastian Brewer was a man of few talents, other than

keeping his true nature private. At fifty-one, he still had a boyish charm and a deep tan, even in these winter months, all thanks to the tanning bed in the equipment room. His family was steeped in old money, and he hadn't earned a penny of his considerable wealth. And he was fine with all of it. He had no connection to them anymore, which was for the best.

"I understand there's been…a complication," he said to his number two as he looked out the tall wall of windows that provided a view of his property.

"Yes, but it shouldn't change anything. Delivery is still set for Monday morning, and there will be ample time to prepare your gift for the big reveal."

"Nothing that can be traced to me…to us?"

"Nothing. The item is in transit to the broker as we speak. She'll be prepped, prettified and ready for the flight, and I've secured sufficient cash to be paid upon delivery. This one should be special," Candy added, a little too lasciviously. Like her partner in crime, she'd long ago surrendered what was left of her soul.

"And the other?"

"Yes. They'll be delivered together."

"Mm, good," Brewer said. "Keep me advised, and make sure the twins eat a good lunch. They're a bit thin and look like they could use a good meal. There've been requests for them, so they'll be in play as well."

"I'll see to it," Candy assured him.

"Please do. Anything comes up, I'll be working on my tan."

CHAPTER 15

POP POP'S HOME
THE GUEST COTTAGE
SATURDAY AFTERNOON

S ITTING AROUND WAITING for updates was driving them crazy. After they'd returned home from their briefing in Gilbert, Curt came clean on the mayhem he'd unleashed on the cottage's drywall. It needed repairs, so they'd gone to the nearby building supply place to get some drywall, putty knives, and copious amounts of spackle. The paint they still had in the garage.

While Curt stuffed some balled up newspaper into some of the bigger holes, Pop Pop cut some fist-sized pieces of drywall to insert into others. Phoenix was pretty good with a putty knife, and she slathered it with precision. Curt had pummeled the wall pretty good, and it would take a bunch of the product to erase the evidence.

"Remind me never to piss you off, Curt," Pop Pop said as he worked on a huge hole.

"Sorry, guys," Curt said. "I guess I let the moment get the best of me."

"Don't need to apologize. I've done the same thing, for a different reason, but the same thing. There's release in that," Pop Pop replied. "Just don't make it a habit," he added with a tired chuckle.

"Yeah, you might want to save some of that Incredible Hulk action for when they catch these bastards," Phoenix said as she feathered in a layer. "God help them if I get my chance."

The three of them worked in silence for several minutes as they considered what would be their individual responses to the situation when the time came. None of them was pretty.

As they waited for the wall paste to dry, the three of them sat on the floor, leaning against the wall, the men each downing a Guinness while Phoenix nursed a Sunny D. All things considered, the wall looked decent—nothing that some paint, and maybe a few strategically placed picture frames, couldn't fix.

Curt stood and ran his fingers over the surface. It was dry enough to paint now, he'd decided. "Hey, hon, would you mind getting the can of flat white latex from the garage when you're done? Stir stick and a couple of brushes?"

"Were you asking me, handsome?" Pop Pop joked, attempting some much-needed levity.

"You wish," Curt answered. "Hon?" he asked, turning to Phoenix as he did.

"Sure," Phoenix said, taking her last swig as she got up off the floor.

"A couple pieces of light sandpaper too please," he added.

"On it!" she said as she exited the cottage.

Curt's stomach growled loudly.

"Heard that…y'know, we've all got to keep our strength up during all this," Pop Pop said to his son-in-law.

"Right. So…"

"So, when we're done here, let's the three of us go get some good grub. Lord knows I don't feel like cooking anything right now, and none of us have eaten so much as a muffin since I don't know when."

"Deal," Curt said, his stomach screaming on cue.

"I know a place," Pop Pop replied.

The one-car garage was packed, pretty much to capacity, but not entirely disorganized. Phoenix's Road Runner occupied the lion's share of it, of course, but wall shelving took up both long walls, and it was chock full of miscellany, including cleaning supplies, paints, assorted file boxes, and the like.

Phoenix glanced over at the now-tainted family decal that still adorned the Road Runner's rear window and knew it could no longer remain. She rifled through a couple of drawers until she found the scraper tool and went to work.

She started with the Gracie dog and worked her way down the stick family until she finished with the crossed-out representation of Rose. Tears dripped onto the glass and her fury was channeled into each scrape of the tool. When no trace of the stick people remained, she wiped her eyes, removed any telltale residue with glass cleaner, and set the spray bottle on the shelf.

Phoenix unfolded the step stool and climbed up to inspect the paint cans. There were many, and some appeared to be twenty years old if they were a day. She moved the cans of tan-colored exterior paint out of the way and saw, behind them, a couple of gallon cans of the flat white interior latex.

She grabbed one can by the handle, and in the process of pulling it out, she lost her balance, grabbing at the rack for support. In doing so, one of the file boxes fell off the neighboring shelf and crashed to the ground, spilling file folders and papers everywhere.

"Dammit, Phoenix!" she hissed as she descended the two steps to safety and to a mess. Most of the box's contents had distributed itself underneath the Road Runner so, after she set down the can, she shimmied underneath the car, laying on her back, as she began retrieving everything.

They'd fanned out everywhere, and it was impossible to discern what the stuff was in the cramped and relatively dark space beneath the undercarriage, so she grabbed random handfuls as she could reach them and hugged the growing pile to her chest as she did. Satisfied she'd gotten them all, she slid back out with the messy stack clutched in her left arm.

"Sheesh!" she said as she dusted herself off and placed the papers, and the now-empty file box, on the trunk of the Plymouth. "What the hell is this crap anyway?" she asked under her breath as she started looking at it.

It only took her a few seconds to realize that this had to be one of the old file boxes that had belonged to her late grandfather, Liam. When he'd passed away suddenly at his home in Pebble Beach, California seven years before, she and Curt had added all his old boxes to their own stuff when they made the move to Arizona that following year. They'd never paid any attention to what was in them, figuring they'd go through it all later—much later. And now, all these years having passed, the time had apparently presented itself.

Most of it appeared to be old case files from Liam's time with the Phoenix Police Department. He'd been a good homicide detective, as well as an arson investigator, with the department before the rug had been pulled out from under him with the discovery of his twenty-three-year-old daughter's charred body amongst the burnt shell of a sketchy mobile home he'd never known she was living in.

As one of the first officers on scene, finding the barely identifiable remains of his daughter—who'd estranged herself from her parents at the age of sixteen—in what turned out to be an arson fire to cover up her murder, he began his slow death spiral that day. It would take him twenty years to complete the cycle, but he'd found more than enough assistance at the bottom of vodka bottles and decades of self-loathing.

Christmas, 1974, it had been.... Phoenix allowed herself the briefest of flashbacks, as it was that very Christmas—on Christmas Eve of that year—she'd been the unwitting witness to her mother's murder, by strangulation, by Roger Offermann, *the Awful Man*, aka *the Pirate*.

It had been a memory she'd blocked entirely for the twenty years that followed. Her earliest memories being adopted at age five by her loving Pop Pop and less-than-loving adoptive mother, before their divorce a few years later. They had changed her name to Phoebe at the time of her adoption, mostly out of caution because there might have still been a very bad person out there, and it turns out there had been.

That is, until Phoenix began reconstructing her mysterious past and set about tracking down the serial murderer who'd been responsible for the death of her mother, Rose, as well as forcing the abortion of Phoenix's would-be twin. It was some heady shit, and she rarely went there in her mind to visit it, but this unscheduled, serendipitous moment had presented itself. And now it was spread all over the trunk of her car.

Memories of being five, escaping the gasoline-fueled trailer park murder inferno on Christmas Eve, clutching her secondhand doll, and running barefoot into the night in her jammies…yeah, you kind of want to block that stuff, if possible.

As Phoenix wiped away her tears and memories of that hell, her mind came crashing back to the present, and another Christmas, just days away. *What's with me and Christmases?* The thought of her own little girl out there—somewhere— in a strange place, with evildoers who had taken her from her family, for whatever nefarious purpose and experiencing God only knows what kind of danger and fear. It was all too much to bear .

She slumped down to the seated position and let the volcano erupt.

"Oh, God!" she cried out as the papers cascaded from her hands. "Show me where she is! Help me—help us—find our little girl, Rose…help bring her back home to us, I beg you!" she bellowed to the universe, to the Almighty. Her sobs were interrupted by the rescue team.

"You okay, honey?" Curt asked, flying into the garage. Both he and Pop Pop had come running in response, and the two of them squatted down to comfort her.

"What's the matter, baby?" Pop Pop asked, flush with fatherly concern. "Did you fall?"

Phoenix just shook her head. Her eyes were closed. "I'm okay," she whispered.

"What's all this stuff?" Curt asked, surveying all the files and papers strewn about.

"Fell off the shelf," she said. "Grandpa Liam's stuff, caught me off guard is all…."

"Let me help with that," Pop Pop offered, scooping up some from the garage floor. Curt kissed the top of Phoenix's head and began picking up the documents from the trunk lid.

"I forgot we even kept this old stuff of Liam's. Anything important in here?" he asked. As he grabbed the next file folder, he got the answer to his question.

On the folder's tab was a handwritten annotation.

A single letter.

In red ink.

The painting could wait, they decided.

Phoenix, Curt, and Pop Pop sat at the kitchen table as they poured over the contents of this new file. This potential gift from Liam...from the other side.

As with many unsolved or cold cases, Liam had made it a habit over the years to keep copies of things that were stuck in his craw. Things that didn't sit right with him. Puzzles with missing pieces. Some were case files from long after he'd retired, as a buddy on the force had occasionally shared some copies with him. And this file, *X*, had apparently been one of them.

It was a hodge-podge of information, especially since it had been terribly reshuffled in its crash to the garage floor, so the three of them set about trying to reconstruct it to the best of their ability. What they had laid out before them on the table was a mysterious collection of news clippings, many going back well over a decade, along with pages of notes written in Liam's neat hand, several copies of Missing Person reports, and assorted photographs.

"Hey, I think I might've found something," Phoenix said hopefully.

"What ya got?" Curt asked, craning his neck to peek at the document she held.

"Child Abduction report. Phoenix PD, dating back to 1997. December 1997," she said. Her brow furrowed. "Late December of 1997—just before Christmas," she added.

"Any similarities?" Pop Pop asked, as he came around to her side of the table.

"I don't know yet, but—wait. Says here…a young girl, eleven years old, abducted from the Saguaro Mall in Phoenix," she said, her fingers covering her mouth as she read from the report. "Jessica Falcon…" she managed, looking at her photograph now. "Just a baby…."

"Anything else?" Curt asked.

"Yeah," Phoenix whispered, too upset to read further. She handed Curt the report and he scanned it to get up to speed.

"Report states Jessica was abducted from the mall's parking lot, in broad daylight, while shopping with her mother and her baby sister," Curt read aloud.

"Jeezus…" Pop Pop muttered.

"And multiple eyewitnesses corroborate the mother's statement that a cargo van, parked near the victim's vehicle, was used during the abduction and then exited the property…" Curt said as his voice trailed off, his synapses working overtime.

"Definite similarities, but—wait, what's that clipped to the back there?" Pop Pop asked, indicating the paper clip.

Curt pulled the item off the clip and stared at it for a long moment before dropping it to the table. His face was ashen.

"What is it?" Phoenix uttered, picking it up. "Good... God," she said, the image branding a scar on her brain. Her head collapsed onto her folded arms and her shoulders heaved.

The color photograph, taken by Phoenix PD at the scene, showed a close-up shot of the victim family's Ford Explorer, with emphasis on the family stick figure decal on the rear window: Father, Mother, Jessica, baby sister, and two cats.

Only Jessica was crossed out.

With a big, red X.

CHAPTER 16

LUCKY PUMP GAS & CASINO
BUTTE, MONTANA
SATURDAY, LATE AFTERNOON

THREE TORTUROUS HOURS north on the I-15 finally presented their best opportunity to water the horses. The road signs indicated the Lucky Pump had a wide range of services, and they had a wide range of needs.

This short jog east into the border land area of Montana should do the trick before backtracking slightly to join the I-90 West and to their destination. Then it'd only be another four and a half hours.

Only.

"The sign says Butt!" Creep announced with a goofy laugh fit for a nine-year-old. "We're in Butt!! Ha ha!!"

"It doesn't say *butt*...butthead," the smaller man replied, shaking his head at his unfortunate sibling's idiocy. "It says the name of the town is *Butte*...as in *beaut*-i-full. *Beaut*-i-ful

Butte. We're in Montana, numb nuts. And only for a quick pit stop."

Creep filed away that kernel of new knowledge as he regarded the facilities they were pulling into. In addition to its multiple busy gas pumps, several painted signs on the brick storefront advertised a deli, liquor store and tobacco shop, and a tiny casino.

"Don't get too excited, Creep. We're not gonna be here long."

"Mama told you not to call me that. My name is Willie, not Creep. It hurts my feel—"

"Yeah, whatever. Don't be such a baby," Dieter said as he scanned the property for both potential threats and opportunities. Gas prices were good, and the volume of cars confirmed it to be a good spot. Many had out of state plates. Maybe even a chance to switch buggies. *C'mon, Lucky Pump, let's see if you live up to your name....*

Dieter pulled alongside one of the empty pumps, choosing an open one where his exit would be unobstructed. He killed the engine and made another visual sweep. No cops, which was good. There were a few families coming and going, thus their pit stops as they went on their merry ways to grandmothers' houses, no doubt. A little busy for his tastes but this appeared to be the only port in the storm.

"I have to go to the bathroom!" the tiny item called out from the back seat.

"Me too! I have to—" the giant blurted out.

"Shh!! Both of you! We will in a minute," the little man hissed. He was about to abandon hope when some movement at the door of the convenience store caught his eye.

Dieter watched closely as a lone, fiftyish, lumberjack type

came through the doors and proceeded toward his vehicle. As the man came closer, it became evident he was headed to the SUV parked at the adjacent island of pumps to their right. And the gleaming red vehicle was a beauty. The next thirty seconds of closer study provided a quick-enough assessment of the situation.

The man replaced the nozzle into the pump's holder and affixed his fuel cap. *Full tank.*

He stuffed a wallet into his left rear pocket and climbed into his otherwise-empty 2007 Dodge Durango Limited. *No passengers.* He started the engine. Dieter knew a little about this vehicle as it had been one he'd considered before settling on the Jeep. *Durango…5.7-liter V8 with four-wheel drive.*

As the Durango started to slowly pull away, it also became apparent that the guy wasn't heading for the exits. Not yet anyway. Instead, he pulled around to the side of the store, near the sign offering FREE AIR. The air-filling station, being off to the edge of the establishment, was obscured from the pumps and the rest of the property.

Dieter pulled out his billfold and handed his brother several twenties. He didn't bother counting it as he kept his eyes on the rear hatchback protruding from behind the sign. "Here. Bring a Pamper with you and get her to the restroom. She can change it herself. She's a big girl," he said as he turned over his shoulder, making eye contact. "Aren't you, sweetie?"

He turned back and gave his brother a stern look. "Five minutes. Use the restrooms, get some sandwiches and snacks—*no Cheetos*—and watch for me. Don't talk to anybody. Keep a close eye on her. I'll pull around to the front doors there. Got it?"

This got a nod of acknowledgement from the big man

as he exited the Jeep, grabbed a fresh diaper, and helped the groggy little passenger down.

"And you," Dieter said, pointing at Rose to emphasize his threat, "you don't say a word to anybody. Don't talk, don't cry, and don't try to get away. If you do any of these things, you'll never see your mommy and daddy again ever! You understand me?"

Tears began to form in Rose's tired eyes. The bad man was now threatening to kill her family. In her foggy, terrified state, she softly nodded compliance as the giant took her by the hand and they headed for the store.

The Jeep pulled away from the pumps and slowly made its way toward the air station. There was only the one vehicle there, and the guy was busy topping off his tires when Dieter pulled up.

"Excuse me," Dieter said, mustering up a fake smile as he exited the cab holding a map.

The man looked up from the left rear tire he'd been inflating and stood. "I'm sorry, you say something? Couldn't hear you with the air."

Dieter approached, scanning the parking lot as he did. "Yeah. Sorry to bother you, but I was wondering if you could help me with my map for a second. Seem to be lost."

"Yeah, sure," the lumberjack said. "Where ya heading exactly?" he asked, closing the short distance. They were shoulder to shoulder now.

"Where?" Dieter parroted, giving himself another second to pull something out of thin air. "Uh, Helena, actually. Grandma's house. Christmas, y'know the drill," he said with the fake smile.

"Okay, you're not too far off," the man said, pointing to

the map. "Helena's about ninety miles north here, probably take you hour and a half, maybe two if the weather doesn't—"

The tire iron to the back of the head interrupted the man's words as he fell to his knees, dazed and bloodied.

"Thanks," Dieter said coldly, taking a nanosecond's pause as he weighed delivering another blow for insurance. He took a step back and felt his grip slacken on the bloodied iron as he regarded the unconscious man lying there. Prior to killing the cop, he'd never had a propensity to violence, and he wasn't enjoying this new side of himself. But there it was. He let out a savage grunt of frustration as he chucked the tire iron back into the Jeep. He looked around to make sure nobody was looking and, satisfied they hadn't been seen, dragged the man's body around to the rear of the store, leaving him hidden behind the Dumpster.

Dieter scurried to the back of the Jeep and took less than a minute to transfer the multitude of Walmart bags and the sleeping bag to the Durango before jumping back into the Jeep. He was going to miss this ride. He'd only had it for a couple of weeks, but it was assuredly hotter than the surface of the sun now.

He did a hurried wipe down of the steering wheel and other surfaces he figured he'd touched. He didn't bother with his brother's grimy prints. He wouldn't be in the system.

This is definitely getting added to the expense report, fucker.

The rear of the property offered a temporary fix as it would buy a little time—hopefully. Where the pavement ended, it was met with a simple curb to delineate the border of the property as well as dissuade anyone from rolling off the embankment and into the tree line below.

As the front wheels came to a stop about twenty feet

from the curb, Dieter put his foot on the brake and ejected his Radiohead CD, stuffing it into his jacket pocket before climbing out and resting a twelve-pack of Dr. Pepper against the gas pedal and letting his precious ride make its perilous journey to the forest below.

He watched long enough to confirm the Jeep effortlessly breached the meager curb and disappear over the edge, generating modest groans of complaint that only he could hear.

Creep held Rose's hand and hefted four plastic bags in the other as they exited the store. Before anyone could get too interested, the red Durango pulled to the curb and the passenger window rolled down. "Get in!" the driver barked. Creep stared blankly, clearly not up to speed.

"Quickly, dammit!" the driver, who was now clearly his brother, barked.

"Whose car is—?" was all Creep could get out before Dieter stormed around to the rear passenger door and all but stuffed Rose inside before snatching the snack bags from his brother.

"Get. Inside. The. Fucking. Car. *Now!*" he hissed in a way that couldn't be misconstrued, even by the Creep.

Fifteen seconds later, the Durango exited the lot.

Next stop: Coeur D'Alene!

CHAPTER 17

POP POP'S
DUSK, SATURDAY

P OP POP HAD suggested the three of them get out of the house for a while and get a bite to eat but Phoenix had waved off his offer in favor of getting to the bottom of Liam's file box. They'd spent much of the afternoon sitting at the kitchen table, and the information they were finding—as troubling as it was—was compelling. They might be on to something, and they were unified in their determination to discover anything that might shed light on where their dear Rose could be.

"What about this?" Curt asked, holding up another incident report. "This one's from Utah, looks like…again, 1997, similar MO."

"Lemme see," Phoenix said, snatching it from his hands. "Provo…where's Provo?"

"Not too far south of Salt Lake City," Pop Pop said. "Big Mormon community there."

"Shocker," Curt murmured.

"Okay, Provo PD report shows a similar modus operandi—sorry, MO—but with one big difference." She continued reading, leaving the guys hanging.

"I'll bite. What's the difference? Why would Liam have this with his other stuff?" Curt asked.

Phoenix unclipped the attached photo and held it so all could see. "Another family's car decal, but with a big-ass family…" she said, pausing to count the family members' stick figures. "Dad, Mom, eight kids—looks like four boys and four girls, three dogs…but look closely," she added, pointing to the third girl in line. She'd been X-ed out, like the others. "This one, and the police report specifies her, was an eight-year-old girl. Caroline Jacobs."

"Jeezus," Pop Pop sighed. "Just like the others."

"Like the others, yes. But like I said, there's one important difference," Phoenix said, looking them both in the eye now.

"What's that?" Curt asked, leaning in closer.

"This kidnapping wasn't successful. Caroline Jacobs fought back. She got away and was able to provide police with their descriptions."

"No shit," Curt said, catching himself. "Sorry. Seriously…."

"Anything else attached to the report? Descriptions? Sketches?" Pop Pop asked.

"Nothing I can see here, looks like there was probably a second page…but let's look through these," she said, handing them each a stack of papers. "See if anything matches. One thing's for certain: this wasn't these assholes' first rodeo."

Pop Pop had excused himself just long enough to duck out to their favorite Mexican haunt, Los Dos Molinos—the one on Alma School Plaza in Mesa. Having served in the military, and as a dad, he knew troops couldn't march on an empty stomach for very long. Which was why he'd brought back copious amounts of pork and beef entrees—and cheese enchiladas for the vegetarian. Large sides of rice, extra beans and fiery salsa rounded out the feast to assure they'd be eating well for a week.

"So friggin' good," Phoenix managed through her mouthful of enchilada. "Thanks, Pop Pop."

"Yeah, thanks, Dave," Curt echoed as he shoveled in his self-constructed carne burrito.

"Dave?" Pop Pop said with a chuckle. "Nobody's called me that in at least five years, probably longer."

"Sorry, just slipped out," Curt said.

"No harm, no foul."

Liam's files still occupied the kitchen table, which was why they were dining on the patio. It was an unseasonably warm night for December, and they'd caught the tail end of a wicked sunset. Pop Pop was pouring some homemade margaritas.

"Curt?"

His cheeks were ballooned out from what appeared to be half a burrito. He answered with an enthusiastic thumbs-up.

"Phoenix?"

"Ordinarily not, but…yeah…hook me up. Please."

"Very well." Pop Pop finished pouring theirs and topped off his own. "A better squad of detectives I could never hope to know," he said, hoisting his heavy, multicolored margarita glass. "Cheers," he said softly. "We *will* bring Rose home safely." His declaration and expression were earnest, as were the others'. This wasn't a celebratory toast.

Their three salted rims came together in a gentle *clink*.

After they finished, they'd have more work to do and as long as Rose was still out there the idea of sleep wasn't even a distant thought.

GILBERT POLICE STATION
RAMAGE'S OFFICE
SATURDAY NIGHT

"Yes...great work. Thank you, Officer," Ramage said, the phone tucked under his chin. His office printer was whirring with an incoming document, and he motioned for his partner to retrieve it. "It's coming off the printer right now. That's very helpful. Yep, roger that," he said, returning the landline to its cradle. "Found the Jeep!"

"Wow...where, pray tell?" Moser asked as she waited the few seconds for the document to eject. "Please tell me they didn't make it to British Columbia."

"Not quite. *Montana.* Damn, these guys have been motorin'. Must've figured we'd be looking for the Jeep. Ditched it in Butte."

"Think they're continuing north? A border run, maybe?" she asked as she handed him the new document.

"God, I hope not. And I don't think so. FBI, state, and local agencies are on alert for anyone matching their descriptions trying to cross into Canada. They've been smart—mostly—thus far, and I'll bet the farm they've done this before. Not ruling it out as a possibility, but my gut tells me they have other plans."

"Okay, so they ditched the Jeep. Any intel on what they might be driving now?"

"Yeah," Ramage replied, scanning the document for specifics. "At the site where they found the Jeep, they also found an assault victim—male—and the owner of a…here it is…a 2007 Dodge Durango…four-wheel-drive…red in color. Stolen. The owner was beat with a friggin' tire iron and left behind the gas station where he'd been inflating his tires."

"Another homicide?"

"Almost. But this guy's in critical condition at Saint James Hospital. Was able to give a brief description of his assailant and the Jeep before he went into surgery.

"A match?"

"A match," he confirmed. "He only saw the short guy, though. The one who clocked him, which means the big motherfucker, and the kid, were probably inside the gas station. Regardless, the stop in Butte tells me—if they're not making a border run to the north—they might be heading west."

"West…like *Spokane* west?" Moser asked.

"Possible," Ramage said as he furrowed his brow. He templed his fingers and spoke from behind them. "If not there, maybe…the panhandle."

POP POP'S KITCHEN
SUNDAY MORNING
1:30 AM

They'd pulled an all-nighter, these three, straining their bloodshot eyes—and what was left of their brains—in their endeavor to finish what was left in Liam's box. They were nearly through it. Pop Pop was asleep at the table. The margaritas had done their job.

Curt abandoned the report he'd been reading and picked up another file paper. It was a Provo PD printout of an artist's rendering per Caroline Jacobs' description of her assailant.

"Found something. From Provo. Sketch of the perps," he said, with renewed energy.

"Let me see!" Phoenix blurted as she leaned over for a closer look. "Jeezus…that one definitely looks like our driver," she said, fully alert now, her hatred festering just below the surface. "A little younger, maybe, but the same guy. Fucker."

"And Chewbacca here, pretty much a dead lock," Curt said, pointing to an entirely reasonable rendering of the Creep. "She obviously got a good look at them."

"Good for you, Caroline," Phoenix murmured. "Tell me again 'cause my memory is toast; when did this occur?"

"Ninety-seven," Curt reminded her.

"And she was…eight, right?"

"Yep."

"Means she'd be about eighteen now," Phoenix said to herself.

"Sounds about right," Curt managed through a cavernous yawn. "Might make a good witness if they catch these guys."

Phoenix turned to him, and her look made it clear he might want to correct that statement.

"*When* they catch these guys, I mean."

"Yep, if she allows herself to revisit that scary memory. Okay, set that one over in the good pile with the others. What else is there?"

"Looks like just the handwritten notes of Liam's on the yellow pad. We've pretty much gone through everything else," Curt said, picking up the note pad. "Liam's jotted down dates and places of incidents he thought might be connected. We've cross-referenced these, and they seem to be solid," he added, as he turned the page. "Also looks like he'd been doing some digging into some anonymous web networks, some background checks here and there, and..." his voice trailed off.

"And...?"

"And he's got a few names he's lined through. Probably eliminated them as suspects. There's another one, though. Just a last name, I'm guessing. Nothing else, except it's circled."

Phoenix rubbed her eyes with the palms of her hands. "Don't leave me hanging."

"Just says ECKS. And, below that, looks like a French word I can't even begin to pronounce."

Phoenix blinked her eyes back into focus and took the notepad from him. "Please repeat the name you just said, again, very slowly...exactly."

"*ECKS*," he repeated.

A few seconds went by as their collective synapses kicked in, then their eyes met.

CHAPTER 18

COEUR D'ALENE, IDAHO
THE CABIN
SUNDAY, OH DARK THIRTY

THE DURANGO'S FOUR wheel drive proved adequate as it wound its way up the incline and around the final turn to the property. It was snowing for real now, and the log cabin was a sight for Dieter's extremely sore eyes.

The property's three beautifully treed acres afforded privacy, yet it was close enough to downtown Coeur D'Alene when it came time for provisions. And it wasn't too far from the municipal airport, which was very important.

Smoke billowed from the chimney of the two-story structure, which meant the wood-burning stove was in use. The two Adirondack chairs on the front porch were unrecognizable blobs that could have just as easily been mistaken for sleeping polar bears, thanks to the snowpack.

The garage building was separated from the cabin and offered a two-car side and a separate garage door for the snowmobiles, tools, and supplies. Dieter instinctively reached up to hit the button on the remote garage opener before remembering his was attached to the visor of his Jeep, which was at the bottom of the ravine and in the tree line back in Butte. *Dammit.*

To make matters worse, he realized his .38 revolver was in the Jeep's glovebox. *Fuck!*

He chalked it up to sleep deprivation and having to go off-script. He wouldn't make those mistakes next time. He made a mental checklist of places to add to his *Fucking Utah* list:

Arizo-nah!

Monta-nah!

The radio had been right about the cold front coming in. The property was in the early stages of getting socked with the white stuff. Dieter pulled onto the flat pad between the house and the garage.

A glance to his right confirmed that his wildebeest of a sibling was still lights-out; his gaping mouth made him look like a largemouth bass, and his forehead rested awkwardly against the window. "Hey," he said, smacking his arm. No response. *I'm way too tired for this shit.*

He liberated the Radiohead CD from his coat pocket and slipped it in the deck. It was only a four-track disc, and it automatically began cuing to the first selection. As it did, he kept the sound muted while he silently shuttled the song ahead to the one-minute mark exactly, where he paused it. He knew this song that well.

Now that it was properly cued, Dieter turned the volume up full and looked over at the unfortunate blob next to him before hitting play. *BOOM!* The shrieking, grunge guitar chords had the desired effect as they savaged the Creep's ears and nearly sent him through the sunroof.

...*I'M A CREEP....*

"WhatawhereamIwhatthe—?!?!" Creep screamed unintelligibly as he thrashed about for several seconds, trying to get his bearings in the dark.

"We're home. Wake up," Dieter said calmly, a smirk on his face as he turned off the car. He climbed out, zipped up his jacket, and stretched his weary body. Creep covered his eyes and winced as the supernova that was the overhead dome light split the night.

Dieter's boots sank into the snow several inches as he crunched his away around to the rear passenger-side seat and opened it. "Okay, Princess," he said, grumpy with fatigue. "Out."

A tiny groan came from deep in the sleeping bag. "I want my mommy..."

"Help her with her jacket while I get the stuff from the back," Dieter commanded as he popped the liftgate and grabbed several bags. He'd left the last of his patience back in Provo.

As Creep watched his brother fumble with the front door key, he climbed out and helped unzip Rose's sleeping bag. "We're here," he said softly through a yawn.

"Where? Where are we?" Rose asked. She'd left the last of her patience back in Gilbert.

"We're home," Creep answered.

"This isn't my home. Where's my mommy and daddy?"

"It's my home," he replied tiredly. "C'mon. Zip up your jacket; it's cold out here."

Rose did as he said and pulled up the hoodie, not because

she was told to but because she could feel the cold slap her face in a way she'd never experienced. Her short legs swung over the edge of the seat, hanging out the door.

"Ready?" Creep held out his hand.

"Wait, please," Rose said quietly. Mindful beyond her years, she took note of her tiny, Uggs-clad feet as they dangled above the foreign, glistening white surface below. She was, with this brief pause, both assessing any threat and marking the moment. This was going to be her Neil Armstrong giant leap—she'd watched the video several times with Pop Pop—and such an experience wasn't to be taken lightly.

Satisfied in the knowledge she wouldn't be in zero gravity, she reached up, taking the big man's hand and took a deep breath before hopping out onto the otherworldly cold powder below. Landing with a soft crunch as her Uggs sunk in halfway, she looked up toward the trees and watched as flurries of flakes whirled around her, dancing every which way.

Any sensation of magic was stifled by her fear and uncertainty.

God must've shaken the snow globe.

Rose's loose-fitting, sheep skinned footwear didn't navigate the snow very well—nor was it designed to, getting stuck in some deep pockets on a couple of occasions. Creep carried her the rest of the way and set her down gently as they reached the front porch. The snowfall was starting to ramp up and they had to get inside. He stomped his boots several times and wiped them on the bristly mat. He looked down at Rose, and after a moment's hesitation, she did the same.

Creep swung open the rustic wooden door and, taking Rose's hand, stepped inside. It closed with a solid thump behind them, at once silencing the winds and the world outside. Other than some creaks and pops coming from the fireplace, it was like stepping into a vacuum chamber.

The big man took off his coat and hung it on one of the wooden dowels created for that purpose. He helped Rose out of her hooded jacket and placed it next to his. It was warm in here.

Rose looked around at this strange place and couldn't help but think it looked like it had been made from her Lincoln Logs, only lighter in color. The entire interior of the home, from the ceilings to the floors, to the staircase, the walls… all knotty, honey-toned timber, actual logs from actual trees, and shiny from the lacquer.

Even the chairs, the tables, most everything seemed to be created from the same forest. Some rustic, panhandle cabin-appropriate decorations adorned the walls. Old, rusted, two-person lumberjack saws, a couple of hundred-year-old looking hunting rifles, even a ginormous bear trap hanging over the couch by the fire. On the other side of the room, the head of an unfortunate and very pissed-off looking grizzly stared down at her from the wall overhead. It was the stuff of nightmares, and her hand gripped the big man's more tightly.

"Well?! Are ya gonna get your ass in here or aren't ya?!" a decidedly unpleasant and raspy sounding voice barked from the next room. Rose looked up at the giant, a concerned look on her face. "It's okay…it's just my mom," he said.

"Your mom?" she whispered incredulously.

"Yeah, c'mon," he said, gently leading her toward the source in the kitchen. As they turned the corner, Rose saw that the mean man from the car was sitting at the table, scowl-ing and, next to him, a morbidly obese older woman taking a deep drag on her cigarette. The large woman had long, wiry gray hair protruding from her wool watchman's hat. She tilted her head back, exhaled a cloud into the air above, and started to say something, but it was unintelligible as it morphed into a frightening fit of coughing, the likes Rose had never heard. *She might be dying.*

The woman caught her breath and smiled. Her teeth looked like Roquefort cheese. She waved the giant over to her. "Willie...how's my Willie?"

"I'm fine, Mama," he said, bending way down to give her a hug.

"Good, baby...good," she said.

Dieter rolled his eyes during this exchange, as it always nauseated him. It had always been this way, ever since they were kids, and it was a far cry from any reception he'd ever gotten. Ever.

Whatever. Fuck.

"And this must be...Rose," the circus lady said as she turned to the little girl. "Oh, look at you...even prettier in person," she said through an ingenuine smile. Just as quickly she looked up at Willie. "Any marks on her? Bruises?"

"No, Mama."

"She's fine. We were careful. Jeezus!" Dieter interjected angrily. "It's not like we're first-timers, ferchrissakes," he mumbled. "Give us a little credit why don't —"

This was met with a sharp, stinging slap to Dieter's face, as this matriarch didn't tolerate disrespect. "You watch your tongue," she hissed before turning back to Rose with her sick version of a smile. It was like she could flick it on and off with a switch. "Come on over here, sweetie. Let's get a good look at you."

At this point, it seems like an opportune time to pause this Hallmark movie moment to make some proper introductions. Cue *Family Feud* theme music.

Meet the Eckses:

Gretl Ecks (formerly known to you as the Troll) and not to be confused with the youngest and arguably cutest Von Trapp Family singer, nor Hansel's gingerbread-challenged sibling. More about Gretl Ecks in a bit.

Dieter Ecks, of course, and the baby of the family, *Willie (Wilhelm) Ecks* (aka Creep), whom you already know. Now, back to our program, already in progress:

"Come here, honey, I won't bite," Gretl said as she ground out her cigarette.

Rose looked up at Willie again and he nodded that it was safe to do so. After a brief hesitation, Rose slowly shuffled her feet as she made her way toward the table, staring at the floor the entire way. She stopped a couple of feet shy of the big woman.

"That's a girl...look at me, honey. Can you look at me? I want to see that pretty face of yours."

Rose lifted her chin a few degrees, enough for the overhead kitchen light fixture to illuminate her delicate features, including the perfect cleft in her chin, and light up all the fiery red and orange tones of her incredible ginger mane.

"Such an amazing child," Gretl said to herself. "Absolute perfection." She turned to look at her two sons. "Good job, boys," she said, making a point to pat Dieter's arm as he didn't often get much praise. He pulled his arm away; he loathed being patronized. Gretl ignored it, her attention going instead to the German-made cuckoo clock on the wall. "Well, it's late—actually it's *early*—and I know everybody must be very tired from the long drive," she said, firing up a bedtime ciggy with a stick match. "Rose, Willie will carry your things and you can sleep in my room tonight, how about that?"

Rose might as well have been invited to sleep in a viper pit, but she was too scared and too exhausted to ask if there might be an alternative arrangement. She nodded weakly, while Willie let out a ten-second-long yawn that nearly shook the house.

Dieter stared straight ahead, avoiding all eye contact, as Gretl labored with great effort to get herself up from the kitchen table. At four hundred thirty-eight pounds, per her last doctor visit a year before, it took some doing. Her youngest son gave her an assist. "Thank you, Willie dear," she said with a strained smile before turning to regard her other one. She almost said something but just shook her head instead. With a firm grip on her industrial strength walker, she shuffled herself down the hallway, leaving a considerable smoke trail in her wake.

Dieter snapped up the key fob from the table, threw on his coat, and huffed out the door. He had to get that Durango into the garage before anyone saw it.

3:15 AM

Rose lay awake, shivering, curled up in a twin bed that was positioned against a wall, lengthwise, in the tiny bedroom on the main floor of the cabin. She wasn't shivering from cold;

the space heater in the room kept it quite warm. She was shivering from a new level of terror and sadness.

This room was where the scary fat lady slept, and she was snoring like a woodchipper. Her queen bed was positioned parallel to, and against, Rose's. Rose would have to climb across the massive woman to get out of the bed.

The space heater's faux flames allowed for some visual information in the otherwise dark room. A tall chest of drawers was positioned against the foot of Rose's bed, and a pile of boxes was butted up against the metal rail at the head of the bed. There was also a cluster of jingle bells hanging from a hook, up high, from the bedroom door, serving as a secondary alert.

The other bedrooms were on the upper level. This was where the kidnappers slept, she knew, because she'd heard them ascend the wooden steps earlier.

Rose's eyes filled with tears. She thought about the threats the bad man had made if she tried to get away. He would hurt her family, and she'd never see them again. And the big, scary lady snoring next to her had earlier hit the bad man. Would she hit her too? *What if she rolls over on me?*

The giant man, Willie, she was still trying to figure out. By all rights, and entirely based on his sheer size and appearance, he should be the one to be most fearful of but, thus far, he had been relatively gentle with her. Still, she couldn't trust any one of them.

She rolled over toward the wall, whispered a prayer she'd learned from her mommy, and quietly cried herself to sleep.

CHAPTER 19

POP POP'S KITCHEN
SUNDAY MORNING
7:05 AM

THERE HAD BEEN precious little sleep happening under these roofs the previous night. Phoenix and Curt had hit vapor lock sometime after 3:00 and, after neatly sorting Liam's documents into piles, crawled off to catch a few hours in the cottage. Pop Pop had probably gotten more sleep than anybody, having spent much of the night faceplanted at the table.

As Pop Pop finished handwashing the margarita glasses and placing them in the strainer to dry, he made a mental note to throttle back on the tequila next time. The coffee maker chimed an impossibly high note, indicating the fourteen cups of industrial strength java had finished brewing. They would be needing every one of those cups this morning, no doubt.

The dogs were enjoying their breakfast. Prick was scarfing down a bowl of the homemade chow Phoenix had been feeding him of late. He was getting up there in dog years but this new food—a hybrid mixture of crockpot-cooked beef bone, chicken chunks, veggies, and quinoa—seemed to be great for him. Luke, on the other hand, was perfectly happy in the corner with his one cup measure of kibble, which was consumed in about thirty seconds.

"Mornin', Pop Pop," Phoenix murmured as she shuffled into the kitchen. "Mornin', babies," she said to the dogs. She was bright-tailed and bushy-eyed and a sight to be seen in her bunny slippers, mismatched ASU shirt, and Minnie Mouse jammies bottoms, along with her towel turban. "Coffee done?"

"Perfect timing, kiddo," Pop Pop replied.

"Praise Jeezus," she said as she went to the fridge and retrieved the carton of half & half and the biggest vessel she could find in the cupboard. "Did Prick get his meds?"

"Mm, not yet; want me to give 'em to him?" Pop Pop replied.

"No worries, I've got it," she said, shaking a chewable antibiotic from the tiny bottle on the counter. Prick had just finished his meal and was only too happy to receive a "treat" from his mama. "Body of Christ," she said, giving him a pat on the back.

"How'd you sleep?" Pop Pop asked, though he already knew the answer, having regarded the stacks of paper on the table. "Sorry I crashed on you guys. Did I miss anything?"

"Um, yeah…you could say that," she said as she dumped three spoons of sugar into the mug and chased it with the requisite amount of creamer to turn her coffee to an off-white. "New shit has come to light," she said, quoting one of their mutual favorite lines from *The Big Lebowski*.

"Mornin'," Curt said as he all but stumbled in.

"Mornin', sweetie," Phoenix said as she took a seat at the table, careful not to disturb the previous night's detective work. "Coffee's ready. Want me to get you one?"

"Nah, I got it, thanks," he said.

"Good morning, Curtis," Pop Pop said, handing him a mug.

"Curtis?"

"Sorry, that's for calling me Dave the other day. Now we're even," Pop Pop said with a chuckle. "I was going to make omelets, guys, who's interested?"

"Not me, thanks. I'll just have cereal. Honey, grab me the Lucky Charms, would you?"

"Sure," Curt said, grabbing the box, a bowl, and a spoon on his way to the table. Milk was already there.

"Mm, thanks," Phoenix said, as she savored her first sip of the enchanting brew.

"How 'bout you, Curt? Omelet?"

"Thanks, but I think I'll make myself a breakfast burrito from last night's leftovers."

"Suit yourself," Pop Pop said as he pulled a carton of brown eggs from the fridge. "Phoenix tells me you guys may've found something in Liam's stuff last night?"

"Yeah," Curt said, as he began littering the counter with several take-home boxes of carnitas, carne asada, and two kinds of beans. He pulled out a large skillet and placed it on the stove. This was going to be the mother of all burritos. "Not sure if Phoenix's told you anything yet, but we found a few reports that show these guys have a history of similar abductions."

"All here in Arizona?" Pop Pop asked, cracking the last of three eggs into a bowl.

"No. Actually, Utah as well, and there may be more. The Utah one wasn't successful, though. Girl got away as they tried to snatch her. She gave cops their descriptions."

"Was it—"

"A match, yeah!" Phoenix said, cutting him off. "Ten years ago, but the renderings were unmistakable."

"Holy cow," Pop Pop said as he whipped the eggs into frothy submission. "Anything else?"

"Yes!" Phoenix said through a mouthful of oats and colorful marshmallow-y shapes. "Here's the best part. Are you ready? Liam had done a little digging around himself, done some hypothesizing of his own. His notes indicate a person of interest. Just a last name but a name. And mention of a place!"

Pop Pop abandoned his project and came over to the table. Phoenix pulled the lined tablet with Liam's notes from the pile and spun it around for him to see. She pointed her finger to the place Liam had circled.

"Ecks? Ecks?... *Ecks!!*" he cried out on its third utterance. "Holy mother of God!" he exclaimed with a look of wonder. He then read what Liam had written underneath the name. "Coeur D'Alene, Idaho!"

"You know of it?" Curt asked as he finished stuffing the oversized tortilla to its breaking point.

"Been there! Long time ago. Beautiful lake. An old Navy buddy of mine used to live up in the panhandle area. Haven't touched base in several years but I think he was working for the Bureau of Land Management up there. I may have to give him a call. Wow, that's great work, guys! Have you shared this info with the Gilbert PD yet?"

"Not yet, but we will. Later."

"Later?"

"Yeah, later. After church," Phoenix said, the idea just coming to her out of the blue. "I think we should go, the three of us. Ten o'clock service."

Curt and Pop Pop exchanged looks. None of them had darkened the door of a church in decades except for Phoenix, whose last time in a church had been her serendipitous visit to the Mission San Xavier del Bac, somewhere in the desert between Tucson and Tubac.

"Church," Curt said to himself.

"Church. Yeah. Look, it can't hurt, right? Christmas is in a couple of days."

The guys were staring at her. "Do it for me, okay? Okay? After breakfast, get dressed, put on a button shirt—both of you—and we'll pray for Rose. And we'll pray for guidance. Because God knows, we need some."

REDEMPTION PRESBYTERIAN CHURCH
SANTAN, ARIZONA
9:50 AM

Hoping they could fly under the radar, Phoenix chose their seats in the middle of a pew, about three quarters of the way back. Curt, dutifully dressed in a clean, button-down shirt, accidentally crushed an elderly man's toes in the process of taking his seat and he was met with a scowl of disapproval. "Sorry, sir…so sorry."

The steps leading up to the pulpit were decorated with

a couple dozen large poinsettias meant to help usher in the holiday spirit. The effect was lost on Phoenix, maybe because she was already seeing red, and her spirit had been severely trampled upon.

Phoenix had sat on picnic benches that provided more comfort but she decided these were likely designed to discourage sleeping during a sermon. As she took inventory of the impressive rack of hymnals and collection plate pledge envelopes, the couple seated in the row in front of them stood and spun around, aiming their high beam smiles at Phoenix and Curt.

"Good morning!" sung the overly-made-up, fiftyish woman with the graying Dorothy Hammill 'do. Her husband, same age, and reasonably attractive in a game show host kind of way, thrust his hand forward, his arm extending well past the sleeve of his gray pinstriped jacket. "Welcome!"

Must be in sales. Cars, probably. It was the toothy grin and the gleam in his eye. Phoenix was slow to reciprocate the gesture but she shook both of their hands in return.

"Hi…uh, good morning," she replied softly. *Not interested in a car today, thank you.*

"We're the Goodmans," the man shared. "My wife, Glenda, I'm Guy!"

Good g-g-grief….

"I'm Phoenix. My husband, Curt. My dad, Pop—*Dave*."

"Nice to meet you," Pop Pop said. Curt just nodded.

"Super nice to meet y'all," Guy said. "Blessings on each of you."

"And you," Phoenix offered, taking note of how odd that sounded coming from her lips.

As Guy turned back around, Glenda's wheels were turning

and she searched Phoenix's face for an extra moment, seemingly communicating something akin to pity, or maybe compassion, before she faced forward as well. *So much for flying under the radar.*

Phoenix was wondering if it had been a mistake to come to church this morning. To venture out in public so soon. Her fragility was high. *They'd better not sing "Amazing Grace" today or I may lose it....* It had been a favorite hymn of her Grandpa Liam's and sung at his funeral.

Another couple, one row behind them, were also standing, looking a bit like fish out of water. Phoenix initiated a greeting with them, as it seemed like the Christian thing to do.

"Good morning," she said to them. They were a younger couple, like themselves; she guessed them to be in their mid-thirties. Both attractive. He was tall with sandy-blonde hair and she had the most amazing array of freckles to compliment her chestnut curls.

"Good morning. I'm Rebecca—Becky," the woman said with a warm smile. "My husband, Rich," she indicated. "First timers at this church, just moved here—well, to Chandler— from California. Nice to meet you." The men all exchanged handshakes.

"Pleasure," Rich said. "The Brysons."

"Very nice to meet you as well," Phoenix said with a half-smile before looking away. Her distraction didn't go unnoticed by Becky, who couldn't help but think she knew her from somewhere.

"Forgive me," she said as she studied Phoenix. "but have we met? You look so familiar."

"I don't believe so," Phoenix said, taken slightly off guard.

"I just have one of those faces, I guess," she added, hoping to change the subject.

"I don't know...I'm pretty good with faces. I've definitely—" Becky managed before she felt a tight squeeze coming from Rich's hand. An awkward moment went by during which Becky's eyes flashed a flicker of recognition. Phoenix picked up on it, as did Curt. Phoenix's smile became a tight line and her eyes spoke of the deep pain that was just below the surface.

"Oh, my—I am so incredibly sorry," Becky said, her voice little more than a whisper. Phoenix closed her eyes and shook her head as if to indicate it was okay. Becky was absolutely mortified she hadn't picked up on the fact that this was the family she'd seen on the TV news. The same woman who had poured her heart out in her absolute worst moment, the couple whose little girl had been so cruelly ripped from them. "I feel so stupid, I should have—"

Phoenix placed her hand on the woman's arm, interrupting the apology. "Really, it's okay. Thank you. We're here to pray for our little girl and, if you're so inclined, we'd appreciate yours as well."

"Oh, sweetie, definitely. We'll be praying for your little girl and for your family. Please know that," Becky replied, her hand resting on her chest. She initiated a hug and Phoenix accepted it before they all sat.

Several other meet-and-greet exchanges were coming to an end throughout the church and the congregation were all taking their seats.

After what seemed like an interminable medley of praise songs, the congregation was asked to take some pine. Phoenix and Curt exchanged looks and she shrugged. *What ever happened to the old hymns? Sheesh....* She consulted the paper program that the usher had given her on the way in. It looked like the sermon was in the on-deck circle after some announcements.

Her mind went to her life-changing five minutes at the majestic anomaly of a church she'd stumbled upon during her soul-searching pilgrimage in the middle of the desert several years before. Those scant few minutes at the historic Mission San Xavier del Bac had provided her with seeds of strength when she'd needed it most.

Perhaps the good Lord could bless her with some now.

As the announcements concluded, the pastor began his lengthy Christmas message. Pop Pop listened with interest, while Curt shifted uncomfortably in the pew. Phoenix closed her eyes and went into a deep place of silent prayer and reflection. As she'd done before, that time in the desert, she silently recited the Lord's Prayer. When she'd finished, she continued praying:

Dear God... It's been a long time since I last checked in with you, I know, but we came to your house today seeking wisdom, seeking strength, and hoping you can help us find...help us find our precious little girl, our daughter, Rose, Lord... I pray, with every fiber of my being, Lord, that you keep her safe...wherever she is...protect her, Lord... Help us find her, help us bring her home safely, and I ask that you restore our precious family, Lord. The family you blessed me with. That's my Christmas prayer... In Jesus's name I pray...Amen....

Her eyes remained closed as a flood of images sprang forth like a PowerPoint presentation: Phoenix holding her daughter for the first time at the hospital, having been blessed with a perfect child of her own—the most amazing of gifts—especially considering the cavalcade of loss she'd experienced in her life up to that point. Her would-be twin sister, a casualty of the abortion that should have included herself as well. Her young teen mother, whom she could barely remember now, taken from her by a murderous demon. Rose blowing out the candles on her sixth birthday. And the white van, driven by the devil himself, speeding away with her daughter, leaving herself screaming, wailing, on her hands and knees in the grocery parking lot.

Phoenix opened her eyes and the pastor paused briefly for effect, hoping his carefully crafted message had had the desired effect. In a soft tone he requested that the congregation remain seated for the hymn. He sank into his own rather ornate chair and the children's choir stood as one, on cue, as the pianist began playing her intro chords to the hymn "Amazing Grace ."

No way.... Phoenix squeezed Curt's hand as it began, hoping to find strength to get through it. After a few bars, the accompanist nodded, signaling to the twelve well-practiced singers, a mix of youngsters ranging from about ten to thirteen years old. The girls outnumbered the boys eight to four, and from the very onset their collective voices blended perfectly. It was truly a joyful noise, and the congregation listened with rapt attention and great appreciation.

"Amazing Grace, how sweet the sound…"

Curt, who'd been struggling to keep his eyes open, was finding the brutally hard oak pew to be a bit tortuous. He shifted his weight a little, willing his bum to survive another few minutes.

The choir continued to sing beautifully and were in the third verse of the song when suddenly, and without warning, Curt began feeling some internal discomfort. His brow furrowed.

Gawd...not now...

He cursed himself for his ill-advised pre-church breakfast choice. He'd never been much of a praying man but he closed his eyes and, focusing every ounce of concentration he could muster, clenched his sphincter muscle tightly, just shy of the pressure required to produce a diamond from a lump of coal. He prayed it would hold until he was outside and not near anyone. But it wasn't enough. The final verse began, a repeat of the first.

"Amazing Grace, how sweet the sound—"

And, right then and there, Curt released a warm ball of gas he didn't realize he'd been holding. It was mercilessly loud and high-pitched, not unlike the sound you get when you do a deliberately slow release of air from the valve of a birthday balloon. It reverberated off the oak pew, which took it to another level, and it was the shot heard around the world.

"—that saved a wretch like me..." the kid choir managed before a smattering of adolescent giggles ran the remainder of the hymn off the rails.

A horrified Phoenix shot a sideways glance at Curt, squeezing his knee. Curt stared straight ahead and quietly cleared his throat. A few impossible-to-suppress giggles came from pockets of the congregation now as well, and if anyone had ever wondered if God had a sense of humor, they'd just gotten their answer.

Curt tried to feign innocence during this, his eyes shifting around, gauging the tsunami of chaos he'd triggered. The man with the sore toes looked knowingly at Curt, his disdain evident.

The choir was toast and, no longer able to contain themselves, noisily found their folding chairs. The pianist shrugged and lowered her head in surrender. The laughter was contagious, and growing, to the point that the pastor felt compelled to return to the podium. Over the involuntary chuckles of the congregation, he motioned for all to please stand as he offered a hasty closing prayer.

"May God bless you and keep you," he said, pausing as he looked directly at Phoenix. "...in the name of the Father, and the Son, and the Holy Spirit... Amen."

CHAPTER 20

PLEASANT HILL, MISSOURI
SEBASTIAN BREWER'S MANOR
SUNDAY, 1:45 PM

MACKENZIE AND REBEKAH Olson had spent the past several hours scrubbing toilets, sinks, and floors and seeing to the manor's considerable laundry duties. With the scheduled arrival of out-of-town guests, each of the bedrooms needed fresh linens and towels, as did the outbuilding that housed the dozen girls who lived onsite. This included the two of them, plus the two who'd be arriving tomorrow.

As they sat at a small table, just off the main kitchen, MacKenzie and Rebekah worked on their second plate of pancakes at the urging of Candy. She'd been tasked with helping them pack on a few pounds as not to appear too emaciated for the visitors who would be traveling a long way to spend "special time" with them. The girls —all of them—hated the "special time." The Olson sisters had seen plenty of that, and their souls were slowly slipping away from them.

"Good job, girls," Candy said. "Who'd like some more?"

Both girls respectfully waved her off. They weren't accustomed to big meals like this. This was a rare treat, but it also was taxing to their digestive systems, and they might get sick if they ate any more. Rebekah was first to finish hers. "Thank you, ma'am," she said. "Yes, thank you, ma'am," MacKenzie parroted upon completion of hers.

Candy regarded the girls closely. They had learned their lessons after that one escape attempt the previous year. Their punishment had been harsh but deemed proportionate to their crimes, as the whole house of cards could have been compromised had they been successful in getting off the property. Each had been thrashed—short of leaving any lasting marks on their bodies—and seen a week of solitary confinement, with reduced rations, while chained to heavy machinery in the equipment shed. They'd emerged, a week later, shells of themselves.

The other onsite "guests," their unfortunate peers, were tending to closely supervised yard work at the moment, which freed up the outbuilding for changing out the sheets on the six tandem bunkbeds and the several hampers of towels. This had since become the twins' bi-weekly duty, as they'd been reformed and deemed the most reliable. They almost welcomed it, as it provided an opportunity to leave the tight confines of their windowless bunker. A tiny glimpse at the sun, now and then, was about the only remaining thread of sanity they had.

"May we be excused, ma'am?" MacKenzie asked softly.

"Yes, girls. Is the laundry finished?" Candy asked.

"Yes, ma'am," they answered in unison.

"Okay. Then after you finish washing your dishes, I'd like

you to get the boxes of ornaments and decorations from the supply shed and decorate the tree in the living room. Same as last year. Look at the picture on the counter if you need to remember how it looked. Understood?"

"Yes, ma'am," Rebekah answered, her eyes cast down. She'd all but forgotten that Christmas Eve was tomorrow; it didn't matter. The previous Christmas, and all holidays since for that matter, had ceased having any meaning. Holidays, it seemed, had become little more than markers for the occasions visiting strangers came to have "special time" at their expense. Though none of the girls would dare express it, each secretly wished they wouldn't live long enough to experience the next holiday.

"Okay then," Candy said. "On your way to the shed, tell the other girls—if they're done with the yard—to come see me. I'll have lunch ready for them here." *And it won't be pancakes.*

"Thank you, ma'am," the girls said, sounding borderline robotic.

"Dismissed," Candy said, waving them off. She had bologna sandwiches to make.

CHAPTER 21

GILBERT STATION
SUNDAY, NOON
SAME MOMENT

OFFICERS RAMAGE AND Moser carved out twenty minutes to refuel. They'd been working almost every waking moment these last three days, Moser reminded her partner, and she'd made an executive decision to duck out and bring back super burritos.

"Got a call from the parents while I was out," Moser said as she unwrapped her lunch.

"Yeah?" Ramage responded, inspecting his burrito. "No onions on mine, right?"

She gave him the thumbs up as she finished her bite. "Right…said they might have come across something from her grandfather's box of old files."

"Her grandfather…as in *William McGinn?*" he replied, half chuckling. "I mean, no disrespect, God rest his soul. I never worked with the man, and I'm told he'd once been a great detective, but there are stories about his drinking."

"Derailed his career, I heard," Moser affirmed as she went for another bite. "Sad."

"Yeah. Sad. And he'd been off the job for a while, so I can't imagine he'd have anything useful to us, but, hey…right now, we're over seventy-two hours into this deal and the clock's ticking fast. I don't have to tell you that," he stressed before diving into his carne asada masterpiece.

"Said they could come in later this afternoon," she added, wiping her mouth and sipping her Coke. "Want me to tell 'em yes?"

"Sure," Ramage replied. "What could it hurt at this point? They mean well and, God knows, any of us would be wanting to help the investigation if it was one of ours that'd been taken."

Moser chewed on that thought, along with her pollo burrito. The very idea of being in that situation made her shudder. She stared at their own file copy of the years-old artist's rendering of the perps. It was a lock when compared against the video images.

"The grease pencil," she said, setting down her burrito.

"What about it?"

"I mean, what's with the X. Is it a taunt? A trademark? Are they just boastful assholes?"

"Probably. Maybe. Might be all of the above. Who knows with these psychos?"

"What else have we got?" Moser asked, back to her burrito.

"Nothing's come in on the red Durango. Nobody's seen it. Which tells me they may've reached their destination or,

God forbid, jacked another vehicle. All agencies are on the lookout. The glovebox of the Jeep, however…"

"Yes?"

"We have the murder weapon, the one used in the killing of Officer Berreth in Utah. Perps were in a hurry, it seems, and left the .38 in the glovebox. They're checking for prints on that one now," Ramage said, taking his final bite. "Gawd, these are good," he added through a mouthful as he pointed to it.

"Good, we need a break on this. Hopefully, if they have something useable, it helps us zero in on these guys. Before it's too late."

"Roger that, partner."

POP POP'S
SUNDAY

Curt had changed his shirt and his pants. His gastric distress had eased but he was still wallowing in embarrassment from earlier. He went about finishing the painting in the cottage. What else was he going to do?

His thoughts went to Rose again, as they did every few minutes, regardless of whatever else was going on. As he perfected the surface with the fine sandpaper and applied the paint, he hoped to God his family could be patched up as well with Rose's safe return.

God, let me know she's okay….

Pop Pop had decided he needed to keep the shop closed through at least New Year's. With everything going on, he couldn't concentrate on the business and, aside from Curt's truck, all customer repairs had been completed. He'd called each of the shop workers, advising them that they'd be receiving paid time off, plus a holiday bonus. He'd already cut their checks, tucked them into Christmas Cards he'd hand-deliver to each—after he put an explanatory CLOSED sign in the shop's window. He was now laying on the bed, taking a much-needed power nap with the dogs.

Meanwhile, Phoenix took some time out to process her thoughts and her resolve. They each had their own ways of dealing. None of them adequate, by any means, but they were the best they had, having had no advance notice that life could so violently pull the rug out from under them. *Again.*

Phoenix's activity of choice was one she hadn't involved herself in in quite some time but it always helped her think, and there was perhaps nothing more therapeutic than creating a mix tape. Well, that and spinning a hundred donuts in a parking lot. Ahem.

As she pulled the last of the LPs she envisioned using for her masterpiece, she placed them with the others—vertically, of course, leaning against the closet door next to the rack stereo system. The wall racks Pop Pop had built in the den/music room years before made it easy to find her selections now, as they were alphabetically filed, as well as categorized by genre of music. The collection itself was impressive, especially considering she'd scored the lion's share of them seven years prior, with one single, sixteen-dollar garage sale purchase from a lady who just wanted to get rid of them all! Add to that, they were all in either mint or near mint condition.

Gold, all of it.

Her prowess as "Queen of the Mix Tape" was legendary and she'd learned it all from the "King" of same, Pop Pop, at an early age. Her soul-searching trip through the desert years ago had been fueled by her mix tapes, and her song selections were always purposeful. As were the order in which they appeared in her playlists. They had helped stoke the fire in her belly, providing fuel to her core as she found the resolve to pursue and avenge Offermann, "the Pirate," her mother's murderer.

She removed the plastic wrapping from a Maxell UD XL-II 90-minute cassette tape, the only tapes she used. She carefully cleaned the stylus, then the record's grooves as it was placed on the platter. This would have to be her personal best, she decided as she strapped on her headphones. She had new dragons to slay. This one called for a white-hot opener, a five-minute burner with intensity to match her resolve, and she had just the one.

As the needle kissed the first groove of the LP, she waited one half second to get past the initial *pop* before hitting the pause button, putting the reels in motion as the recording began. The volume unit meters danced, and she cranked up her headphones' volume.

Her skin bristled with the opening power chords and headbanging percussion of Judas Priest's "You've Got Another Thing Comin'."

And they did.

CHAPTER 22

THE CABIN
SUNDAY AFTERNOON

THE ODD FOURSOME was seated at the table, finishing up a very late breakfast. Er, brunch. They'd all slept in well past noon. All but Rose, that is, as she'd finally drifted off to sleep around 7:00 and slept fitfully for the few hours until the big lady had groaned loudly in her effort to extract herself from the bed.

The members of the Ecks family each presented in their thermal jammies and slippers, while Rose had been provided a terrycloth robe that was two sizes too big for her. It had been the perfect size for the last girl. And the girl before her.

An interesting familial portrait this would have made as the adults stuffed their faces with all the trappings of this German-style breakfast. Several varieties of cheeses, breads, sliced meats, and fresh fruits littered the table.

Rose's eyes were downcast, as were her spirits, as she picked at her fruit.

"Stop playing with your food," the big lady said as she stuffed a massive cheese-laden bite of bread into her own mouth. "You need to eat that, Rose. You need to eat everything on your plate," she added, talking through her mouthful.

Rose didn't want anything bad to happen to her family, so she dutifully ate the berries. Willie let loose an accidental thunderclap of a belch, which drew a scowl from his mother and a headshake from his sibling. "What do you say?" Gretl asked with an admonishing tone.

"E'scuse me," Willie said shyly, looking around the table.

"Lovely," Dieter said under his breath. He wiped his mouth and pushed his plate away.

"Dieter, I need you go into town and pick up some things. There's a list on the fridge," Gretl said. She wasn't asking.

"Not sure that's a great idea to be driving that Durango around right now," he answered. He was trying to weasel out of that chore, but he was also right. The law would surely be on the lookout for it once they'd found its owner—not to mention his own Jeep at the bottom of the ravine. That Jeep had still had the new car smell, and he was pissed about that.

"It's not a lot. Just a few things. Take the snowmobile, go to the country store. We'll figure out the car thing later."

Dieter pushed himself away from the table, his only response being a slow, deliberate nod to acknowledge what she'd said as he got up and went up the stairs.

"Willie, I want you to bring some water and a plate of breakfast downstairs when you're done. Plastic utensils only! Then take a shower. Wash your hair. You look like a hobo."

"Yes, Mama," he said. "Can I be excused?"

"May."

"What?"

"May…"

"It's December, Mama," her confused son replied.

"*May…may…maaay* I be excused," she barked under her breath. She shook her head, silently wishing Willie had had the same educational opportunities Dieter did growing up. She regretted that Dieter had been pressed into helping with Willie's homeschooling needs for several years once her health had made it increasingly difficult for her to do it alone. Dieter had hated the role, and the responsibility, she knew. The resentment was always on-deck with Dieter, and it was no small wonder Willie hadn't become the first homeschool shooter.

"May I be e'scused, Mama?"

"Yes, honey. Clean up this stuff before you take your shower, sweetie," she said.

"Yes, Mama," he said as he got up from the table, leaving Rose to pick at her bread.

Gretl watched her giant boy lumber away and allowed herself a moment to consider his plight. She could never be upset with her Willie for too long, and it wasn't his fault his umbilical cord had deprived him of oxygen. He'd been nearly thirteen pounds at birth and delivering him had been akin to driving a bus through the eye of a needle.

As her boy went about noisily washing the porcelain plates, Gretl's focus shifted to the pine hutch hugging the wall directly behind where Willie had sat. The Hummel figurines needed dusting, she noted. So did the arrangement of small, framed family photos on the shelf below.

There was a lot of history on display here, including several of Gretl in her youth. As she studied the frontmost black-and-white image of a budding ballerina, about Rose's age, she found it hard to imagine that she had once been a true beauty herself. Though the photo couldn't convey its colors, her long hair had exhibited a range of ginger tones, not too unlike Rose's.

The next frame to the right displayed another capture from happier times: Gretl, in her late teens, her long hair in a perfect ballerina bun. An early theatrical photo, it presented a gorgeous ballerina posing on stage, in Fifth Position—her arms and hands elegantly fixed overhead, standing with feet turned out so the front foot's heel was touching the back foot's toe—and looking as graceful as the swan she'd hoped to portray. She would enjoy a brief reign as a respected ballet dancer with great promise in her native Germany.

With the arrival of her second child, Willie, any hopes of that career path—not to mention her body—quickly became kaput.

Gretl shook her head, casting away thoughts of what might have been. It didn't matter now.

Her eyes settled on another framed image, this one in color, and taken several years later: her late husband, Thore, a jeweler. A slight and bespeckled man with closely cropped hair, he wore a simple gray suit, a thin black tie, and a serious expression. In the photo, he ignored the lens; his attention was elsewhere, as it had often been in the years they'd had together.

Thore....

Thore Ecks had moved the family from their home in Lübeck to the United States, settling first in Utah and later Idaho. The cabin had been lovingly constructed in the hopes of bringing a bit of the homeland to their domicile in Coeur D'Alene.

Thore's untimely death from a slip and fall at an Opal mine he partnered with had left the boys fatherless when they were young. He left Gretl with some money but as time passed, she found out it wouldn't last forever.

Gretl essentially threw in the towel as her health continued to decline. It became harder and harder for her to leave the house, which made any kind of employment impractical. Dieter's childhood had been cut short as he was forced to become the man of the house. In addition to the usual chores, he'd been saddled with teaching his brother and being a nursemaid of sorts to his health challenged mother. He took the reins reluctantly, and he'd harbored his hatred ever since.

Years later, with the advent of the new frontier called the World Wide Web, Gretl eventually stumbled upon a very dark and sinister corner of the internet. It was indeed dark. Pitch dark, and nothing short of a black hole.

Strangely, she hadn't found it to be repulsive. Maybe initially she had, but the more time she spent there she became oddly drawn to it. Perhaps drawing on her own childhood experiences of being molested by both her father and two uncles had provided context, and the conduit. It became a fascination to her as she started reading the perverted posts, studying the geography, analyzing the dynamic, assessing the need, and wondering who was supplying all these young children to meet the increasing demand.

Gretl had always been a quick learner and, after a few successful abductions and deliveries under her considerable belt, she learned how to carve out her own little, twisted, decidedly evil family business. It was a service industry, and when the boys became old enough to help, the Eckses were in business.

And the money was good.

Rose's fork fell noisily to the tile floor, snapping Gretl back to the present.

"May I be excused?" Rose asked shyly, politely, and hoping not to be backhanded.

"Yes, hon. C'mon, let's get you washed up and dressed."

As they got up from the table and slowly made their way down the hall, Rose's gaze went to the other closed door. She had seen the big man go in there earlier. There were more stairs behind that door, the one that went down. It had been dark, she'd noted, and you could see no light at the bottom of those stairs.

Yet someone was down there.

CHAPTER 23

POP'S AUTOMOTIVE

THE 11"X14" HANDWRITTEN sign was readable enough, he'd decided. Pop's penmanship was better than average, and he'd used a large, chiseled-tip marker on cardstock, making it legible from behind the door's glass pane without customers having to get out of the car.

He hoped the community would understand the need to close the shop for the coming week—longer, if necessary—but he knew he couldn't keep it shuttered indefinitely.

He just needed his little angel home safe. Nothing else mattered.

He'd already dropped off his employees' Christmas cards, each containing their paychecks. He climbed back into the cab of his F-150 XL, started it, and paused to surf through the contacts on his phone. It had been a long while, and he hoped the number he had was still good. Worth a try. He pulled away from the parking lot. The phone picked up on the fourth ring.

"Murphy," the husky voice said.

"Murf?"

"This is Wayne Murphy, yes. Can I help you?"

"Murf, man, long time. It's Dave. LaFlamme...."

A moment went by before recognition kicked in. "Flamer?"

"Haven't been called that in a long time, but yeah, man," Dave said, bringing as much cheer to his voice as he could muster under the circumstances, but he wasn't convincing.

"Dave, *the Flamer,* LaFlamme...well, I'll be," he said with a chuckle. A moment later a change of tone kicked in. "Damn, man, I, I read something in the paper yesterday...tell me that wasn't about your people," he said, his concern evident.

"I wish I could tell you it wasn't, but it was...and it is. We're in a world of hurt over here, as you can probably imagine, Murf," Dave said, pulling to a stop at the red light. "My daughter's little girl. Rose...my angel."

"Damn sorry to hear that, brother," Wayne said softly. "What's it been, a coupla days?"

"Day three, but it feels like a year. Clock's ticking big time. Local police tell us she's crossed state lines already. FBI's involved. All the agencies. We're worried sick, and, well, we're at our wit's end. Feeling utterly helpless, just hoping our baby's okay and we can get her back safe, y'know..." Dave said, his voice trailing off. "Fuck," he whispered to himself.

The signal changed to green, and he accelerated through the intersection and down a road he didn't even recognize. The silence at the other end of the line was deafening.

"Murf, look, I didn't mean to lay that on you, man. It's been a long time, and I apologize for not keeping in better touch, but—"

"What direction the police think they might be traveling?" Wayne Murphy interjected. "You're still in Arizona, right?"

"Yeah, in Gilbert. Still got the shop here. These guys—two of 'em—were reportedly traveling north out of Arizona, through Utah and beyond."

"North. Beyond Utah...."

"Yeah. Some new information indicates their destination could even be Idaho..." Dave said, half regretting making the call. As a rule, he hated to impose on anybody, and his entire life he'd always tried to be self-sufficient, to handle things on his own. To be the strong one. Not involve others unnecessarily. It was just his way. But sometimes in life, the situation calls for throwing out a Hail Mary. Was this one of those?

"Idaho."

"Yeah, I seem to remember last time we checked in with each other—what's it been, ten years, maybe more? You were doing some work for the Bureau of Land Management up there somewhere."

"You're right about that. I was. I mean, I'm retired now—not by choice, but I had to go on disability on account of bustin' up a leg pretty bad—but still in Idaho. Settled a little north of Coeur D'Alene...around Post Falls. We went fishing there that one time, remember?"

"Sure do," Dave said as he took a right turn to get off the road he was on. *Where the hell am I?* "Beautiful place."

"God's country," Wayne said resolutely.

Dave looked around to get his bearings and came upon a landmark he hadn't expected to see here. The tall sign was familiar but he'd never approached it from this direction before. It indicated he was at the Oasis Market. At the scene of the crime. He pulled over to the curb and caught his breath.

"Still there?"

"Yeah, sorry, uh, just took a wrong turn," Dave said, his

eyes scanning the near empty parking lot, picturing Phoenix's Road Runner, the white van, their little angel enjoying a cookie while she stood in the shopping cart.

"What's your info tell you as far as where in Idaho they might be headin'?"

"It may be a long shot, Murf, but there's a possibility they might be coming to—or already be in—the Coeur D'Alene area. Might be wrong about that, but it's the best we've got at the moment."

Another pause on the line allowed Dave to replay the horrific abduction scenario vividly in his mind as he sat there studying the grid. *My God!*

"How can I help?" his former Navy chum asked. "I might be busted up a little, but I've got time. Tell me what I can do, Flamer. I wanna be there for you, and maybe I can be your eyes on the ground here."

Dave couldn't believe what he was hearing. This offer of help was the closest thing to a lifeline they'd had, and he might be grasping at straws but he had to grab on to something. Anything. He closed his eyes and let a moment pass before responding because he didn't know how to. Dave realized that if they hadn't stumbled upon Liam's notes referencing Coeur D'Alene, another ten years might've gone by without reaching out to this good friend. He felt guilty as hell. *Fuck.*

"Murf, you're a saint to ask. Really. You've always been the closest thing to a brother I've ever known, and we go way back. But I—"

"Talk to me, Flame. No bullshit, buddy. What do we know? Idaho's a big state. Eighty-three-thousand square miles, give or take. Coeur D'Alene's about sixteen point eight, if memory serves, which narrows it down. Narrow it down a little further for me if you can. What else you got for me to work with?"

Dave digested the figures Murf rattled off. He knew better than to make a move without further consulting law enforcement but he was at the end of his rope. Rose was still out there, scared, in mortal danger, and at this point he was desperate. He blurted it out.

"Only a name. And, again, it's only a guess, based on a hunch and little else, but—"

"The name, Flamer. What's the name? Give me something to work with here, buddy."

"Ecks."

"X. Like marks-the-spot, X?"

"Ecks," he repeated before resorting to the NATO phonetic alphabet they both remembered from their Navy days: "*Echo. Charlie. Kilo. Sierra… ECKS.*"

"Roger that."

CHAPTER 24

POP POP'S
MOMENTS LATER

PHOENIX WAS FINISHING up her mix tape when she thought she heard another knock at the door. She emerged from her cave and made the short walk down the hall.

"Sorry to bother you, hon, but with everything goin' on, we thought you might just like a break from cooking right now," the matronly neighbor from across the street said. She was a sweet lady, sixtyish, and could often be seen in her yard tending to her cactus garden.

"That is so sweet of you, thank you so much. Yeah, we haven't felt much like cooking lately. Bless you," Phoenix said, taking the large Pyrex dish and placing it on the counter, out of view of the neighbor, next to the other six casseroles.

"It's tuna…hope you like tuna," the woman said as she started to turn back down the drive.

"Love it," Phoenix lied. "Thanks again for your kindness,"

she called after her. She was truly thankful for all the warmth the neighbors had shown, and she was sure her men would enjoy all the casseroles that had rolled in thus far. *Maybe someone will bring a vegetarian dish.*

The cellphone in her hip pocket rang and she recognized the funky ringtone as the one assigned to her Pop Pop: "Papa Don't Take No Mess" by the Godfather himself, James Brown.

"Wassup, Pop Pop? You done with the rounds?"

"Yeah, kiddo. Hey, listen…have you talked with the detectives yet about what you found in Liam's files?"

"Not really. Only mentioned we might've found some pertinent info. Not sure, but Ramage didn't sound overly excited. Anyway, I told him we'd come by the station. Why?"

"I don't know. I'm just wondering if…maybe…we might want to sit on that most recent revelation—the name, especially—a little bit before we pass it along to law enforcement agencies and they send in stormtroopers to make a play that could jeopardize Rose's safety. What do you think?"

"You make a good point, Pop Pop, but what else do we have? I mean, if we just sit on our thumbs and nobody pursues it, then what? We don't even know if it's a good lead or not, and we don't have the luxury of time. Right?"

"Right," Pop Pop replied softly. He sounded distracted.

"Pop Pop, is there something you know that I don't? If there is, tell me right now because we all need to be on the same page. What are you thinking?"

"Remember I mentioned I used to have an old Navy chum that I'd visited once, several years back?"

"Idaho, right? That guy?"

"That guy, yes. Well, I got a wild hair and gave him a call a little while ago. Hadn't talked to him in well over a decade,

171

but we chatted, and he verified he still lived in the panhandle area up there."

"Yeah," Phoenix said. *Go on.*

"Well, he felt compelled to ask if there was anything he could do to help our situation. Be our eyes and ears there if nothing else."

"He's a cop?"

"Not a cop. But he's retired BLM up there. Knows the area, probably better than just about anybody."

"Okay, good to know. How does he help though, exactly? He doesn't have any other information to go on," she said. Her brow furrowed. "Does he?"

"Just a name," Pop Pop replied softly.

"A name."

"He pressed me for something to work with. I gave him the name. Said he'd look into it."

"Wow, okay," Phoenix replied, her feeling of concern out-weighing her hope. "And you can trust this friend—what's his name again?"

"Murphy. Wayne Murphy. And yeah, I can trust him. We've literally saved each other's lives a while back, so I'd say, yeah. A story for another day. I'll be home in a little bit, and I'll make the three of us some dinner. Discuss things further."

"Uh, I think we've got dinner covered."

RAMAGE'S OFFICE
MOMENTS LATER

Detective Ramage returned the phone to the cradle. He looked over at his partner, at the adjoining table, revisiting the case files for the hundredth time. "O-kay..." he muttered.

"Don't tell me," Moser said, looking up from the report she was reading.

"They're not coming in now. Said she'd misspoken about coming across new information."

"Huh...okay. She sound all right?"

"Yeah, I guess. I mean...yeah."

"Believe her?"

"Sure. Why wouldn't I? She wants her little girl back and I can't imagine her withholding anything to prevent that from happening."

"Probably right," Moser said, closing the file folder and rubbing her eyes. "Guess that frees us up to get out of here, right? I mean, nothing new coming in from the field at the moment. I love what you've done with your office, and don't get me wrong, I love your company, but I think we need to get the hell out of here, be with our peeps, with our dogs, with our fish...have an adult beverage or two, and look at this mess with fresh eyes tomorrow. Tomorrow...on Christmas Eve...ahem."

"You're right. Keep your phone nearby but yeah. Let's call it a friggin' day."

THE CABIN
SAME TIME
SUNDAY, DUSK

Dieter brought the snowmobile around the last corner as he made his way up the long driveway and pulled alongside the cabin's front porch. He cut the engine. The snow was frozen to his face, his goggles, his wool beanie. He looked like a friggin' Japanese snow monkey and he cursed the weather as his gloved fingers awkwardly wrestled with the bungee cords that held the grocery basket to the rear of his buggy.

He carried the basket up to the porch and stomped his boots on the front door mat as he looked out above the tree line. He had a flight to make tomorrow, and the weather was...less than ideal. Kicking the door closed behind him, he set the basket on the kitchen table and went back out into the elements to garage his ride.

Down the hall in the bathroom, Gretl was still in her jammies. This wasn't unusual as, during the winter months, she pretty much lived in her jammies and a robe. Spring and summer, you'd likely find her in a muumuu. Never a pretty sight, regardless of time of year. It wasn't like she ever had visitors—at least adult ones—so she rarely felt the need to get *dressed* dressed. Besides, it was a bitch trying to find Levi's 501s in her size.

"There, that's better. Don't you think?" she asked, a cigarette dangling from her lips as she finished brushing the six-year-old's freshly washed and styled hair.

Rose studied her reflection, trying to see through the considerable smoke. She let out a cough and nodded shyly. Gretl picked up the curling iron and made a few adjustments to Rose's mane before turning it off and placing it on the counter, next to another full ashtray. Another blast of hairspray completed the toxic cloud, rendering the tiny space uninhabitable.

"All done, princess," she said, her voice sounding especially husky as she ground what was left of her grit into the ashtray. "Christmas Eve tomorrow," Gretl reminded her cruelly.

As the smoke dissipated, Rose gazed at the "princess" and couldn't help thinking she'd been denied her time to shine as the Christmas Angel in the school's musical. The past several days had been a whirlwind of fear, loneliness, and sadness. *How can tomorrow be Christmas Eve?*

Unseen by Gretl, who was putting away the hairspray and brushes, tears rolled down Rose's tiny cheeks. All she could think about was her mommy and daddy and her Pop Pop. And Luke. And Prick. And Angus, the bird. And missing Gracie. She didn't like these people, and she didn't like being away from her family and her home. And her Christmas.

Life in the snow globe was definitely overrated.

Willie sat in the robust wood and leather chair. It was the same one his mother sat in when she was doing her computer "business" at the desk and was rated at five-hundred pounds.

Other than the dim desk lamp, the room was dark. The heavy red drapes were closed, blocking out any moonlight, or daylight, disallowing any reference to what time of day or night it was. It was the way his mother insisted when there was a "guest" in the cage. It kept them literally in the dark as to how long they'd been there. She had tried to explain this tried and true business model to him, but he didn't really understand it, and felt stifled by the darkness.

The desk lamp's pool of light spilled over into the enclosure enough so that Willie could see the eight-year-old girl's eyes when she turned them his way between bites of the peanut butter sandwich he'd brought her. It had been served on a paper plate as to not take any chances on them cutting themselves. Same went for utensils as they were always cheap plastic ones, and only when the meal called for them, which was rare.

He had dutifully refilled the cage's plastic dog bowl with fresh water, using the freestanding dog washing sink. This sink also made it easier for his mother to supervise the occasional sponge bath.

They weren't *savages*.

The girl in the cage had only been a guest there for twelve days and nights—not counting travel time from Portland, where they'd bagged her—but even he could notice how feral she now looked. Willie knew his mother would be taking her out of her small, locked enclosure after their own dinner. He knew this because he'd heard his mother and brother saying this girl would be sent away tomorrow. With Rose. And his mother always made them pretty before they left.

Willie looked over to the stairwell going up to the main level. It was short, with only eight steps, but he'd seen how difficult the process to go up and down it was for his mother. It usually took her a good ten minutes each way, and she could almost always smoke an entire cigarette with each passage. She relied on the wooden railings and kept one walker on each floor rather than carry it up and down.

It was why he liked to help. He wanted to be a good boy.

Willie turned away as he heard the child inhaling the two boiled eggs he'd peeled for her. He'd never had a pet of his own, but he imagined this is what feeding time would sound like. He didn't much care for this part of the job. Or much for any part of it anymore. His thoughts went to the lady he'd seen on TV in the motel room.

Deep down, in the bowels of his sasquatch soul, he was beginning to feel bad about things.

CHAPTER 25

MEANWHILE...
IN SILICON VALLEY
SUNDAY, 6:05 PM PACIFIC TIME

BING CROSBY WAS crooning from the high-end Bang & Olufsen CD player as William "Will" Masters polished off his second eggnog and placed the empty glass on the bathroom counter next to his dopp kit. Other than those toiletries, his duffel was packed and ready for the trip to Pleasant Hill. *Almost forgot.* He tossed a half dozen condoms into the kit.

He regarded his fit physique in the mirror. A boyish fifty-six, his impressive head of wavy hair having long ago turned platinum, he still had his movie-star good looks.

This would be his fourth Christmas spent at the Manor and his "charitable contributions" had assured his longstanding reservation was in good standing. It had become a twisted taboo tradition, after all, and he looked forward to these two-day festivals of debauchery.

Time away from family at the holidays wasn't an issue anymore. Since he'd divorced his fourth wife, Crystal, five years before, he had no one to answer to. No more lying or explaining his need to be away. She'd been handsomely compensated in their settlement, and it hadn't adversely affected his impressive portfolio in the slightest.

As the founder and former CEO of BrowzMasters Corporation, a Palo Alto, California-based software company, he'd amassed a considerable fortune and, with that, the freedom to do whatever he pleased, with whomever he pleased, and whenever he pleased.

BrowzMasters had been one of the early pioneers in internet security. The applications he and his team had developed had come into favor by top corporations, the U.S. military, and web surfers who valued a private experience. As a result, many who dwelled in the darker corners of the web were evangelical users of his products as it made their activities that much more difficult to trace.

It had also proved an opportune calling card as it served as an introduction to "Richard Atkinson" in Missouri, owner of the subterranean playground he'd come to enjoy so much.

A private plane would serve as his chariot to Shangri-La tomorrow. He smiled at his reflection again, unapologetically. He'd worked hard his whole life, and he deserved to have some fun. Even Bing seemed to sign-off on it.

It's beginning to look a lot like Christmas.

OUTSIDE DALLAS-FORT WORTH, TEXAS
SUNDAY, 8:10 CENTRAL TIME

Patrick Felice sliced away another bite of his imperfectly cooked rib-eye steak as he sat alone at his table at the Sirloin Depot. He'd asked for it medium rare, and it had come to him medium *well*. He was starved and too tired to pursue it, so he decided to go with it. The baked potato was on point. So was the young server. *Now she's medium rare.* He took a sip of the house merlot and sighed.

He enjoyed his position as Superintendent of Schools. He also enjoyed the winter break—as much, or more, than any of the thousands of students in his stewardship.

Despite his best efforts, which amounted to ten minutes on the treadmill three nights a week, he'd become a chubby bureaucrat. At sixty-three years old, he looked forward to his retirement in June, having served, by all appearances, a respectable forty-plus years in public education. Well respected by his colleagues, students, and parents alike, he had clawed his way to the top of the ladder, progressing from intern to tenured teacher, vice-principal to principal and, after jumping through several more hoops, eventually became Superintendent of Schools.

Both of his parents had been teachers. His mother, Susan, had taught kinder for twenty-two years before succumbing to brain cancer, and his father, Anthony, had braved the high schoolers as a science teacher until his retirement. He passed away the following year.

The field of education, naturally, seemed like a good fit for young Patrick and he dove in with both feet as soon as he could earn his credential.

It was during his third year of teaching, while still in his early twenties, and at his first assignment at a small school outside of Garland, that Patrick—*Mr. Felice*—began taking closer notice of the fourth graders in his charge. It wasn't all his students, but rather the young girls that captured his attention. They tended to develop more quickly than the boys, and—especially during those hot Texas summers—their young, budding shapes became impossible to ignore.

Still, he never acted on his impulses. He'd come close on several occasions, certainly, but he'd managed to keep himself in check. He didn't fancy finding himself labeled as a sex-offender for life, nor did he relish the idea of prison.

So he'd dug deep and soldiered on, rechanneling his energies into becoming an award-winning educator, and in this manner moved up—way up—in the education hierarchy.

He'd found an early outlet, first through pornographic printed material via some old copies of *Playboy* he'd found in the back of his father's closet. *Dad!* Then it had morphed into the digital realm with the onset of the world wide web. But after many years, it no longer was enough for him. It had become oddly dissatisfying and he'd eventually discovered that really dark corner. The pitch-black one, where he could better indulge his fascination with the younger ones, the underage ones. The forbidden fruit.

Like others of his ilk, he maintained his anonymity through BrowzMasters software. It was the layer of protection he and the legion of other sickos relied on to exist in this world undetected.

It was also how he'd come to find out about the Manor, a different kind of playground entirely and unlike any he'd ever seen in his four decades in the school system.

A lifelong bachelor, Patrick Felice had nobody at home to answer to. With no kids of his own, and two less-than-close younger siblings who'd long ago migrated to the East Coast, he only had one person to buy a gift for: himself.

And it was in the form of a two-day trip to Missouri. It wasn't Thailand, but he could wait till summer. He had his tickets already.

He gestured for the waitress to bring the check. She glanced over and nodded but seemed too busy to serve a smile with it. It'd be reflected in her tip.

He'd have his dessert tomorrow.

TAMPA, FLORIDA
SUNDAY, 9:15 PM EASTERN

It had been a long day at the salt mine for Preston Talbot, MD. A renowned cardiovascular surgeon, Doctor Talbot's open-heart procedure today had taken every minute of the five hours he'd estimated it to. But the patient survived. Barely.

His patient, a highly stressed and decidedly unhealthy-for-his-age, type-A real estate broker and a Class-A Asshole, was only fifty-one years old. Hot wife. Three little kids at home. Successful as hell. Talbot would be surprised if the guy ever saw sixty unless he made some major lifestyle changes. But who was he to judge? If he wanted to be a repeat client, fine with him. He had plenty of patients in that category, and business was good.

It was getting late, and the lengthy procedure had necessitated blowing off any hope of lunch. He enjoyed the last bite of his sensible, heart-friendly dinner, which consisted of a grilled, skinless chicken breast, fresh spinach salad, and some quinoa. He accompanied his meal with a glass of exquisite French chardonnay and pushed his plate to the side of the table.

Talbot was dining alone tonight. His wife, a youthful forty, was twenty years his junior, and had flown, along with their two teenaged kids, Leidy and Mandy, to her sister's family's home in Cincinnati. They'd be there for a week, and he'd promised he'd join them on Wednesday. Funny, but the past two years had been like that too.

What am I gonna do, fly twenty-two hours each way to Bangkok? He couldn't take that much time away from the hospital, nor his family. And, even in business class, it was excruciating. He'd already made the pilgrimage to Thailand on three occasions, and it was all he could think about. That's where he'd initially met a couple of the guys he'd be seeing this weekend.

The Manor assured discretion and a place to fulfill his twisted fantasies for a couple days. He needed to blow off a little steam, and he had a flight to catch tomorrow.

CONNELLY TOWNHOUSE
BALTIMORE, MARYLAND
SUNDAY, 9:22 PM EASTERN

Congress was in recess, and would be for another eleven days, which meant it was hunting season for the semi-honorable Congressman Martin Connelly.

A left-leaning Independent, Connelly was in his third term as a Representative in the U.S. House, and legislation he'd introduced—and seen passed—a few years back had been very helpful to the tech industry. And Will Masters of BrowzMasters was one who liked to return favors.

Thus, Congressman Martin Connelly quietly enjoyed some under-the-table perks. His campaigns were well financed thanks to contributions from the likes of Masters, and others, and the upcoming "hunting" trip was at his kind invitation.

Was it a true hunt? Not by any stretch of the imagination. This was a tiny, manmade, freshly stocked, and guaranteed-catch lake. All he had to bring was his pole. *Ahem.*

Connelly's carefully crafted image was as a vocal proponent of child safety laws. Whether it be cracking down on child trafficking, safer toys, or more nutritious school lunches, he was publicly all for it and a leading voice on the House floor.

A lifelong bachelor, he was a highly respected representative of the great state of Maryland. He was an expert at playing the game of public perception and, if eligible, would win an Academy Award for Best Performance by a Bad Actor.

Connelly set his wheeled carry-on bag by the front door. He checked the deadbolt, climbed into bed, and after confirming his alarm was set, turned off the lamp on his nightstand. He fell asleep with a smile on his face and visions of sugarplums.

CHAPTER 26

MURF'S PLACE
HAYDEN LAKE, IDAHO
SUNDAY, 6:55 PM PACIFIC

WAYNE MURPHY HAD long enjoyed his little slice of paradise. He and his late wife, Doris, had fallen in love with it at first sight, twenty-six years ago. Their shared love of fishing had made this the perfect place to settle down. There was, arguably, nothing more serene than sitting amongst the trees, baiting your hooks, and seeing what species of fish responded that day. Depending on the time of year, and what had been stocked, the lake might be teeming with bluegill, rainbow trout, cutthroat trout, yellow perch, white crappie, both large and small mouth bass....

Unfortunately, it seemed more and more people were discovering this beautiful area, just north of the Spokane River, since it was an easy commute from Coeur D'Alene and not far from Spokane itself. The damn airport was only forty-five minutes away.

Setting down his fork, he savored the last bite of his trout dinner and let out a sigh. He missed Doris terribly. He took a long pull from his new favorite beer, a Belgian-style white beer from the Selkirk Abbey brewery in Post Falls. *Doris would've liked this one.*

His two-bedroom cabin home was plenty big, especially now that he lived alone. The emptiness made it feel cavernous to him. He bussed his dishes to the sink, gave them a rinse and put the bones in the trash so the cat wouldn't get them. He decided he could wash dishes later. First, he had to cross-reference a couple of county records he'd found in the archives.

It seemed, if these old records were still current, there was somebody of interest who had once been living in the Coeur D'Alene area. The name on record was one Thore *Ecks.*

Deceased. *Damn. Maybe some kin still around?*

He looked up at the kitchen clock. A little late to be knocking on strangers' doors, certainly, but he wasn't sleepy, and he figured it couldn't hurt to have a stealthy look-see. After topping off the cat's kibble bowl, he grabbed his ski parka, cellphone, cane, and the truck keys. He had good snow tires.

Nice night for a little drive.

POP POP'S
SUNDAY, 10:15 PM

Curt turned sideways, hugging the wall in hopes he didn't knock off any of the ornaments as he squeezed his lumber-jack-like frame behind the artificial Douglas Fir. With a grunt and considerable effort, he stretched out his arm until he managed to reach the button on the power strip. With a flick he turned off Christmas. It felt more like Halloween than Christmas anyway. Evil spirits were out there and at play, and they had their little girl.

As he passed by the seldom-used gas fireplace, he paused to regard the large, hand-sewn stocking that hung next to the three adult ones. It was emblazoned with Rose's name, a fabric applique of an angel and another of a snow globe. It had been a recent purchase at the holiday craft fair in Mesa—a stock-ing Rose had picked out for herself—and Santa had stuffed it full of their precious angel's favorite toys and candies a couple of hours ago.

The Christmas tree and stockings; the gifts they'd liber-ated from the Road Runner's trunk and since wrapped; and the tiny, pink girl's bicycle Pop Pop had spent too many hours assembling—and cussing at—this evening…it was all they could do to keep their sanity and their collective hope alive for Rose's safe return. They couldn't surrender their family Christmas, nor their faith. If they did, the bad guys won.

Curt resumed his position, spooning with Phoenix, curled up on the oversized leather sofa in the mostly dark family room. She had exhausted her supply of tears tonight, and her hundreds of prayers were already out there, floating around somewhere, in hopes the seeds made purchase.

Curt stroked his wife's glow-in-the-dark hair gently and wrapped his massive arms around her tiny frame. She had always loved that, as he tended to generate as much heat as any fireplace could ever aspire to. She let out a sigh. Her faith and her hope were being tested, and she wasn't sure if she'd get a passing grade. She knew they needed a miracle at this point.

A telltale rattling sound came from the cut-crystal candy dish on the nearby end table. It was one of those dishes where you kept the good treats, not the arguably inferior treats like candy corn. Dove milk chocolate *Promises* were found here, and Pop Pop kept it stocked year-round. Despite your best efforts, you could spend an hour trying to stealthily replace that lid, but you might as well have been manning the cymbals in the orchestra. It might even be rigged to an alarm system.

"Luke! Leave it!" she called out. Luke reluctantly pulled his nose away from the treasure and awkwardly joined his humans in a dog pile. "Oomph!" Phoenix uttered as he climbed up. "Come here, baby," she said, including the furry shepherd boy in the group hug Prick had initiated an hour before.

With Rose missing, the dogs were clearly off. The humans were off. The whole world was…off its axis right now. *Lord, give me something.*

Pop Pop's phone display lit up as its lame factory ringtone let out a shrill musical alert. He jolted awake from his adjoining recliner. "Wha—?!" It took five rings for him to get reoriented. It was long-distance, and a caller he recognized. "Murf!"

This instantly got Phoenix's and Curt's attention. They quickly sat up, shooed away the pooches, and looked over at Pop Pop.

"Murf. What are you doing up, buddy?"

"Well, you know me, Flamer. Still a night owl. Hope I'm not callin' too late."

"No, man. We haven't been keeping regular hours around here of late," Pop Pop said.

"Suppose not," Murf replied softly.

Phoenix waved her arms to get Pop Pop's attention and whispered loudly, "Speaker!"

"Dave, you asked me to look into the name you gave me and—"

"Hey, Murf, sorry to interrupt. Gonna put you on speaker, okay?" he asked, nodding to Phoenix as he did.

"Yep," Murf responded, and he was now loud enough for all to hear.

"Okay, what were you saying?"

"Since we talked, I've been doing a little checking around up here, poked around some of the old city and county records—I've got a buddy still works there. Looking for any names that matched the one you gave me."

Phoenix got off the sofa and went over to Pop Pop's chair, hovering over his phone.

"Anything?" Pop Pop asked, taking his Lazy Boy out of recline mode as he sat up.

"Not sure. But there's one old record with a name match. A man by the name of—and I know I'm probably butchering the pronunciation—Thore Ecks."

"Thor…like the superhero, with the hammer. Thor."

"Maybe. All I know is the spelling's *Tango Hotel Oscar Romeo Echo*. Last name Ecks."

"Okay," Pop Pop replied, scribbling the name on a note pad. "Where's he live, Murf? Could he be—?"

"Doubt it. Deceased, I'm afraid," Murf said bluntly.

"Damn," Pop Pop muttered. Murf could hear the defeat in his friend's voice. "So, we're back to square one?"

"Not sure about that yet," Murf replied.

"Mr. Murphy. Hi, it's Phoenix, Dave's daughter," she interjected, hoping to cut through the cryptic responses.

"Awful sorry to hear about your troubles, miss," Murf said, mustering up some until-now unheard sensitivity. "Really am...."

"Thank you. And thanks so much for your help, by the way," she said.

"Least I can do," he replied.

"So, this Ecks guy is no longer living, you said. Do we have anything else to go on?" she asked, not even trying to hide her desperation. She closed her eyes as she spoke. "*Anything?*"

"Well, it might be something and it might be nothing, but I'll tell you what I *do* know," Murf said, pausing to take another look through his field glasses. "I'm sittin' in my truck right now, a little ways off from a property address that was listed for this Ecks fella."

"You're there? At his old house? Right now?!" Phoenix pressed urgently.

"Yes, ma'am. Can't see too much from my position 'cause I don't want to spook anybody, but there's somebody living there. More than one, I think. Smoke comin' from the chimney, coupla lights are on. Seen somebody pass by a window a coupla times. Somebody's definitely home."

"Could be anyone living there now though, right?" Pop Pop jumped in, a reluctant devil's advocate.

"Could be. But there's a bunch of mailboxes sittin' at the

bottom of the hill, before you head up the driveway here. Care to guess the name on the box?"

"*Jesus…*" Phoenix muttered, her hand to her mouth.

"No, that ain't it," Murf answered.

Pop Pop rubbed his eyes, trying to muster up some clarity of thought. "Murf…."

"Yeah, Flame…."

"Listen, buddy. Like you said, this could be something or it could be nothing, but—for right now—let's just play this like it's *something*."

"Roger that. What do you want me to do?"

"Murf, it's Curt…Phoenix's husband," he said more loudly than necessary.

"Yes, Curt."

"I'm thinking we throttle back for the night and think this through," Curt said, searching the eyes of the others in the room. Phoenix and Pop Pop both nodded their agreement.

"So, you don't want me to call the—"

"God, no," Phoenix said, cutting him off. "Murf, we don't want to spook these guys—if it is indeed these guys—and, as you know, we don't want to risk our little girl's safety. No police. Not yet. Please." Her eyes were wide now.

"Understood," Murf confirmed. "Guess I'll head back down the hill, and we can talk in the morning. They're not going anywhere tonight. Make sense?"

"Yes," came the chorus of three.

"Roger that," Murf said.

"Say, Murf," Pop Pop said, jumping in. "You gonna be around? Not going anywhere to be with family, being Christmas and all?"

"Nah. No family to be with, really. I'll be around. Just me and my cat."

"Okay. Remind me how far you are from the Spokane airport," Pop Pop said, exchanging looks with Phoenix and Curt.

"Forty-five minutes, give or take, depending on weather. Why do you ask?"

"When we get off the phone, I'm going to inquire about available flights for tomorrow morning. If I can find something, how would you feel about having a little company?" Dave asked, his face a grimace.

"Been a long time, Flamer. Circumstances aren't the best, but I'd love the company. All of you. Call me in the morning, let me know what you find out."

"Roger that. Thanks again, buddy."

CHAPTER 27

THE CABIN
MONDAY MORNING, 8:15 AM
CHRISTMAS EVE

THINGS WERE FAR from "holly jolly" at the breakfast table, but not for the lack of foodstuffs.

Gretl shuffled around the kitchen in her heavy robe and slippers as she plated the last of the pan-fried bacon that had been draining on a cutting board laden with paper towels. She had prepared two full packages of it because her little Willie liked bacon.

She carried it over to the table and set it down next to another platter containing a mountain of breakfast potatoes. Scrambled eggs; yogurts and a few Danish cheeses; and some good German bread and assorted marmalades rounded out the menu.

Rose yawned, picked at her raspberry yogurt, and kept her eyes down—that is, when she wasn't sneaking sideways glances at the closed door down the hall.

Willie gleefully grabbed eight slices of the bacon with his sausage fingers and put them on his plate. He'd already dished himself enough potatoes and eggs to feed a small army. Dieter stared at him with the usual disgust.

"You'd better eat all that, Creep," Dieter said. His brother looked back at him cluelessly.

"How many times have I told you not to call your brother that!?" Gretl barked as she took her seat. "Pass the potatoes," she said angrily.

"I don't like it when he calls me names, Mama," Willie said as he passed her the dish.

"See?" she hissed, letting the urge to bitch-slap her eldest pass. "Can't we all just get along? It's Christmas Eve, ferchrissakes!"

Dieter rolled his eyes and crunched on a piece of well-done bacon. His gaze went to the window. There was snow coming down now, but not as heavy as before. He took a sip of his coffee. "Got to go online, check the weather report," he said as he stood and pushed in his chair.

"You've hardly eaten any breakfast," his mother said through a mouthful of country taters.

"Eat later. Got to make sure we're not grounded."

"Suit yourself. Hey, if you're going downstairs, might as well take a plate of food with you, and plastic utensils. She'll be hungry."

Dieter was loath to give his mother the satisfaction of a verbal reply, so he begrudgingly grabbed a paper plate and threw a few spoonfuls of potatoes and eggs on it. From a drawer, he produced a plastic knife and fork and held them out for Gretl to see before he headed down the hall.

Rose watched as he disappeared behind the stairwell door and noisily took the steps going down.

She'll be hungry.

PHOENIX SKY HARBOR AIRPORT
MONDAY MORNING
CHRISTMAS EVE

They wouldn't all be sitting together, which was far from being a dealbreaker. It was nothing short of a miracle that Pop Pop had been able to find them seats at all on such short notice. Miracles such as this came with a hefty price tag as the airlines took advantage of last-minute holiday bookings where they could add opportunistic price hikes to the fares. And, knowing you can't put a price on family, Pop Pop had ponied up without any hesitation.

It was 8:20 a.m. and they were bed-heading it. They had barely made it to the gate in time for their 8:55 flight, and boarding was now underway. Other flights had been available, starting as early as 5:20 a.m., but that wasn't an option with all the pieces in play.

As it was, they were lucky the next-door neighbor's college-aged daughter, April, was home for the holidays and willing to take care of the dogs. And the bird. They'd used her before on one occasion and she was trustworthy. Being as it was such short notice, Pop Pop had offered her an insanely generous one-hundred dollars per day, which she had more than gladly accepted.

Pop Pop and Curt found their respective seats, just behind the wings, Pop Pop's on the left side of the plane and Curt's across the aisle. Each of them had only packed a small carry-on bag, which they stuffed in the overhead.

The only other available seat on this flight went to Phoenix, and she was riding First Class for the first time. Pop Pop fastened his seatbelt and looked up the aisle toward the First Class section. Phoenix leaned into the aisle and turned toward him, flashing a big thumbs up before buckling herself in. She pulled her cassette Walkman and headphones from her bag as she planned to escape into her music once they were airborne.

Curt shifted his large frame in his insanely cramped seat, trying to find a position where his kneecaps wouldn't suffer too badly. It was only about a two-and-a-half-hour flight, nonstop.

Pop Pop turned his gaze out his window. The flight attendants were demonstrating the important safety features of this aircraft, but his mind was elsewhere. He wasn't sure what the game plan was yet, which wasn't his style. This knee-jerk, seat-of-your-pants operation—if you could even call it that—went against all his Navy training. But the clock was ticking and had been for some time. They were winging it, and that's when mistakes can happen.

All he knew was that Murf might have stumbled upon a potential lead, and they hadn't had many of those. He'd also generously opened his place to them and would be keeping a stealthy watch on Casa Ecks to the best of his ability until they rendezvoused that afternoon. After that, all bets were off. He had to hang onto hope though.

Pop Pop exhaled from ballooned cheeks as the plane taxied to their holding position on the runway. Across the aisle, Curt closed his eyes. He'd be asleep as soon as they were airborne. It happened every time.

In the front of the plane, Phoenix closed her eyes and clutched her tape player tightly as she silently recited the Lord's Prayer.

The jet engines began to roar, the aircraft vibrated as it gained thrust, rocketing down the runway as it reached the requisite groundspeed and, with a steep lift, became airborne. She looked out the window and watched as the airfield and surrounding areas shrunk to miniature size, like something from Disneyland's "It's A Small World" attraction.

Leaving Phoenix.

They'd be sharing the sky with thousands of other flights today, but four were noteworthy:

Leaving Baltimore/Washington

Leaving Dallas/Fort Worth

Leaving San Francisco

Leaving Tampa

GILBERT POLICE STATION
RAMAGE'S OFFICE
CHRISTMAS EVE, 9:05 AM

Officer Ramage had tried. At the suggestion of his partner, he'd managed to spend a little time at home with his fish but, try as he might, he found he couldn't turn off his mind. Not with the clock ticking on this case. He had to come in. Besides, his fish sucked as company.

He sat at his desk and pulled the lid off his tall Circle K coffee, dipping his old-fashioned cake donut into it as he reread the report from Butte for the tenth time. He glanced over at the printer. Nothing new had come in.

As he went to pull the donut from the hot java, the soggy piece cleaved off, polluting his French roast with a thousand small particles of doughy crap, ruining the start of his day.

"For fuck's sake!" he yelled out to the empty office. Stuffing the remaining donut half in his mouth, he replaced the coffee's plastic lid and placing the vessel upright in his empty trash can and punched a number into his cell. It rang several times before going to voicemail.

"Hey, partner. Uh, Merry Christmas. Listen, uh, against better judgment I decided to come into the office. Nothing new to report, so kind of a waste of time, but sitting around at home's just not my style. Anyway, I'm thinking I might pay a little visit to the LaFlamme residence, see how they're holding up. Still kind of curious as to why they'd said they might know something then changed their story. Anyway, I'm reachable if you get this, but don't feel you need to call back. Hope you're having a cool yule, Moser. Later."

Ramage looked at his watch and switched off the lights. He decided he'd make one stop on the way.

Showing up unannounced on Christmas Eve was decidedly uncool, so he hoped the poinsettia he'd bought from the sidewalk vendor might be a nice gesture. He shifted the plant to his left hand and knocked on the front door, making the dogs go ballistic. As he waited for someone to answer, he looked over at the driveway. LaFlamme's truck was still parked there. Nobody was responding to his knocks, so he walked up the driveway and peeked through the garage window. *Road Runner's gone.*

"Hello?" a voice called out. Ramage spun around. It sounded like a woman's voice, and it had come from the front of the house. He scurried back toward the source. As he arrived at the porch, the door was open and a tall, leggy nineteen-year-old blonde disarmed him with her smile.

"Oh, hi…um, I'm sorry, I must be at the wrong house," he said, almost stammering as he looked around to get his bearings. "I'm sorry to bother you, I was looking for David LaFlamme."

"Good morning. Yes, well, you're at the right address. I live next door—well, visiting family—on semester break. I'm just watching Mr. LaFlamme's place," she said. Again, the smile. He had a Glock on his hip, yet he was clearly outgunned.

"Oh. I didn't know they were going away," he said, which was the truth, since he'd asked them to remain available for more questioning if necessary. He returned his personal best police officer smile. "Did he say how long he'd be gone? Where he was going? Did they all—?"

"All three of them, yes. Left early this morning. Said they were visiting a friend, not sure where, and didn't say how long, sorry."

Ramage's brow furrowed momentarily. "Hey, no problem. I was just in the area and wanted to wish them a Merry Christmas. Uh, would you mind telling them I stopped by? Here's my card, and please tell them this is from me," he said, handing her the plant.

"It's beautiful. I sure will…" she looked at the card, then back to him, "…Officer Ramage."

"Great. Thanks. Well, if you happen to hear from them, would you mind calling me at that cell number? Really appreciate it."

"Sure thing, Officer. Merry Christmas," April said, beaming her Colgate-commercial smile. He stared for about three seconds longer than was appropriate then nodded. He hoped he wasn't blushing as he turned and walked back to his car.

Where did you guys run off to?

CHAPTER 28

THE CABIN, 10:05 AM

GRETL WAS SHOWERING down the hall, leaving Willie to supervise Rose at the kitchen table while he washed the dishes and put the leftovers away. Dieter had come back up from the basement and gone outside. And back inside. And outside. He'd been out there for a while now, doing God knows what.

Willie put the plates back into the cupboard and regarded the lonely little girl with the sad expression. She was holding a Hummel figurine that portrayed a little girl and her dog. The girl in the figure looked a lot like herself.

Willie set the dish towel on the counter and went to the ceramic cookie cannister sitting atop the fridge. He reached in, pulling out two wrapped treats and joined Rose at the table. He set one down in front of her. She looked at it, then at him. "What is it?" she asked.

"It's good. It's Marzipan," he replied with a smile that told Rose he probably hadn't seen a dentist in recent years. "It's from Germany. Where I used to live. Try it." It was like two first-graders sharing treats from their sack lunches.

Rose looked at it with interest. It was about six inches in length and thicker than the candy bars she was accustomed to. She rarely turned down a treat and as she picked it up, it felt both heavy and girthy in her tiny hand. She slowly peeled away the blue wrapper on the milk chocolate-covered confection. "It's chocolate."

"Chocolate outside. But it's marzipan. From Germany. Better than just regular chocolate," he promised as he watched her inspect the almond-rich delicacy. It was the good marzipan. The best, actually, as it was manufactured by the one and only J. G. Niederegger GmbH & Company, in his old hometown of Lübeck.

Rose put it up to her nose, noting it smelled more like the hand lotion her mommy used than like chocolate, but took a bite. Several seconds went by as she did a taste analysis, while big Willie watched for her reaction.

She swallowed, and her sour expression made her disappointment clear. She turned to Willie. "I don't think I like nazzi palm," she said.

Willie's smile slowly vanished. "Marzipan," he corrected. "You don't have to eat it. I thought you might like it," he said softly. A dejected little boy.

"Thank you though. You're nice," Rose said. "Nicer than that other man."

Willie looked back at her and recouped part of his smile. He couldn't remember the last time he'd been complimented. For anything. And this little girl was the closest thing to a friend he'd ever had—at least in all his years on this side of the pond.

"I don't think he has Jesus in his heart," she added. "He's mean, and I don't like the way he treats you."

"He's my brother," he said, resigned to the fact, and to his lot in life. He opened the red wrapper on his own bar, which was the same as hers but covered in dark chocolate. He bit off a large piece and chewed it noisily while Rose watched him.

"Who's downstairs?" she asked bluntly, stopping him midway through his chew.

"What?"

"Downstairs. Somebody's down there," she said, drawing on her detective skills. "Who is it? Do you have another brother? A sister?"

Willie shook his head slowly. He wasn't sure he was supposed to say anything. This was new territory for him, and above his mental pay grade. "No," he said softly, returning to his candy.

Rose wasn't satisfied with his non-answer. "Who is it then?" she probed further.

Willie swallowed his bite and set the candy back down. He looked down the hall for a moment, then looked down at the table. His comfort level had been breached and the bad feelings he'd had before were returning. He shook his head in response to the feeling and to her queries. It was his nonverbal reply indicating he didn't want to talk about it. He looked out the window and watched the snowflakes coming down lightly. His brother had been out there a long time, it seemed.

"Willie!" the hoarse voice bellowed from the other end of the hall. "Bring me my slippers, son!" Gretl called out, followed by another round of hacking.

"Yes, Mama," Willie said, getting up from the table.

"Stay here," he said softly to Rose, before disappearing down the hall.

Murf set down his Bushnell binoculars and took a long pull from his thermal mug. He had his wipers on, intermittently at the moment, which helped with the snowflakes, but if it got much heavier, he might lose his line of sight to the house. And he didn't want to kill his battery.

He'd seen one figure, a rather short man, make a few trips between the house and the garage building, where a vehicle was parked inside. It was hard to determine a make and model, but it appeared to be red. Maybe a Dodge. Not sure. The man had also pulled something out of the house and been futzing with it for a while. He couldn't discern exactly what though. Appeared heavy, whatever it was, as he'd had to drag it. He looked at his watch and did some mental math. He hoped the weather didn't get worse, for two reasons: he needed to keep eyes on this house, and Flamer's group would be driving a rental over here from Spokane. *They're Arizonans. Probably not too used to driving in this stuff.*

Murf took a bite of the onion bagel he'd been neglecting and lifted the binoculars for another look. He watched the man go back inside. He could barely see shit at this point, and the cold sure wasn't doing his bum leg any favors. Weather permitting, he'd stay for as long as it takes, but you never knew what mother nature might bring. And you never know what's going on behind closed doors.

THE MANOR
PLEASANT HILL, MISSOURI
1:55 PM CENTRAL

Candy had spent the past hour making tweaks to the Christmas tree decorations in the main room. The twins had done a decent enough job with the spacing of ornaments—after all, they'd had a photo of last year's tree for reference—but the embellishments she'd added really made it pop. She stood back and admired her work.

This wasn't like just having a few inconsequential cousins over for an obligatory eggnog. Things had to be taken up a notch as there were some very wealthy and influential guests arriving later, and it had to be perfect. Their host would accept nothing less.

MacKenzie and Rebekah had finished washing the windows and had been asked to bring several items up from the supply building, per Candy's written list. These items included, but were not limited to, the designated bottles of wine and champagne, cheeses; and desserts and assorted snack items. They had been provided with a sturdy wheeled cart for this purpose, and they had previously demonstrated a willingness and trustworthiness to take on this chore.

"Looks lovely," the voice said, startling her. She spun around to find Sebastian Brewer standing behind her, regarding the tree and the newly festive ambiance of the room. "Even nicer than last year, Candy. Well done," he added.

"I'm glad you approve. Yes, I think so too," she said with a proud smile. She was a perfectionist. That's why he'd trusted her with the details.

"Should be a nice night for a party. Not sure if it'll be nice enough to spend any time outdoors, but let's put out the patio warmers and have the girls bring plenty of wood for the fire pits. Just in case."

"Will do. Flights should be airborne by now. Hoping the Idaho one's able to beat the storm."

"Mm," Brewer muttered. "Hoping so. If not, don't pay the bonus we'd talked about."

"Okay. I'll monitor the weather reports. Roger's got the schedules and they'll be shuttling guests as they come in. The Escalades have been gassed and washed. Everything's on track. I'll make sure all the girls are ready."

"Good. Good. It sounds like we're in very capable hands—*yours*—so I think I'll take a walk, then have a tan session before my nap. If I'm not up by five, please wake me."

"You've got it," Candy said, giving him a peck on the cheek. As he closed the front door behind him, she went to the window and watched him begin his stroll along the tree line. As he disappeared on to the walking trail, she consulted her own "to do" list. Most everything had been checked off but there was one very important item that couldn't be overlooked.

She went to the closet and found the two-step folding stool, utilizing it to retrieve something from the top shelf. It was heavy, so she took great care in lifting it down. As she descended the steps with it, she noticed the item was slightly dusty. Not surprising, considering it was only used once a year, and only for these annual parties.

She placed it on the counter, next to the kitchen sink, and prepared a bath of mild suds. The cube-shaped box had twelve-inch sides and was constructed of thick, rose-colored, heavy-duty, translucent glass. After a careful cleaning with a soapy sponge and a thorough rinse, she dried it with a soft, lint-free towel. The finishing touch was a few spritzes of glass cleaner and a wipe down to remove any streaks.

This box had an important role, as it did every year, and would be placed atop a festive table runner on the long entry-way table, surrounded by a few decorative pinecones, just beyond the front entrance door. Guests knew of its existence, as well as its purpose, and all agreed to comply with it. After all, it was for *all* their protection.

Upon landing, each would power down their cellphones and remove their batteries. They would remain powered down until they were airborne again, two days later. Until then, they'd go in the box immediately upon arrival at the Manor.

No phones, no cameras. Those were the rules here.

SPOKANE INTERNATIONAL
ARRIVALS, CURBSIDE
12:10 PM PACIFIC

Phoenix and Curt stood at the curb just outside, the three carry-on bags at their feet. Pop Pop had told them to watch for him to pull around in their rental, a white Chevy Tahoe. He'd gone with Enterprise rental since he was a veteran, and had scored an upgraded unit with a built-in navigation system. They'd need one where they were going.

Phoenix squinted as she tried to discern the makes and models of the myriad of SUVs making the rounds, all seemingly picking up happy family on this Christmas Eve. Lots of Subaru lovers here, she noted. Out of the pack, a larger vehicle emerged. White and with a giant, brushed-gold Chevy emblem. It had to be him. She waved, which got a flash of the headlights in acknowledgement as it approached. The Tahoe pulled to the curb in front of them and the passenger window rolled down. "Toss the bags in the back and hop in," Pop Pop said.

"Yep," Phoenix said as she and Curt popped the liftgate and inserted the bags. Curt offered to take the rear seat, but Phoenix insisted that he ride "shotgun" since he was the much larger of the two, and she'd flown first class already.

"Got the GPS. Good," Curt said. "Okay, gimme a quick second to punch in the address your buddy gave us." Pop Pop nodded agreement then turned his attention to the highly stressed airport security guy in the yellow vest. He didn't envy this guy's job, especially on a crazy travel day like this. The guy scowled and blew his whistle, waving them on. Pop Pop waved, trying to buy another few seconds.

Curt pushed another button on the infotainment panel and a flashing icon appeared. "Okay, got it. Good to go!" he said, as Pop Pop engaged his blinker and pulled into the stream of cars, each filled with people who were having a better Christmas than they were.

Guaranteed.

X

Murf's phone vibrated from its perch atop the dashboard. He'd wisely turned off the ringer as to not alert anybody up at the cabin. Sound traveled out here. He set the binocs on the passenger seat and looked at the display.

"You made it," he said, rubbing his face with his free hand.

"Thus far anyway, yeah, man," Pop Pop replied. "Headed east on 90. How're you doin'? You still on site there?"

"Yeah, still here. A few snow flurries have made it difficult to see much, but I did see one fella. Short guy. Making trips in and out of the home. It's a log cabin."

"I'm sorry, did you say a short guy?"

"Appeared to be. Shorter than me, anyway, and I'm five-ten. This guy was several inches shorter than me, from what I could tell. Why, that important?"

Phoenix whispered loudly, "Speaker!" Pop Pop glanced at his phone and pushed the button, allowing them all to participate.

"Murf, one of the guys the authorities are looking for is approximately five-six, medium build. He's been seen with another man, much taller—the guy's a monster by comparison. Way bigger than me. Any sign of anyone matching that description?" Pop Pop asked. Concern was written all over his face as he drove.

"No. I haven't seen anyone else clearly. Other than seeing somebody walk by a window a few times. But from where I'm parked, and with the snow, it's difficult to see much more. You want me to move in closer? I'd have to do it on foot, if so."

"No, Murf. Stay where you are. If these are the guys, we must assume they're armed, and very dangerous."

"Did you see a little girl, Murf?" Phoenix interjected, a desperate Hail Mary query from the back seat.

"No, miss. Not yet, but I'll keep my eyes peeled."

"What about a vehicle? Did you see what they might've been driving?" Curt asked.

"Hard to make out the year and make, but the guy made several trips to an SUV parked in the open garage. Red. Dodge, maybe, but not sure."

Dave shot a look over at Curt, then to Phoenix in the mirror.

"Look, Murf, I think we're still about thirty minutes out, per the nav system. Stay put, brother. We'll call you when we get to that mailbox you told me about, okay? Call me back if anything changes."

"Roger that," Murf said, and the call ended.

Seconds later, the large green road sign welcomed them to Idaho. This shit was starting to get real.

MOSER RESIDENCE
EAST MESA, ARIZONA
12:25 PM

Bethany Moser pulled the tray of saguaro-shaped sugar cookies from the oven, much to the delight of her little four-year-old elf, Darla, and placed it atop the gas stove's burners to cool. They'd already baked a similar sized batch, but of the more traditional Christmas tree variety. Darla was chomping at the bit to decorate them, and Bethany was looking forward to this mother-daughter bonding experience with her.

From the opposite kitchen counter, her cellphone came to life. "Don't touch the trays, honey, they're still very hot. Mommy has to take this call for a second, then we'll ice the Christmas trees, okay?"

"'Kay, Mommy," Darla replied, spinning circles in her bare feet.

"Moser," she answered, walking the few feet to the dining area.

"Merry Christmas, partner."

"Hey, Jeff. Merry Christmas to you too, partner. I was just about to check in with you. Wassup?"

"Eh, not sure. Maybe nothing. But I can't help but think something might be brewing. Just a gut feeling."

"Huh. What's your gut telling you?"

"Like I said, it might be nothing. But I made a stop by LaFlamme's place earlier. Brought them a plant, one of the red ones."

"Poinsettia?"

"Probably. Listen, when I knocked on their door, they weren't home. His truck was there but the orange car was gone."

"Could've gone out for brunch or something. Not entirely unusual in and of itself. Christmas Eve and all."

"True. But a neighbor girl answered their door. Said she was watching their dogs, and their place, while they were gone."

"Gone. Like, *gone* gone?"

"Uh-huh. She didn't know where they went off too, or for how long. But yeah. Gone. Out of town. Seem weird to you?"

"Maybe. I dunno. What do we know about other family members? Think they—?"

"Mm, not sure, but I don't think they just up and took a sleighride to grandma's—if there even is a grandma—especially considering everything going on. Doesn't feel right. Maybe I'm reading into it, but I don't think so."

"Hm...and nothing new coming in from any of the agencies this morning?"

"Nope. They're watching border crossing points, airports in Great Falls, Glacier, Boise, Seattle. The Highway Patrol, hell, *everyone's* out there looking out for the red Durango. But we seem to have lost the trail after Butte."

"Mommy, can we do the frosting now?" the elf asked, pulling on her mama's apron.

"Couple of minutes, honey," she said, covering the mouthpiece.

"Aww...."

"Sorry, Jeff," she said.

"Hey, it sounds like I might be interrupting something there," Ramage said. "That's important too."

"It is, but I can still come into the office for a while if you think—"

"Nah. Listen, you enjoy your time with the little one."

"Okay, thanks, partner. If anything else comes to mind— or to gut—don't hesitate to call me back. Promise?"

"Promise."

"Merry Christmas, Jeff."

"Merry Christmas, Bethany." As the call ended, she couldn't help but take notice that this was the first time he'd ever called her by her first name.

She placed the phone next to the coffee machine and

spun around to her daughter, mustering all the excitement the moment called for. "Who's ready to decorate some cookies?!"

"Me!!!"

"Okay, let's start with some green frosting. Then we can add sprinkles, okay?"

"Yay!"

As she retrieved the premade icing from the pantry, Officer Moser's thoughts went to the concerns Ramage had raised. *Where would they go?*

CHAPTER 29

THE CABIN
12:40 PM

DIETER STOMPED HIS feet several times, entered the cabin, and closed the front door with a thud. "Fucking Idaho," he muttered through clenched teeth. He'd never liked it here and was working on his accelerated exit plan. And it wouldn't include a trollish mother or an oafish sibling.

He could hear the whir of the hair dryer coming from down the hall and looked at his watch. She'd been in there forever, he knew, because she always washed her hair afterward, and in the sink. Creep helped her out with that once or twice a week, depending on when she decided to shampoo the rat's nest. His nostrils flared as he noted a strong peroxide odor.

Coloring that shit again...? Why, for fuck's sake?

Dieter shook his head and opened the door to the basement, his boots clomping each step on the way down into the dark pit. The computer's screen was glowing, and the weather website was still on the screen. He plopped down into the desk chair and refreshed the browser, waiting several long seconds for it to update. It looked like he might have a narrow window of decent weather if he moved on it. His attention went to the edge of the browser's open window. There was the edge of something else. *Another open window?* He clicked it and his face froze.

The Yahoo! Mail window took center stage on his screen, and it showed a mailbox with a familiar name. It took him a few seconds to recognize it: *Phoenix Martinsen.* His brow furrowed and he cocked his head slightly as he saw a tiny checkmark icon, along with a confirmation that said, *Your Message Has Been Sent.* "What. The. Fucking...*fuck!*" he barked.

He went to the Sent mailbox and a new email popped up. It was sent to Phoenix Martinsen, from herself. It was brief, and poorly written, but damning as hell:

Mommy. Itts Rose mommy. I mis you and daddy. I am in the sno and scarred . thees peepl are not nise can you find me and bring me home .

I luv you . xoxo

Dieter pounded the desk as he jumped up from his chair and spun around, his eyes searching the dark space. He stormed over to the cage in the corner and grabbed the padlock. It was still locked, and he could make out the outline of the girl, crouched in her usual corner.

It was a couple of quick strides to the staircase landing and the single light switch. He flicked it on, and the caged girl cowered from the naked bulb's brilliance, like a vampire at sunrise. "Where the fuck are you?" he hissed, before changing his tone to sound less threatening. "Come out where I can see you. You're not in any trouble," he lied.

A quick look under the desk, under the dog sink, and inside the cabinets told him she wasn't down here. "Where'd she go?!" he screamed to the cage. "Tell me where she is!!

The girl looked back at him with wide eyes that broadcast her level of fear. Dieter burned her with a hateful stare for a second longer and decided she didn't know. He bounded upstairs, taking them two at a time.

At the landing to the main floor, Dieter could no longer hear the hair dryer. He whipped around the corner to the kitchen where he saw Creep just staring vacuously at the empty table. "Where's the girl?" he demanded. Creep looked back at him blankly. "You had one fucking job!!"

"I'm sorry," he said softly, his head hanging down now.

"You are way beyond *sorry...*" he said in a tone that conveyed his utter disgust. "Go outside, right fucking now, and look on the side of the garage. The *side* of the garage, you hear me?! See if she's there. *Go!*"

Willie's eyes began to moisten. He turned, grabbed his heavy coat, and went outside. Dieter watched until his brother closed the door behind him. *I'm so done. With both of you.*

He gave the main room a quick scan before bolting down the hall and into Gretl's bedroom. No sign of the girl, only a beached whale beginning a nap. Gretl's eyes opened and she blinked rapidly. Her son was standing over her, a wild, panicky look on his face.

"What's going on?" she asked, managing to prop herself up slightly on one elbow.

"Your precious Willie lost her! That's what's going on!"

he answered. "I'm gonna find her and we're gonna fly out of here. Now!"

"You're not going anywhere—and definitely not flying in this shit," she commanded. "You find her and put her in the box with the other. We'll wait out the storm. Don't you be a stupid—" Their loving conversation was interrupted by a loud metallic clunk and a howling, bloodcurdling scream coming from outdoors.

"What was that?" Gretl asked, her eyes wide with alarm.

"From the sound of it, I'm pretty sure that was your precious little Willie," he said, an until now unseen level of evil on his face.

"Out of my way!" she demanded as she labored—and failed—to lift her mass from the mattress. "Help me up, you idiot!" That was the final straw for Dieter.

He pushed her back down, straddled her and, grabbing a pillow, stuffed it into her face and leaned his palms into it while putting his weight behind it. She flailed her arms and her legs kicked as she screamed her muffled protests. He leaned in harder, bucking like a bull rider at the rodeo. "You don't get to call me an idiot," he said in a hissed whisper. "Not anymore, you...sorry...excuse...for a...*mother*."

Gretl tried digging her nails into his forearms, but her strength was diminishing. Dieter could feel it and hear it. "Mmmmfffff."

"So long, farewell, auf Wiedersehen, goodnight... Adieu, adieu, to yieu and yieu and yieu," he sang softly, maniacally, as the life slowly left her body. "Mmmmffffff" came from the backup singer.

He waited several seconds to confirm the kill and to process the finality of the event, then stood and spun down the hall. He quickly bounded upstairs and did a quick sweep.

Little shit must've gone outside.

The front door flew open, and he spilled out onto the porch, pulling on his wool cap and quickly zipping his snow coat. With a quick glance, he scanned the perimeter then, looking down, he saw a trail of tiny, round, Uggs-shaped footprints leading off the porch and heading toward the garage building. He also heard a deep moaning coming from that direction. It sounded like a wounded grizzly, but he knew it wasn't.

As he rounded the corner, he confirmed the source. Amazingly, his brother, Willie, had done what he'd been asked, for once, and gone exactly where he'd been told to: where he'd buried the bear trap.

The bear of a man had fallen to his knees in the bloodied snow, his right leg nearly severed from the fierce bite of the trap, his face frozen in a nearly silent scream. Standing next to him was a little redheaded girl, her face made ugly by tears, snot, and an expression of abject horror. "Help him!!!" Rose screamed.

Dieter just looked back at her through dead eyes. Seeing his brother in such pain almost made Dieter feel bad—but only for a nanosecond, before the feeling instantly passed. He felt nothing now. For any of them. His only thought now was getting this delivery done. He'd decided he would be done after this one.

Willie's giant chest heaved involuntarily several times as he gathered air for another primal scream. It came out as a low, rolling, desperate wail and as it began to lose its power, he stared into the expressionless face of his sibling, the one who had sent him to his death. There was a rare moment of understanding between them, and Dieter just marked it with a shrug.

The pool of red-stained snow was getting bigger as Willie continued to bleed out. It wouldn't be too much longer, Dieter decided. He definitely wasn't one to stick around and have a final kumbaya moment. He lunged forward, startling Rose as he grabbed her by the waist and stomped over to the Durango waiting in the open garage. Popping the rear hatch with his free hand, he set Rose inside the cargo area. Rose screamed her panicky protest as he closed the hatch behind her.

Rose's movements were restricted due to the new confines, made smaller by the metal dog barrier Dieter had installed behind the back seat. She wasn't going anywhere, and he wasn't going to fuck around with her squirming free-range in the back seat.

Dieter climbed in and started the Durango, its exhaust joining the snow flurry to create a sizeable white cloud.

Murf lowered the binoculars, his jaw slacked in response to what he was witnessing. "Holy Mother of God," he muttered in disbelief. His heart began to race, and he could feel his blood pressure rising. He jumped at the sound of his cellphone's ringer and answered without looking at the display.

"Flame! That you?"

"Yeah, Murf. Look, we're here—at the bottom of the hill, by the mailboxes. Hit some serious traffic with a jackknifed truck and didn't have cell service for a while. Anything going on up where you are?"

"You could say that, yeah!"

"Talk to me, Murf!"

"Wait one…" he replied, trying to get another look through the binocs.

Phoenix's cellphone lit up in her hand. Its display showed

an email icon. She scrunched her brow as she went to her mailbox and saw the one new message. As she opened it, she noticed it was from herself, and the construction of the message immediately told her it was written by a first grader. *Her first grader!* Her hand went up to her mouth and she let out a shriek. Pop Pop's eyes went to the mirror and locked into hers. "What is it?"

Curt spun around in his seat and, having only seen that expression on her once before— while they were being pursued by the Pirate—knew it was something bad. "Phoenix! What is it, baby?" She couldn't answer because her air had been snatched away. Curt grabbed the phone from her hand, and it took him two seconds to know what he was looking at. "Jeezus," he said, before looking over at Pop Pop. "It's... an email...an email from...Rose!!"

What?! Pop Pop took the phone and stared at the tiny screen with disbelief. It *was* Rose, and she'd remembered how to log into her mommy's account, as he'd shown her. *Good girl!*

Murf set down the binoculars; he couldn't really see much now. "Did you say something, Dave? Kinda garbled if you did." The wipers were doing a less-than-adequate job of swatting away the flakes. He thought he could make out something new. It appeared to be a couple of dancing lights, bobbing and weaving behind the veil of snowflakes. *Headlights?*

"Listen, Dave, something's starting to go down up here. Visibility's for shit right now, but I was able to make out two men. The short guy from before and that big motherfucker you described. I think the big one might be hurt. The little guy climbed into the SUV, and it looked like he had a child in tow!"

"Fuck!" Dave said through clenched teeth.

"Rose???!!!" Phoenix screamed from the back seat. "That's my Rose!!!" she yelled, emphatically. "Did she look okay?! Please, God—!!"

"She looked okay, from what I could tell. Wait one," Murf said, squinting through the windshield. There were headlights coming his way. "Dave, I think they're coming down the drive, not sure if they've seen me yet, but...whoa...shit...shit...shit!!!!"

Dieter scowled as his headlights lit up the shape of Murf's truck. He deliberately cranked the wheel to the left, delivering a powerful blow to Murf's driver door and nudging him a few feet. Rose rattled around in the Durango's cargo space as she screamed out.

The loud crashing sound could be heard through the phone, followed by a moaning sound. "Murf!! Murf!! What was that??!!"

Several seconds went by before Murf could retrieve the phone from the floorboard. He shook his head and a quick look to the mirror confirmed he had a trickle of blood coming from his forehead. "He rammed me! Motherfucker just rammed me as he went by!!" Murf yelled. He tried starting the truck, but the starter just whirred in protest. He looked at his cracked driver's side mirror and saw the Durango's taillights disappear, but not in the direction he'd envisioned they would.

"Murf, are you okay? How bad is it, buddy?" Dave asked urgently, his eyes scanning the area outside his own rental vehicle, while visualizing a life and death situation he didn't have eyes on. "Murf?"

"Yeah...yeah, I'm here. Fucking truck won't start!" he said, smacking the dashboard with his free hand. "Not sure, but I think the Durango may've turned off the main driveway I'm on and gone down another way."

"You don't see him?"

"Nah, not in this shit. I'm pretty sure there's another driveway though. Not coming your way. And I'm dead in the water here!"

Pop Pop rubbed his face and his long-dormant military training kicked in. In the course of about five seconds, he evaluated the scenario and its moving parts: his friend was up there, immobilized and probably hurt, and an obviously violent criminal was escaping—with his granddaughter—down a road he had no intel about, and in weather conditions that made it impossible to see. He had to make a tactical decision right now, under fire, and it had to be the right one.

"Murf, hold on. Stay in your vehicle. We're coming to you—right now!!" Dave said, as he slammed the Tahoe into drive, pulled away from the mailboxes, and turned on to the snowy driveway.

"Roger that. I'm not goin' anywhere," Murf said.

Pop Pop's wipers were working overtime and his eyes were straining to make out the edges of the road as they chugged up the drive in silence. Phoenix was softly sobbing from the back seat while Curt's outwardly stretched left hand tried to comfort her. Several seconds went by before Murf's voice came back on the line. "I'm sorry to let you down, partner," he said softly, steeped in failure.

"Don't go there, Murf," Pop Pop said as he approached the final turn. He could see the truck now and it was clearly immobilized. He pulled up alongside Murf, jumped out, and stomped over to the crushed door. He tried the door handle, but the collision had rendered it impossible to open. Murf motioned for him to come around to the other side, which he did.

"Gawd, Murf…your head. You're bleeding. How do you feel?" Pop Pop asked, doing a quick triage of the situation.

"I'm…I'm good, I think," Murf replied.

"Okay, you think you can walk?"

"Think so," Murf guessed. "Yeah."

"Okay, I'm gonna help you out. Take it slow. Capische?"

"Capische." It was their shared one word of Italian from a port of call visit long ago.

"You're gonna get in the Tahoe, next to Phoenix, and we're gonna go up to the house. See if we can find anything that'll help. Okay?"

"Roger that," Murf replied, his response acknowledging that there would be no ambiguity as to who was now controlling the movements of this ship. *Flamer has the Conn.*

As Murf labored to get into the rear seat, everyone exchanged looks and nods of acknowledgement. There was no time for proper introductions. Pop Pop climbed in and grabbed his phone, knowing he had to alert police to be on the lookout for the Durango. "Dammit!!" he hissed, as his phone surrendered to the whiteout.

"Mine's the same," Curt said, staring at his display. "All circuits are busy!"

"Hold on, guys," Pop Pop said, as the Tahoe lurched up the driveway toward the cabin, their four heads bobbing. As they made the final turn and came to the landing, they got their first glance at the cabin. The chimney was billowing smoke. The garage door was still open. And there was a bright red pool of blood originating from the side of the garage building.

"What the hell?" Pop Pop muttered as he pulled onto the flat slab and cut the engine.

"Doesn't look good," Murf said.

"Oh, my God!" Phoenix said, horrified at the sight. "Looks like somebody's over there!"

Curt got out and opened Phoenix's door for her. Pop Pop jumped out and leaned back into the cab. "Murf, you can stay here. We're just going to take a quick look around, see if we can find out anything."

"Hell with that. I'll be right behind you," Murf replied, swinging his legs out the rear door and testing them. "Go."

Curt and Phoenix trudged their way through the powder, over to the side of the garage. They immediately regretted not having time to shop for proper winter gear before leaving home. Arizonans didn't tend to keep such things on hand, and it wasn't even on their radar.

A moment later, Pop Pop joined them. They all three stood there, freezing in their grossly inadequate layers of clothes, looking in horror at the giant of a man, now reduced to a mortally wounded beast, trapped, rendered helpless, and slowly freezing in a pool of his own blood.

Snow had already begun to stick to his torso, and to his face, but not to the point where he was unrecognizable. This was the man from the market; Phoenix was sure of it. The others recognized him as well, from the security footage they'd seen.

"It's him," she said, shivering, as she blew some warmth into her fingers. Her emotions were whirling. This was one of the monsters who'd taken her child, and she reserved a hatred for him that only someone in her position could feel. She also looked into the wide, glassy eyes of the creature kneeling before her. There was something else in there, but she didn't know what. Then he blinked. "Jeezus!!!"

"He's still alive," Pop Pop said. "But just barely; he's about bled out."

Phoenix took a step forward, keeping out of arm's reach, as she leaned in closer to the man. "Why?" she asked. He blinked again and his eyes met hers. He now recognized her as the lady on TV. "Why did you take my daughter? She didn't do anything to you! Who is she with?"

A few moments went by, and Phoenix noticed his bluing lips starting to quiver. "Tell me where they went!! Please…" she begged.

A raspy, remorseful whisper escaped him. "I'm s-sorry…" he managed before his eyes closed and he was gone. Phoenix collapsed to her knees in the powder, just outside the bloody patch. "NO!!!!!!!!" she wailed to the sky, not out of sympathy, but at being denied her answers. Curt reached down and helped her up, while Pop Pop ran over to the main house.

Murf was on the porch, and seeing the door ajar, they went inside together. With an economy of movement and time, Pop Pop ran from room to room. A quick scan of the main room revealed nothing other than a telltale discolored and empty spot on the wall where the bear trap had likely hung. The kitchen was next, before bounding up the stairs to the upper level. Other than evidence of two beds having been slept in, nothing. As he came back down to the main level, he nearly collided with Murf.

"Anything?" Murf asked.

"Not yet, you?" Pop Pop replied, half out of breath.

Murf shook his head, then gestured toward the hall. "After you." Pop Pop made haste down the hallway and turned into the next bedroom, stopping in his tracks at the sight of an enormous person laying prone, arm dangling down to the floor, face underneath a pillow.

He approached the bed, watched for any signs of breathing coming from the muumuu-clad figure. Seeing none, he slowly lifted the pillow. He was greeted with a death mask expression, one of bulging eyes and a tongue grotesquely hanging from the mouth. It was a woman, he confirmed. "What the hell?"

He spun back around to see Murf had joined him. "I think I remember her," Murf said, looking down at the expired person on the bed. "Pretty sure I remember dealing with her once a while back. Something about a permit, maybe. I think this might be your *Ecks*."

Pop Pop took this into consideration as he left the room and, seeing nowhere else to explore, tried the closed door that was mid-hallway. It opened to a dark space and there were dimly lit steps leading down.

"Pop Pop! Where are you!" Phoenix called out from the main room.

"Over here!" he answered. "Hallway!"

She found him there at the landing going down into the dark. "What's down there?" she asked.

"Don't know yet. Looks like a basement space; going to check it out. Found a dead woman in the far bedroom."

"What the hell happened here?" Curt asked, having now joined them.

"Good question. Come on," he said, leading the way. "Watch your step, guys."

As they got to the bottom step, they could see that the light was coming from a computer screen atop a desk. Outside of that, they couldn't see much else. "Look for a light switch, guys," he said as he crossed to the desk. A moment later, the room exploded with light coming from the exposed bulb. Phoenix joined him at the desk but something else caught her eye.

"My God!!" she gasped at the sight of the crudely constructed metal and wood cage. Pop Pop followed her gaze and ran up to the structure. He grabbed the padlock and looked further into the small space. A dog bowl half filled with water, an empty paper plate on the cement floor, and a young girl hunched in the corner.

"It's okay…" Pop Pop whispered to the girl. "It's okay. We're not going to hurt you," he said. The girl looked a wreck; she was clearly terrified and had obviously been maltreated.

Phoenix looked at the girl and tamped down the cocktail of emotions she was feeling. "My name is Phoenix, and we're going to get you out of there, okay?" she managed, her voice breaking at the sight of this young prisoner. *Had Rose been kept in this…kennel from hell?*

"Look around for something. A key. A saw. Bolt cutters. Something," Pop Pop barked, while Phoenix noisily rifled around the desk drawers, then the cabinets adjacent to the sink. Curt pulled on another drawer, and it came off its track, crashing to the floor. Screwdrivers, a hammer, assorted hand tools were strewn across the deck. There was also a long-handled tool he recognized as a set of bolt cutters. "Found cutters!" he exclaimed, rushing back over to join Pop Pop and Phoenix at the cage.

"What's your name, sweetheart?" Pop Pop asked the girl, making small talk while working on the forged-steel lock. It was a heavy duty one. "Can you tell me your name?"

"Cindy," the girl said softly. She hadn't had many opportunities to talk in recent weeks, and her voice was quite weak. "Cynthia...Cynthia Elise Shannon," she repeated, a little louder, using her full name.

"Cynthia Elise Shannon...that's a very nice name, honey. We're going to get you back home, okay?" Pop Pop replied, directing his energy to the cutters as they snapped the lock free and it fell to the floor.

With Pop Pop's help, the frail looking girl slowly emerged from her tiny prison and stood, shivering—both from the cold and from fear. "You're going to be okay, Cindy."

"Cynthia, honey..." Phoenix said, coming in closer and initiating a hug. "Did you see another girl here, sweetie?" she asked, doing her best to punctuate the question with a nonthreatening smile. Cynthia nodded.

"Was she about your age? A little younger, maybe? Red hair, honey?" Another nod. "Do you know where she went?" Phoenix asked. This got a head shake to the negative. Cynthia's eyes searched the room in a panicked state. "Are they coming back?" her voice trembled. "I want to go home now," she managed as tears began cascading down her cheeks.

"The bad people...no, they aren't coming back, sweetie. We will get you back home to your family, I promise," Phoenix assured her, then turned to Pop Pop. "I need to check something." Phoenix spun back around to the desk, took a seat, and started in on some computer forensics.

Pop Pop looked around and saw a small, woolen blanket in the corner and wrapped it around the girl's shoulders, giving her a comforting hug as they joined Phoenix and Curt at the desk.

The first open browser window was all weather data, so

Phoenix minimized it. The next one looked very familiar as it was a Yahoo! Mail mailbox—*her own!* She caught her breath with the next click, as the screen displayed the same message she'd received on her phone earlier.

"Oh, my God…Rose was sitting right here!!" she gasped, her fingers now touching the screen, as if her daughter was somehow inside it. Curt put his arm around her shoulder, leaned in, and stared at the screen. He kissed the top of her head. "We're gonna find her, honey!" *Please let us find her!*

Phoenix clicked on the last open browser window, and it filled the screen. "Jeezus!"

"What is it?" Pop Pop urged.

"Looks like a website for…a local airport…Coeur D'Alene. That's where we are, right?!"

"It is," Murf said, a new participant to the conversation. It had taken him some effort getting down the steps, but he had. "God, I hope he's not trying to fly out of here in this shit."

Phoenix looked over to the notepad to the right of the keyboard and saw some scribbled words and numbers. She struggled to make sense of it and held it up for Murf to look at.

"He's a damn fool," Murf said, his eyes trained on the gibberish only he understood.

"What you got?" Curt asked.

"I'm guessing it's a flight plan."

"A flight—?" Pop Pop started to say.

"Know anybody in Missouri?" Murf asked, pronouncing it *Missou-rah.*

Three head shakes told him his answer. "Do you know where this local airport is? The one they're going to?!" Phoenix asked urgently.

"I do," Murf said with a nod. "It's where I keep *my* plane!"

CHAPTER 30

MEANWHILE...
PAPPY BOYINGTON FIELD
COEUR D'ALENE

THE DURANGO WAS parked behind the hangar and Dieter had engaged its child safety locks to assure his passenger would stay put while he finished de-icing his Cessna 172S.

He'd done a safety walk around the craft, assured it was fully fueled, and he'd warmed the engine with an electric pre-heater. Another flurry would likely come any moment, and he had to get airborne before it socked him in.

Dieter had long hoped to trade in this single-engine Cessna for a twin turbo prop, but he hadn't had the scratch necessary to make the upgrade. As of today, he no longer had to worry about splitting the proceeds of his upcoming payday with anybody, making him one step closer to accomplishing that.

Satisfied with the status of the Cessna, he checked the

flags for indications of crosswinds and studied the runway. He'd have to leave right now.

With a sense of urgency, he strode back to the Durango and grabbed a small duffle and two coats from the passenger seat, then went around to the rear hatch and popped it open. Rose's knees were under her chin and the cold winds blowing in caused her to shiver.

"Put this on," he said, handing her the tiny coat. She put it on without hesitation. He took her hand, helped her down, and slammed the cargo hatch. "Come on, we've got to hurry."

"Where are we? Where are you taking me?"

"Don't you worry about that," he said, grabbing her hand and leading her aggressively along the side of the building. Her little legs had to work double time to match his strides, and she was falling behind. "Walk faster!" he hissed, as the aircraft came into view.

Rose stopped. She planted her feet as soon as she saw the tiny airplane. Dieter pulled her arm sharply and she let out a tiny scream. "Come. ON!" he yelled. But she resisted.

"No!!!"

He didn't have time to play games. With his free hand, he grabbed her by the waist and, with her legs kicking in protest, he huffed toward the Cessna. He tossed the duffle in the back and stuffed Rose into the rear seat, buckling her in. As she looked around the cramped cabin in terror, Dieter produced a syringe and plunged it into her arm. This elicited another scream of protest, but it was short-lived. It would be a long flight and he wasn't going to deal with a whiny, flailing brat for the next five-plus hours. He'd need every bit of concentration on piloting this craft, and conditions were far from optimal.

He climbed into the cockpit and fired up the engine. He checked his instruments, his flaps, and then his instruments again. He'd be flying a little over 1,100 nautical miles at a speed of 177 knots—not factoring in any headwinds—at an altitude of 9,000 feet on a heading of 110 degrees. He'd have to stop to refuel, and it would be two hours later at his destination, but he figured he'd still arrive there in time to collect his "bonus."

He put on his headset as the engine spun noisily, vibrating the tiny craft. It was go time. He rolled the plane into position, stopped, and made final checks. He revved the engine to speed and roared down the runway. He could feel the crosswinds playing with him, but he was committed now. Reaching groundspeed, he pulled back on the controls and was aloft.

Just me, and Santa's sleigh, flying in this shit tonight....

THE AIRFIELD
ABOUT THIRTY MINUTES LATER

As the Tahoe circled around the back of the hangar buildings, the first thing they saw was the crimson Durango. It stuck out like a very sore thumb against the white surroundings.

Pop Pop pulled over and turned to his new co-pilot, Murf, who was now riding shotgun.

"This the one?"

"Nah, pull up to that next one there. I keep her in that

one," Murf replied. His expression registered his concerns as he studied the ever-changing flurries.

Pop Pop pulled ahead and stopped behind the next building. He turned to Murf. "What do you want me to do? Just tell me how I can help prep."

"Just grab any gear you might have with you—the less, the better, 'cause we've got five of us now, and it's a four-seater," Murf said as he opened his passenger door and stepped down with a limp.

Pop Pop's eyes went to the rearview mirror. Sandwiched between Phoenix and Curt was young Cynthia. In the interest of time, and her safety, they sure as hell weren't going to leave her alone in the cabin, and they couldn't wait with her for any hypothetical help. They had to find Rose before they lost the trail completely. "All right, will do," he said as Murf closed the door behind him and started toward the hangar.

"You heard him," Pop Pop said to his crew. "Just the essentials. Phones, your coats. Bring Cynthia's blanket. Anything else stays behind. Let's go!"

As they all climbed out, Phoenix felt the lump in her jacket pocket. It was her cassette Walkman and tiny headphones. Another pound of weight wouldn't hurt, she decided.

Inside the hangar, Pop Pop and Curt did as Murf instructed, assisting with wheel chocks and records, and providing the muscle to help jockey the bird out of the nest and into position.

"Beautiful aircraft, Murf," Pop Pop said, studying the twin propellers. "What is it?"

"Piper. The PA-44 180 Seminole. Turbo prop. Don't usually take her up on days like today, unless I hafta, but sometimes you gotta do what you gotta do, I guess," Murf replied, as he checked under the wings.

"It'll be all right…right?" Curt asked, his concerns not very well hidden.

"Guess it'll have to be," Murf said, as they got her engine warmed up and he checked the fluid levels. "She's a fine girl. Flown a lot of miles in her. I trust her. I trust her more than that Cessna, that's for sure," he added, before realizing he'd just expressed doubt in the smaller aircraft their little girl was now a captive passenger in.

"How long, once we get airborne?" Phoenix asked, trying not to dwell on his last comment.

"It'll be windy as hell, but I'd say four, four and a half hours, give or take."

"And the Cessna?" Pop Pop asked. "How long would you say?"

"Probably more like five and a half, or so, I'd guess. He's got a head start on us, and we've both got a stop to refuel, but we've got a more efficient aircraft. By the time we get airborne—and we'll have to get a move on that—it might be roughly equivalent."

Phoenix, Curt, and Pop Pop exchanged looks. "Go ahead and throw your stuff in there," he said, indicating the small cargo area behind the seats. "Might as well turn your phones off right now and save the batteries. Won't do you any good in the air. And make sure everybody takes a potty break 'cause once we're up there, you're shit outta luck."

"Roger that," Pop Pop said. "You heard him. Ladies first. Phoenix, take Cynthia with you. Curt and I will go after."

"C'mon, sweetheart," Phoenix said, putting a comforting arm around the young girl as they walked to the restroom. She wished somebody would put a comforting arm around *her*, though it probably wouldn't do much right now. Phoenix had only made two trips by plane in her whole life—the first being to and from Hawaii for their honeymoon, and today's leg to Spokane. She'd already decided she didn't like flying, and this next flight—in that tin can—would cement that assessment.

Murf urinated a steaming stream, right there on the runway, then walked around the aircraft. He checked the condition of the tires, inspected the underbelly, the wings, the propellors. He looked over toward the hangar building. He'd already closed the large hangar doors. He waved at the four passengers now running toward his position. "Let's go!"

They huffed their way to the plane and Murf helped each find their seat. Phoenix offered to sit on Curt's lap since they were short a seat, but Murf fashioned a small seat out of a duffel and coats. She and Cynthia would trade off between that and the leather seat, he instructed.

"Five people in a four-seater isn't ideal, I know, but weight wise you girls count as one. Let's buckle up."

Murf assisted with the seatbelts and handed each adult a headset, instructing them on the proper use of the talk switches, as this would be how they communicated once in the air.

After each passenger had given him a thumbs-up, he climbed into the cockpit and put on his own headset. "Can you all hear me?" he asked, speaking into the mic.

A chorus of yeses and more thumbs-up gestures served as confirmation. Murf flicked switches on the impressive instrument cluster as Pop Pop observed from his co-pilot seat. The engines revved and instrument readouts danced in response.

The headsets helped drown out some of the engine noise

but it was still louder than Phoenix had expected. With the engine noise came an unsettling vibration. She had visions of rivets and screws popping off in protest.

This is nothing like first class!

"Here we go, everybody," Murf's metallic voice announced through the headsets. "Try not to puke in my pretty airplane, if you can avoid it," he laughed.

The twin engines roared louder as the pilot gave a thumbs-up and they began to roar down the runway. Murf had a firm grip on the wheel while Phoenix had a firm grip on her seatbelt. Pop Pop gripped his armrest, while Curt had a firm grip on his bowels.

As for Cynthia, this was her very first time on an airplane, and her eyes were shut tight. She didn't have headsets like the others, only the earplugs Murf had given her to wear. She hummed to herself to alleviate the panic building inside her.

Nobody else could hear her, but as the Piper took to the skies, she hummed a pitch-perfect version of "Amazing Grace."

How sweet the sound.

CHAPTER 31

MEANWHILE...
MOSER RESIDENCE
2:55 PM

RAMAGE WAS SEATED at his partner's kitchen table, enjoying a glass of milk and conducting a taste test at the urging of little Darla. Platters of both varieties of cookies were on hand, and the little girl studied him as he finished the saguaro-shaped one.

"Mm... oh, my goodness. It's so hard to decide. I liked the Christmas tree one and this one about the same."

"You have to pick one though," Darla said with a giggle. The ingredients and recipe were identical, the only difference being which cookie cutter had been employed.

In the interest of time, he made an executive decision. "I like the cactus one the best!"

"Yay! Me too!"

"Best cookie I've ever had...ever," he said with a wink.

"Okay, honey. How about you go to your room and play with your new puppy while the adults talk, okay?"

"'Kay, mommy. Bye, Uncle Ramage," Darla said, skipping down the hall.

Officer Ramage watched her disappear into her room. "Uncle Ramage?" he asked with a chuckle.

Bethany Moser shrugged. "It's easier for her than *Officer* Ramage and, besides, she almost considers you family," she replied with a smile as she set the cookie platters back on the counter. "Get you anything else?"

"Nah, I'm good, thanks," he said, polishing off the remaining milk in his glass. "So you got a puppy?! Huge responsibility."

"Not a real puppy. Like I'd have the time and energy for that! No, Darla's been working me hard over getting a dog, so I relented and met her halfway. It's a Fisher-Price deal. Get this: you plug it into your computer, install some software, then select your kid's name and pick a name for your puppy. The more you interact with the pooch, the more it grows—which sounds borderline creepy—and I think it stops growing after, like, four days. This is Day One, so I hope she doesn't get bored and just toss it in the toy box on Friday with her other stuff. Hoping to teach her a little responsibility before she gets the real deal, you know?"

"What'll they think of next, eh?" he replied, shaking his head. "Better hope it doesn't poop, too."

"I know. So. What's going on? You mentioned the dog sitter at the Martinsens'. Anything else going on?"

"I swung back by the office after and nothing solid coming in from anywhere. Nobody's had eyes on the Durango. No other flares in the air. Which tells me they're probably dug in...wherever that is. Best guess is still Idaho."

"A white Christmas up there, I'll bet."

"Yeah. Weather's turning to shit, and communications have been spotty up and down the panhandle, but local agencies in Coeur D'Alene report a couple of emergency calls coming in earlier today. A couple of tries to local police that got disconnected, and one panicky 911 call that aborted."

Moser leaned back against the counter, her brow scrunched. "Anybody dispatched?"

"Last I heard, they'd triangulated the calls and were sending someone in response."

"You think it could be—?" she began to ask.

"I'm a firm believer that anything's possible, and considering the last few days' events, we can't rule anything out. I mean, the mother, Phoenix, tells us the other day that they may've come across new information, then they call us back a little later and say, *oh, sorry, my bad.* Now, they're gone. Left in a hurry, according to the house sitter. Didn't take the dogs. Left no info as to where they went, who they were visiting, for how long, nada..." he replied, rubbing his eyes.

"I just hope to God they're not going rogue on some knee-jerk hunch *or* on any intel they didn't choose to share with us. In either scenario, if that's what's happening, things could go south real quick. Not only for the case but, more importantly, for everyone's safety. Gawd...."

"Yeah..." Ramage said. His phone vibrated. He held up a finger and answered. Moser studied his expression as he listened. "No shit! Dammit...no...good work, absolutely...and I appreciate the heads up. Hell of a thing...yeah...and you say there's a vehicle sitting halfway down the driveway to the property? Uh-huh. Registered to a Wayne...wait one..." he said as he gestured for something to write on. Moser brought him a note pad. "Wayne…Murphy…yeah… And you say there're two deceased onsite?" He scribbled more notes.

Moser's hand went to her mouth. Hearing only one side of the conversation was torture for her. She tilted her head as she made eye contact with Ramage. "FBI's just arrived? Uh-huh. Okay, I know you have your hands full up there, Officer. Let me know when the bureau's weighed in, and please text me his or her contact info. Yeah…yeah… Merry Christmas to you too." He ended the call and set down the phone. "Jeezus…."

"*Deceased!?*" Moser pressed. "Two? Who? How? Where?"

"Yeah. Listen to this: one of em's the big guy! Found him stuck in a fuckin' bear trap. Unbelievable…and the other, a woman—appears to be sixties—in a back bedroom of the log cabin there. Likely homicide—appears to have been suf-focated. Nobody else there. Open garage tells us somebody split in a hurry, and the car down the hill appears to have been rammed…signs of red paint on the door. Sure looks like they took off in the Durango. Tell me if you think I'm reading into things." He looked her square in the eye and she held his gaze for a long moment.

"What do we know about this—what's his name—*Murphy* guy, with the truck?"

"They're checking that now. So, let's look at the moving parts still in play, to the best of our knowledge: we've got somebody named Murphy, who's unaccounted for, add to that LaFlamme and the two Martinsens, who may be attempting some Nancy Drew/Hardy Boys kind of shit, one remaining perp, the short guy, and Rose. Am I leaving anybody out?"

"I don't think so. I just counted six. Murphy's truck is out of commission, right? Perp and Rose, likely in the Durango, headed God knows where. If they're out on the road, we should have eyes on 'em. Which leaves LaFlamme, the two Martinsens, and Murphy, possibly together, but where? And in what? Gawd, I'm not cut out for this long-distance stuff. I wish—"

The whole table vibrated. "Ramage!" he answered urgently, grabbing the note pad again as he listened. "Okay...you found what!? Yes...yes...okay...not really, but okay...yeah. Holy crap!" He circled the last word he'd jotted as Moser came around to look over his shoulder. "Man...no, great work, Agent Muro. This is *huge*...yeah...roger that. I understand. Call me back!"

Ramage set down the phone and circled the word one more time before looking up at his partner. His expression telegraphed a thousand things all at once. "Federal agents found a treasure trove of info in a basement there. What looks like a large, recently evacuated cage in a property without any pets. An unlocked computer with a fresh email, *written by Rose*—which puts her there at the house—and an apparent flight plan!"

"Flight plan? In that weather?!"

Ramage nodded, and held up the notepad with the word he'd circled:

MISSOURI

THE PIPER SEMINOLE
OVER NEBRASKA

They'd left South Dakota airspace behind, and the fuel stop at Sturgis had checked three more important boxes for Murf and his weary crew: the all-important potty breaks, procuring basic snacks to replenish very empty tummies, and the cleaning of vomit from the second row of leather seats.

Phoenix had been the first to toss her cookies and only managed to get half of it into the air-sickness bag. As is often the case, this had a powerful effect on her young seatmate, Cynthia. As one who had never experienced air travel at all, the combination of being tossed around in a four-seater tin can, while being buffeted by winds, hit her hard. Add to that, suffering the singularly triggering aroma of fresh vomit in the seat next to her, and she'd launched moments after Phoenix. At least hers had been in the bag. But it didn't matter.

Curt, bless him. He didn't stand a chance, and he'd never even found a bag.

Thus, cabin cleaning had added a good twenty minutes to their schedule.

Murf keyed his mic. "About an hour out, guys, barring any more weather anomalies."

Pop Pop looked over at him and nodded. The back row nodded as well, trying to put a brave face on this leg of the journey, even though it seemed like an eternity. Phoenix looked out her window and saw a whole lot of nothing. Her nostrils flared. *My kingdom for a can of Glade.*

X

THE CESSNA
LEE'S SUMMIT, MISSOURI
TEN MINUTES LATER

Despite a better patch of weather and good visibility coming into Lee's Summit Municipal Airport, the crosswinds were tossing the tiny Cessna about on its approach to Runway 11. To the casual observer, one might think the pilot at the helm of this craft was drunk off his ass.

Dieter wrestled with the controls, making small corrections as he aligned the trajectory of the craft with the rapidly approaching landing strip stretched before him. The kid was stirring in the back, but he had to direct all his attention to the task at hand.

Three...two...one....

The chirp of rubber and the thud of contact were welcome sensations as the Cessna kissed the strip, hard, and made its way down the runway before turning toward the hangars.

This is the last damn time.

He rolled to a stop and cut the diesel engine. The silence was bliss. He looked over his shoulder toward the rear seats. The item was still groggy, which was good, securely strapped in, and no worse for the wear. She might be hungry but at this point, catering this gig wasn't in his job description. They'd have food where she was going.

Dieter shut down all systems, climbed out and set his wheel chocks. He gave the fuselage a light tap with his palm as if to say "good job" as he walked around to the door. He looked over toward the hangar area and noticed three small, executive aircraft, and a couple of black Cadillac Escalades. Another small craft was lined up with the runway, making its approach.

"Wake up," he said to his tiny passenger. Rose was completely disoriented and let out a big yawn as he unbuckled her. She sat up and looked around the tiny cabin of the airplane. "Where are we? Are we going flying?"

"Already did. But we're going to a party now," he said, which was technically true. "Come on, I'll help you out."

As Rose emerged from the fog of her sedative, a violent image crashed through. "Willie's hurt! Willie's bleeding…he needs help!" she gasped as new tears sprang forth.

"It's okay…Willie's going to be fine. He called me a while ago and is feeling better," Dieter said with an eerie calm. He felt nothing—certainly not remorse—and lying about his brother's status served to remind him that he was now free of the responsibility for him. "We'll call him later, after we get to the party."

Rose furrowed her tiny brow. She wasn't buying it, but she believed in miracles. Dieter lifted her down to the deck, closed the aircraft's door, and took her reluctant hand as they walked toward the assemblage of planes and SUVs.

As Dieter and Rose got closer, one of the Escalades was pulling away and heading for the exit. Standing by the remaining vehicle, its driver, Roger, seemed preoccupied with watching the executive plane that had just landed and was taxiing toward them. Roger was sharply dressed in a navy-blue suit and holding a clipboard. He nodded his acknowledgement as they joined him.

Next to him was a well put together woman, fortyish, with stylish, platinum blonde shoulder-length hair and a black suit. In her heels she towered over Dieter, but then, most people did. She smiled broadly, a friendly, perfect smile that she directed mostly to the young girl.

"Hello...you must be Rose!" she said, offering her hand.

"How do you know my name?" Rose asked, unsure about her.

"Oh, well...we've heard good things about you, sweetheart," Candy said, dripping sweetness. "There are people who want to meet you, and we're here to take you to a party!"

"A party?" she asked incredulously.

"Yes, a party."

"I don't *want* to go to a party...I want my mommy and daddy. I want to go home!" she declared, her bottom lip quivering and fresh tears on deck.

"It's a Christmas party, honey," Candy replied. "With lots of presents!" she lied. *Enough with the twenty questions...we're going to be late.* She had to close the sale. "We'll take you home after. You'll see your family then. First, our friend, Mr. Roger, will help you into your seat, honey," she added, gesturing toward the waiting SUV. Rose looked back at Dieter, then to Roger, and walked to where he was standing. He set his clipboard on the roof as he helped her in.

"And..." Candy began, directing her attention to...the delivery man. "You must be—I'm sorry, I don't think I know your name, forgive me."

"That's not important, really, so long as you have the cash we agreed upon," he replied. Dieter was nothing if not consistent. He wasn't big on pleasantries, and he wasn't about to start now. "You have it here?"

Candy flashed a smile that disappeared just as quickly. "Certainly. It's not *here* here, but we do have it ready for you at the main house. We're going there now, and I assure you you'll be more than happy with the bonus we've added for your troubles. Thank you for your prompt service. If you'll follow me, we'll get you seated. We have one more party who's just arrived, so we should be underway momentarily."

Dieter nodded, then glanced over at the new plane. It was a sleek, blue and white, turbo-prop executive craft and its pilot was shaking hands with the passenger he'd just delivered. This new arrival seemed to reek of self-importance, Dieter thought. He looked a little familiar, even, probably because Congressman Connelly made it a point to get as much TV airtime as possible.

"This way, please," Candy said, gesturing Dieter toward the Escalade, before peeling off to greet the next guest. "Congressman! So nice to see you again!"

CHAPTER 32

THE MANOR
THIRTY MINUTES LATER

ROGER AND THE other shuttle driver, Dennis, had dropped off their guests at their respective destinations on the property. The adult guests had been delivered to the grand main entrance doors while young Rose was taken to the bunk room, where she and the others would be showered, groomed, and dressed for the party.

Roger inspected the inside of his Escalade to assure no guest items had been left behind. Satisfied that they hadn't, he went to retrieve his clipboard from the dashboard.

Only it wasn't there. A quick look underneath all the seats came up empty, so he approached Dennis, who was doing a similar sweep of his vehicle.

"You happen to see an extra clipboard, Den?"

"Extra clipboard…nope, just mine," he said, holding it up in his left hand. "I'll let ya know if I see one though."

"Yeah…thanks," Roger said, more than a bit concerned as he pocketed the keys and exited the garage building.

The VIP guests each exchanged hugs and pleasantries with Candy, who was now wearing a Santa hat and serving as the party hostess. As they came into the foyer, each of them dutifully followed established protocols by removing their phones' batteries and placing all electronics into the glass cube that sat on the entryway table, just inside the door.

Roger and Dennis stood behind, in the driveway, next to the guests' belongings they'd be delivering to their respective rooms once they'd been assigned them. Roger couldn't help but obsess about the missing clipboard, but he'd retrace his steps after delivery of the bags.

As guests progressed from the foyer and into the elegant main room, they were met, one by one, by the weekend's gracious host: the man they all knew as Richard Atkinson. Dressed for the occasion in a white tuxedo, he seemed to channel Mr. Roarke from TV's *Fantasy Island*. His festive necktie and matching handkerchief were a Christmassy-red, and his tan was impeccable.

"Congressman, welcome to the Manor," Atkinson said with a toothy smile and an extended hand.

"Richard, such a pleasure to see you again. Thank you for your kind invitation," Connelly said, gripping the host's hand and turning on the schmooze. He had a gift for it, and it had served him well all these years. "You're looking fit."

"Thank you. You as well. I've been doing a little circuit training since we last saw each other."

"I may have to follow your lead on that," Connelly replied, looking around at the festive décor. "Place looks great,

Richard. You've outdone yourself this year!" the schmooze master added.

"Thank you. We have fun with it, and we do it all for you. When you're ready, Candy will show you to your room and we'll have your belongings delivered there. Same room as last year, Congressman. You seemed to enjoy that one."

"Perfect. Perfect," he replied with a smile, a hint of bad boy sneaking through.

"In the meantime, please, enjoy a festive cocktail or two," Atkinson said, gesturing to his servers. Two trays of drinks materialized, delivered by none other than the twins, who had been ordered to dress in Thing One and Thing Two costumes, and with fuzzy blue wigs, straight out of Dr. Suess. "You remember the twins from last year," Atkinson said with a twisted smile. "MacKenzie and Rebekah, you remember the Congressman."

"Yes, sir," they said in lockstep unison. They dutifully mustered their best half-smiles, though they each harbored deep hatred for the man after the way he'd degraded them the year before. The twins extended their trays toward the congressman, and he eyed them lasciviously before selecting a glass of champagne.

"Thank you, Thing One...mmm...and Thing Two... mmm, look at you two..." he said with long, lecherous looks at each before they walked away and returned to their appointed queue as the next guest arrived.

"Doctor Talbot!" Atkinson called out. "Welcome to the Manor...."

Similar pleasantries were exchanged with the arrival of Will Masters and Patrick Felice, and the twins quietly made the rounds, assuring the guests were getting properly lubricated.

THE AIRFIELD
RUNWAY 11
A BIT LATER

The Piper had made a somewhat more graceful landing than the Cessna, thanks to diminishing wind gusts and a slightly more skilled pilot. As Murf taxied the craft toward the hangar building, he noted that there wasn't any other flight activity to speak of, other than the four outbound craft he'd noticed on the way in. The only other plane on the tarmac was a Cessna 172S. *Might be....*

He pulled the Piper over to the tarmac and cut the engines. With a bit of effort, Pop Pop extracted himself from the cabin and assisted the pale-faced crew in the back seat. Their expressions were grim as each tried not to think about the possibility of throwing up again. Phoenix thought about kissing the ground but decided against it.

"You can power up your phones now, see if you get a signal," Murf said, sliding the tether of his binoculars around his neck as he placed his wheel chocks and closed the cabin door. "Welcome to Missouri...or, as I like to call it, *Misery*," he said with a tired chuckle.

"Got a signal!" Phoenix chimed.

"Me too," Curt confirmed.

"That's good, 'cause we don't have wheels and have no idea what to do next," Murf said.

"You think we're in the right place?" Pop Pop asked as they walked toward the hangar.

"It would seem so. That Cessna there tells me he's still here. Somewhere."

Phoenix walked closer to the tiny plane and attempted to

peer through the windows, looking for any sign of Rose. She couldn't see any tangible evidence but her mama's intuition was strong. "She was here. Rose. We've gotta find out where they went!" she called out.

"They can't be that far ahead of us," Pop Pop concurred. "What do we have to go by?"

As Phoenix walked back to join the group, her foot kicked something, and it scraped along the rough pavement. Reaching down, she picked it up and inspected what appeared to be a clipboard. Two documents were affixed to it, and she squinted to get a better look.

"Well, what do we have here?!" she said, looking up with a wry smile.

The clipboard's documents proved to be a godsend. It was a treasure trove of information, and more than they could have wished for. Aircraft tail numbers, flight originations, arrival times, passenger names, and a business card reflecting the name of the shuttle driver and location.

"Thank you!" Phoenix said, directing it to the sky. She turned to Curt. "Honey, call a cab company, tell 'em to send a vehicle with room for five passengers."

"Okay…where should I tell 'em we're going, exactly?" he replied.

"That's for us to know and the cab driver to find out once we're on our way," she said, folding the documents and stuffing them in her pocket. She took another look at the business card. *And thank you, Roger….*

CHAPTER 33

THE BUNKHOUSE

WHILE CANDY WENT about softly blow drying Rose's incredible mane, the older girls took care of their own, and each other's. The windowless bunkhouse had, in addition to its twelve bunkbeds, a bathroom with four doorless toilet stalls and an equal number of vessel sinks spread about the long counter that ran along a far wall.

"Hurry up, girls," Candy said as she fine-tuned Rose's bangs with the curling iron. "We only have a few more minutes until the party. Your costumes are laying on your beds. Snap-snap!" She sounded more like a stage manager prepping girls for their grade school musical than the grooming pimpstress she really was.

None of these former innocents were even close to being of legal age, and their childhoods, cruelly plucked from them, seemed like a distant past. They applied their foundation, mascara, and lip gloss until they didn't recognize themselves any longer.

That's what the "daddies" liked.

X

A COUPLE OF ACRES AWAY

A dark green Ford minivan pulled off the main road and onto the entrance to a very long driveway that led to the address Phoenix had provided the driver.

"You must have some pretty rich family," the driver said, smiling broadly as he turned to Pop Pop, who was riding shotgun. Pop Pop couldn't help but notice the guy was missing several teeth. Getting no reply from him, or anyone else in the van, the driver turned to Curt in the back seat, as he'd been the one who'd called. "You want me to take y'all up to the house, right?"

"Uh, no. That's all right. Thanks, though. We kind of want to surprise our cousins. We can walk the rest of the way," Curt replied.

"Suit yourselves," the driver said. "Okay, ride from Lee's Summit to Pleasant Hill, five passengers, Christmas Eve surcharge…let's call it eighty bucks, even."

Pop Pop dug out his wallet and handed the man a one-hundred-dollar bill. "Keep it. Merry Christmas."

"And a Merry Christmas to you fine people. You sure you don't want me to wait around in case nobody's home?"

"No, we're pretty sure they'll be there. Can't wait to see their faces," Phoenix interjected, selling the holiday gathering story a little harder as they exited his vehicle. "Thanks!"

"Bless y'all!" he said as he slowly pulled away and went back the way they'd come. They all watched until his lights disappeared.

"Damn, it's dark out here," Curt said.

"Language," Phoenix said, ever the protective mom, as she nodded her head toward the youngster in their charge.

"Sorry," Curt murmured.

Pop Pop tried to get a feel for the terrain. Other than what the intermittent moonlight provided when it peeked from behind the clouds, there wasn't much visibility out here. It presented a challenge for them, but it was also a blessing as they didn't want to broadcast their presence. "Let's go. We'll follow this tree line here. Stay on the gravel surface. Turn off the ringers on your phones and keep 'em in your pockets. We need stealth right now."

"Roger that," Murf said, pocketing his.

"Mine's good," Curt said as he stashed his.

"Same," Phoenix said. "Let's do this."

As they crunched along the gravel road, the only other sound they heard was the hoot of an owl. Several minutes went by before anyone spoke. It was Pop Pop. "Hold up. Anyone else hear that?"

"Hear what?" Murf asked. The group stopped in their tracks.

"Listen," Pop Pop said, holding up his hand. Off in the distance, the unmistakable sound of music was wafting through the trees. It was a low, pulsating hip hop beat, just enough to piss off an owl and signal a party in progress. "That."

"Yeah. Shitty taste in music," Curt uttered.

"*Language*," Phoenix reminded him. She turned to Cynthia. "You okay to walk, sweetie?"

"I'm good," she replied softly. "Hungry, though."

"I know...me too. We all are. We'll see if we can get something to eat at the house."

"'Kay."

"Guys, it's whisper voices from here on. Music aside, it's very quiet out here, and we've got to be mindful of that," Pop Pop reminded them, his own voice a whisper. This got four silent thumbs-up responses.

"I'll try not to slow y'all down too much," Murf said softly as he limped along.

"Slow and steady wins the race," Pop Pop whispered back, giving his fellow vet a supportive pat on the back.

"Roger that."

The ragtag group walked in darkness until they came to the end of the tree line, where they got their first real view of the Manor off in the distance. Pop Pop held up his clenched fist shoulder high, and the group froze. As they did, the full moon decided to emerge from its hiding place, lighting up the grounds and themselves, like somebody had just flipped on the light switches at a football stadium. Pop Pop gestured for everyone to jump back into the cover the tree line provided.

"We're more exposed out here, and as long as the moon's playing hide and seek, we'll have to use the tree line to our best advantage," Pop Pop whispered, making eye contact with each. He pointed in the direction of the outbuildings as they were closest to the trees. "We'll follow this trajectory. Stay close, watch my signals, and keep low."

Everyone nodded. The moon disappeared again. Cynthia was almost enjoying this game and she gave a thumbs-up as Pop Pop led the way. Phoenix was right behind him.

"What's the game plan, Pop Pop?" Phoenix whispered.

"I'll tell you once we have one," he whispered back, punctuating it with a wink. He engaged Phoenix in a longer gaze, assessing her in an instant. "You good, kiddo?"

She had on her game face. "Yeah. I'm so good...."

X

Dieter stood in the corner of the main room, taking in the scene as he waited for Candy to return with his promised cash. As he munched on some finger food the blue-haired girls had offered from their trays, he couldn't help but think it rude that he had to wait. He had come a long way, kept his part of the bargain by delivering his item on time, and he should be compensated accordingly. *Where the hell is she?*

A laugh from across the room redirected his attention to the familiar-looking guy he'd seen on the tarmac. The charismatic, self-important dude with the bullshit smile and a laugh to match. That's when he figured it out. *CNN! Congressman-somebody-or-other! What an asshole.*

Thing One materialized with her tray, which held one remaining champagne flute. She offered it to Dieter, and he grabbed it as she walked away. There was no way he'd be making the return flight tonight, he knew, so he might as well have a celebratory drink. *It's Christmas Eve, fer chrissakes. Whatever....*

MacKenzie met her twin in the kitchen. They both had empty trays, and they'd blown through the bottles already, which necessitated another run to the supply building. Rebekah grabbed the wheeled cart and the two of them exited the house, proceeding down the path to the outbuildings.

From the edge of the trees, Pop Pop watched as two figures emerged on the path, coming their way. "Murf," he whispered, gesturing for the binoculars. Murf came up alongside him and handed them over. Pop Pop toggled the focus until the two young-looking girls came into crisp view. "What the—?" he whispered to himself.

"What ya got?" Murf whispered back. Pop Pop handed him the optics and he had a look for himself. "Must be some party."

"Okay, listen up. We've got two unknowns approaching. Stay put, heads down. I'm going around the back of the building to see if I can find out anything," he told his crew in a hushed tone. Four thumbs acknowledged his orders, and he crept silently along the side of the outbuilding. Phoenix gestured to Murf, asking for a peek through the binocs, and he obliged.

Pop Pop sidled up to the structure and put his ear to the wall. Nothing. A moment later, he could hear the cart's rickety wheels approaching the building's one door. Next, the sound of a key as it found the lock and the door squeaking open as they pushed the cart inside.

Pop Pop shimmied down the wall, slowly, his back to the building, as he looked for a window in hopes of getting a visual. There appeared to be one at the far end, as light was coming through it. He approached the opening and kept his head down as he reached it. The window was a small square, about a foot in diameter, but it was set in the wall at his eye level. He peeked over the ledge slightly.

He could see several steel racks, each laden with boxes of various items. Some were cleaning supplies, others paper goods, foodstuffs, cases of wine and assorted liquors, and—against the far wall—what appeared to be a locked white cabinet with a red cross stenciled on it. *Medical supplies.* The two attendants came into view, and he ducked down. He waited a few moments before risking another peek.

At first glance, he could swear he'd been transported into a Dr. Seuss book, as he'd read them to his granddaughter countless times. These costume-clad figures were both girls, and young ones from the look of it. Definitely early adolescents: he guessed them to be about ten. *Maybe.* The blue wigs made it difficult to discern. *Are these girls being held here against their will?*

The clanging of bottles brought him back to earth. He watched as the two of them restocked the cart with champagne, red and white wines, and bottles of hard liquor. He crept down the side of the wall toward the door they had entered and paused a few feet away.

From her vantage point, Phoenix could now see Pop Pop poised near the entrance. She had watched the two go in and she too was puzzled by their appearance. They were young, certainly, and their expressions made them seem almost zombie-like. *Maybe they know where Rose is....* She lowered the binocs and handed them to Curt. The moon disappeared again.

"Be right back," she whispered, then broke into a sprint.

"Wait! What—?" Curt managed on deaf ears. She was already gone. "Dammit, Phoenix!" he said to himself in a pissed whisper.

Fifteen seconds later, Phoenix reached the corner of the building, padding quietly to a position behind Pop Pop. He spun around and his expression told her he wasn't pleased to see her here. "What part of *stay put* did you not understand?" he whispered sharply.

"Sorry, but I couldn't wait any longer. Besides, you're going to need me," she replied.

"And how's that, exactly?"

"Not sure, but you will. I saw the girls go in. Just the two of them?"

"Yeah…" Pop Pop replied. He was past being pissed off for being disobeyed, and he knew he probably would have made the same choice in her shoes. "I don't want to startle them. There's no telling how they'd react to seeing me, and we can't risk having them alert others. Any suggestions?"

"Can you give me a boost to the window? I wanna see something."

The two of them slithered back to a position below the window. Pop Pop put his ear to the wall and could hear the rattle of bottles. They were still loading the cart. "Ready?"

"Ready," she replied as he cradled his fingers to create a step for her foot. She hoisted herself up to see over the ledge. The girls were indeed still loading the cart and, more importantly, her eyes hadn't been playing tricks on her. She studied them for a moment longer before jumping back to the ground.

"Any brilliant ideas?" Pop Pop asked.

"Just one," she replied. Her determined look told Pop Pop it was worth considering.

"I'm all ears."

CHAPTER 34

THE PARTY

RICHARD ATKINSON WAS making the rounds, checking in with his distinguished guests to make sure everyone had everything—and everyone—they needed.

Candy was parading her troupe of young darlings amongst them, dangling the red meat in front of a small but hungry crowd of high-level pervs. She'd dressed the girls all in matching outfits—all Christmas themed—and all as sexualized little girl elves.

All save one: the Angel, Rose. Dressed all in white, her costume was layers of chiffon and lace, adorned with silken wings and a sparkly halo attached to a six-inch riser from her satin headband. Her mane was coiffed in a perfect display of cascading curls and its fiery brilliance was even more amazing than it had appeared in the video clip they'd seen a thousand times.

She held Candy's hand as she walked with the others, and she had a strong feeling something was very wrong. This was unlike any Christmas party she'd ever seen, and she wanted her mommy and daddy.

Rose was the grand prize, and the four main players considered each of the nine young girls as they slowly paraded before them like beauty contestants in the swimsuit competition. It was a depraved bastardization of an innocent theme, and the hosts had reached new lows in their presentation this year.

Each girl dutifully followed the path, pausing before each of the four "daddies" and executing slow, provocative turns as they'd been instructed to. The congressman's jaw hung open a bit more than the others', and each girl secretly hoped they wouldn't end up with him. Not that the others were any better prospects. They tried not to think about what was to come a little later. They tried not to think about anything at all.

The men were silently tallying their choices, each making note of the numbers pinned to the back of the girls' costumes. No names would be used here, only numbers, and the Angel had a **1** affixed to her.

Candy carried a round fishbowl into which the guests dropped their written selections as she came to them. Each guest was allowed three choices and knew from previous years that there might be sharing involved in some instances. As before, this would be a two-day affair and it was a target-rich environment. Nobody ever went away unhappy.

As the bowl was waved in front of the tech guru, Will Masters, he dropped his tally into it and, a second later, another folded piece of paper. His wink to Candy told her he would like to make a "contribution" to the host's favorite charity. The generous check also assured he'd get first dibs, and his tally had a big **1** on it.

Candy finished collecting tallies from Dr. Talbot, Congressman Connelly, and Superintendent Felice before placing the bowl atop the fireplace mantel. She walked over to the delivery man, standing alone in the corner. His mouth was drawn in a tight line and his body language told her his patience had been exhausted long before.

"If you'll follow me to the study, I have something for you," she whispered into to his ear. Dieter's posture straightened and he responded with a slight nod. *It's about fuckin' time. What a bunch of sick fucks.*

He followed the hostess down the hall, and she opened the second door. As she entered, she turned on a desk lamp and walked over to another door, a closet. She turned to Dieter and her expression told him he didn't need to watch what she was doing. He looked away as she opened the door and began spinning a combination of numbers on the robust safe.

Dieter's eyes scanned nearby shelves while she did this. Framed photos of the tanned guy littered the shelves. Tanned guy with the congressman. Tanned guy with the doctor guy. Tanned guy with the dweeby superintendent, and the other guy. There was even a photo of tanned guy with the President of the United States. *What the hell?* Candy's voice brought him back to his purpose for being here.

"I think you'll find everything is in order," she said, handing him a leather satchel. Her cold smile was all business. Dieter took the satchel and unzipped it wide enough to see a mountain of cash, all bundled and in crisp hundred-dollar bills. He reached in and stirred the bundles around, doing some quick mental math to make sure he hadn't been shortchanged.

"We were under the impression you'd be delivering another girl tonight as well."

"Uh, she wasn't feeling well," Dieter said as he inspected another bundle.

"I see...perhaps when she's feeling well enough to travel, you might make a return trip."

"Yeah, maybe so..." he replied halfheartedly, trying not to be distracted from his count.

"Are we good then?" she asked, gauging his expression.

"We are," he replied, giving the noisy zipper a firm pull. He looked back at her. Her smile was gone, and she'd mentally moved on.

"Very well. If you'll just see yourself out," she said as she gestured toward the door. "Merry Christmas," she added without any attempt at cheer; she'd forgotten the meaning behind the sentiment decades before. Dieter had as well, and he only nodded a response as he walked out.

THE OUTBUILDINGS
SAME TIME

Phoenix waited for cloud cover, then made haste back to the rest of the group waiting at the tree line. Murf lowered the binocs as she arrived. "Anything interesting?" she whispered.

"Not especially," he said. "Most of the activity appears to be happening inside. How 'bout at the big shed there?" he asked, indicating the outbuilding she'd just come from.

"A couple of girls, making a supply run, from the look of it. Not sure if they live here, or if they have a choice in the matter, but they're young. They're not aware of our presence yet."

"Anything else? How long do we have to wait here?" Curt asked, his patience wearing thin. His stomach growled loudly.

"We're making it up as we go," Phoenix replied. They were all beyond exhausted, and she didn't want to sound snippy. "I need to borrow Cynthia," she said to the adults before turning to their young rescue. "That okay with you, honey? Want to come with me?" Cynthia nodded.

"Good. Okay, guys. Wish us luck…gotta get back," Phoenix whispered. She looked up at the sky; the moon was still obscured. "Here we go," she said, her arm hooked around Cynthia's. As they sprinted across the open area, the music coming from the house suddenly became louder. It was as if somebody had opened a door.

Murf raised the field glasses to get a better look, and his suspicion was confirmed. Somebody was exiting the house, and it sure looked like…the short guy. *Shit!* The door closed behind him, restoring the throbbing hip hop to a slightly reduced level of mayhem.

This didn't go unnoticed by Phoenix as they neared the outbuilding. The moon rematerialized just as they padded to a stop next to Pop Pop, around the corner from the supply room's open door. "Company's coming," she whispered loudly, out of breath. "The little bastard!"

Pop Pop's brow furrowed, and he peeked around the corner toward the drive. It was him, and he walked to the middle of the driveway, where he stopped, his phone to his ear. *Calling a cab.* Pop Pop turned back to the girls. "Okay,

I think we've got to make our move—whatever that looks like—right now. Let's hope this works."

Phoenix glanced back toward the driveway. The short man was standing there, messing with his phone. *Waiting on a cab.* She turned to her young companion. "I'll bet you liked Dr. Seuss when you were younger," she said, mustering up an excited smile, which got a smile and nod from Cynthia in return.

Dieter's phone vibrated an alert and he looked at his display. It was the taxi company with an estimated arrival time: *20 MINUTES.*

Ay. With twenty minutes to kill he didn't feel much like standing there, and there was light coming from one of the outbuildings down the drive. Curiosity got the best of him. He picked up his bag and began a slow stroll toward the shed.

Phoenix said a silent prayer as she watched the man closely. They needed to divert his attention elsewhere. Pop Pop found a medium-sized round stone and hurled it in the direction of the garage building, several feet away from the unwanted guest. It did the trick as it landed noisily. His head turned toward the sound and he began taking steps in that direction. Pop Pop gave her the thumbs-up. *I've still got it!*

Phoenix took a deep breath and, with Cynthia by her side, crept into the open doorway of the supply room. The twins' heads turned as they registered new visitors, and the looks on all four of their faces was priceless.

"Hi, girls," Phoenix said in a loud whisper as she took a step closer to the twins. She hoped her smile would convey her friendly intent, as the last thing she wanted to do was render alarm. Rebekah Olson set her wine bottle down slowly, her mouth agape. MacKenzie froze in her tracks. Both were doing a threat assessment at the sight of these two strangers.

"Who are you?" Rebekah asked in a normal voice, looking from one face to the other.

Phoenix held her index finger up to her lips in a shushing gesture. "It's okay, we're friends. My name is Phoenix, and this…is Cynthia. We're here to help you," Phoenix replied. Cynthia nodded. "What are your names, girls?"

The twins exchanged looks, wondering if it was okay to answer that question. MacKenzie took the lead. "My sister is Rebekah, and I'm MacKenzie," she said shyly.

"Listen, MacKenzie, I need to ask you: are you all right? Do you live here? Has anybody ever hurt you?"

Another exchange of looks preceded their nods in the affirmative. "Are there other girls here with you?" Phoenix probed. More nods. "Can you tell me," she asked, retrieving her phone from her hip pocket, "have you ever seen…" she paused, pushing another button. "…this girl?"

She held the screen so they both could see the close-up photo of her daughter. "Is this little girl here?" she asked, searching their expressions for any glimmer of recognition. She looked at their faces, going from one to the other. Neither shook their head no. They each looked up from the photo to Phoenix and their eyes told her yes before their nods did.

A tiny gasp escaped Phoenix and her heart skipped a beat. She put her phone back in her pocket, mustering up another half-smile. "This girl is my daughter, Rose. Do you know where she is?" she asked them, more a plea than a question. "It's very important. You won't be in trouble if you tell me."

Two nods. *Praise Jesus!*

Phoenix clamped her eyes shut for a moment and took

a deep breath before opening them again. She let the smile return to her face as she asked the question. "Would you like to play a little game?"

The short man abandoned the mystery noise and, satchel in hand, resumed his stroll toward the supply room. Pop Pop had been watching his every move and based on the man's pace, estimated he'd be there in two minutes' time. He ducked back out of sight. *Come on, girls!*

Another minute went by, and Pop Pop could hear the approaching steps. He listened intently, gauging their proximity. He'd be there any second and he couldn't risk him seeing them. As the footsteps came to a halt, next to the open door, Pop Pop made his move.

His survival training was easily summoned as he spun around the corner, using the element of surprise along with his superior size and strength, as he cupped his left hand over the short man's mouth and grabbed him like a mannequin, lifting him off his feet noiselessly and, with little effort, to a position around the dark side of the building.

The captured man's limbs flung about randomly but he was no match for the much stronger and taller Pop Pop. He needed to be incapacitated, and quickly, before he gave away their position—or worse. Pop Pop delivered a non-lethal blow to the back of the short man's head, which instantly rendered him limp. The satchel fell to the deck.

Pop Pop did an instantaneous assessment and determined he had a few minutes while the man was unconscious. After frisking him for any weapons, he carried the limp form, and the satchel, over to the tree line, arriving next to Curt and

Murf. "Look familiar?" he asked, out of breath and already knowing their answers.

"That's the fuck!" Curt said a little too loudly as he lunged toward the small man.

Pop Pop held up an arm to block Curt's advance. "Watch your voice," he hissed. "And I know what you're thinking, but now's not the time!" he whispered back earnestly. He set the heap down at his feet while he removed his belt. "Give me your socks," he demanded of Curt.

"My socks?"

"Just give them to me. Please," Pop Pop said. He let out a grunt as he lifted the limp form to the standing position and leaned him against the nearest young tree, one that was strong enough while also being small enough for his purposes. "Hold him up," he said to Curt. Curt joined him at the tree and handed Pop Pop his socks while he did as he'd been asked.

Pop Pop made sure the unconscious captive's feet were touching the ground when he wrapped his leather belt around the man's neck and cinched him against the tree, allowing him to still breathe. Satisfied he'd immobilized him, he stuffed Curt's socks into his mouth. "Shoelaces."

"Use mine," Murf volunteered. "They're longer, and leather, and I'm not doing any running anytime soon."

Pop Pop nodded, and after Murf removed his bootlaces, he used one to tie the man's wrists behind him and the other for his ankles. Curt walked up to their prisoner, and it was all he could do not to murder him right then and there. He turned to Pop Pop. "I can stay here and watch him."

Pop Pop shook his head. "Not sure if that's the best idea… we need him alive—for now. Besides, I need you with me. Murf, you okay with keeping an eye on this asshole?"

"Thought you'd never ask. I'll be fine. He decides to give me any sass, I've got two more socks—and some undies—he can suck on."

"Roger that. Curt, you're with me. Let's go," Pop Pop said, in full combat mode now. The moon was tucked away where he wanted it and their work was far from over. They sprinted across the grounds, taking a position on the side of the building.

Curt turned to Pop Pop, since he obviously had a plan. He hoped. "What's the play?"

"It's still fluid," Pop Pop replied as he peeked through the window.

"What you mean is: *We're making it up as we go.* Tell me I'm wrong."

"Something like that, but Phoenix's come up with what might be our best option. And we don't have a lot of them," he said, gesturing for Curt to follow him.

The two men turned the corner and entered the supply building, startling the twins into tomorrow. Pop Pop smiled, holding up his right hand in a gesture of friendship as the girls cowered behind Phoenix.

"It's okay, girls. They're with us. They're the good guys," Phoenix assured them. Curt seemed every bit as startled as the twins, as Phoenix was now wearing a Dr. Seuss outfit and had tucked her red hair underneath the blue wig. As had Cynthia. *Thing One and friggin' Thing Two!* The twins were now wearing Phoenix's and Cynthia's duds.

"What the—?" Curt turned to Pop Pop. "This is the plan?"

"If you have a better one, tell me real quick, because it's game time," Pop Pop answered, his expression deadly serious. Curt shook his head.

"Okay," he said to Curt. "Find me a crowbar or some bolt cutters. Let's see what's in the medicine locker." As Curt searched the shelves for tools, Pop Pop turned to the twins. "Girls, we are here to help you. Now, I have a couple of questions to ask: are there more girls up at the house? If so, how many?"

"Nine, I think," MacKenzie volunteered.

"Jeez," Pop Pop muttered to himself. "Okay, now, how many other people—how many adults are up at the house?"

MacKenzie tallied them silently to herself. "I think seven."

"You're sure?"

"Yes. One lady...and six men," she said before looking away. Even thinking about them disgusted her.

Pop Pop turned to Phoenix. "Let's assume there are now five men since we just bagged one of 'em. Plus the woman. Add to that the nine girls, one of which...well..." his voice trailed off. "Lots of moving parts."

"The girls say there's a video system behind that locked door," she said, pointing to a partitioned wall at the back of the room. "Might give us a better lay of the land."

Curt returned with a beefy crowbar. "Found one."

"Good work. First things first," Pop Pop said to him. "We need to see what's behind that door." Curt nodded, jammed the tool into the door's edge, leaned into it, and set about destroying it. Two minutes later, what was left of the door popped open. He turned to the group. "Got it."

MacKenzie was holding up her key ring from which dangled three keys. She shrugged.

"Oh, well." Curt muttered, flicking on the light switch. An overhead bank of fluorescent lights blinked to life. Seconds later, so did a console of small TV monitors and a keyboard.

Pop Pop and Phoenix hurried over and peered at the dozen tiny, black-and-white screens.

"Jeezus," Phoenix muttered in shock. There appeared to be six unoccupied bedrooms, as well as a well-populated main room. Pop Pop quickly started assessing the headcount. There were indeed five men in the main room, plus the blonde woman MacKenzie had spoken of. To their collective horror, it was the sight of seeing eight young girls dressed as sexy elves that began to get the blood boiling. "Oh, gawd...do you see her?" a panicked Phoenix asked the men. "Where's Rose? God...."

"There," Pop Pop said, choked with emotion, as he pointed to the tiniest of them all. The angel. She was sitting on the lap of one of the men and holding a stuffed toy. Phoenix's hand was over her mouth, holding back a scream of rage. Curt stepped away from the console. He was seething and battle ready. "We've gotta get in there. *Now.*" This wasn't open for discussion.

"Agreed," Pop Pop said. "The medicine locker's first. Pop that lock, see what's there." Curt didn't need to be told twice. Five seconds later, the lock crashed to the floor and the cabinet door lay open. Pop Pop pushed away the gauzes, scissors, and the rest of the stuff that would be of no help to them.

He began rifling through the medicine bottles. Aspirins and cold remedies were tossed aside. "Here we go," he said, holding up an unopened pill bottle. He scanned the details quickly, then turned to Phoenix, who was now standing next to Cynthia at the drink cart. "Take these with you. Give each of those bastards three of 'em. Four even. The woman, too, if you can. Curt and I will come around the back of the house. Unlock the patio door. Got it?"

Phoenix looked him square in the eye and nodded. This was the moment of truth. He looked back at her, and they both understood the danger they faced. "Got it," she affirmed. "Be careful," she said, hugging Curt. "You too, Pop Pop," she added.

"I will. Did you think I was gonna let you have all the fun like last time?" he winked, then turned to Curt. "Bring the crowbar with you, just in case. Let's go." And they were gone.

Phoenix turned to the twins. "Girls, listen. We're going up to the house. I'm sure they're wondering what's been taking you so long with the drinks. We'll take it from here. You can watch the TVs if you want. Close and lock the front door behind us. Okay?"

MacKenzie and Rebekah both nodded, and a very faint smile spread across both of their faces. It was the first time that had happened in over a year, and tears cascaded down their cheeks. Phoenix and Cynthia engaged them in hugs.

As Phoenix hugged MacKenzie, she felt a couple of lumps in the jacket the girl was wearing. Since it was her own jacket, Phoenix knew them to be her phone and her Walkman tape player. She took both items and smiled, tucking the phone into the spandex of her ridiculous outfit and wedged the tape player on the cart amongst the bottles. And they wheeled the cart out into the night.

Rebekah dutifully closed and locked the door behind them before joining her sister at the monitors for the entertainment that would be starting shortly.

CHAPTER 35

WHEELER AIRPORT
KANSAS CITY, MISSOURI
SAME TIME

CONSIDERABLE BUREAU AND local resources had been dispatched to the Charles B. Wheeler Downtown Airport: two FBI helicopters, six black FBI Chevy Suburbans, ten special agents, and two units belonging to the Kansas City Police Department. And they were all sitting there, waiting.

The open browser on the Ecks' basement computer had listed this as a flight destination, and there was no indication the Cessna had been here or would be anytime soon.

"Dammit!" Agent Muro cursed to the sky. "We're in the wrong damned place." He motioned for his partner, Agent Anderson, who scrambled over from the airport office. "Anything?"

"Yeah! Looks like the perp was fucking with us. Either that, or he changed his plan. But there's a report of a

Cessna matching the description and tail number over at Lee's Summit."

"Where the hell is that?" Muro needed information fast and was in no mood to play Twenty Questions.

"Lee's Summit's thirty miles due south from here," Agent Anderson replied.

Muro looked at his watch, nodded, then motioned with a spinning finger gesture to his pilots and drivers indicating they were wheels-up. *Dammit!*

THE MANOR
THE KITCHEN
SAME TIME

The hip-hop was still blaring as Candy entered from the main room carrying the fishbowl. She placed it on the long counter, laden with platters of finger sandwiches and snacks. The clanging of bottles got her attention. She turned to see Thing One and Thing Two unloading items from the cart. They had their backs to her and were placing the liquor onto the counter next to them, adjacent to the patio door.

"There you are! What took you so long, girls?" she asked, not hiding her annoyance. The clanging of bottles continued without an answer. "Girls? Did you not hear me? I'm talking to you!" she said firmly as she approached them. Still no response. Candy put her hand on Thing One's shoulder and spun her around. Thing Two turned around to face her as well. "I asked you—"

Candy's brow furrowed. For a moment she wondered if perhaps she'd had too much champagne. She blinked rapidly, nervously, as she tried to figure out this anomaly. "You're not...."

Phoenix smiled back at her and shook her head. *No, we're not....* Cynthia smiled as well, her hamster cheeks full of the several finger sandwiches she'd been scarfing down.

The smallest flicker of recognition registered with Candy just as Pop Pop's large hand materialized from behind her, covering her mouth. Her eyes went wide as he carried her out through the patio door to where Curt was waiting. Curt had turned off the burners on the patio heaters. It was dark out there now.

"Wait here. Keep a close eye on things. I'll be back in a few," Pop Pop said to Curt as he dragged Candy off into the dark, toward the garage buildings.

"Need any help?" Curt asked.

"Negative."

Candy's legs kicked and her fingernails found Pop Pop's neck and arms, drawing blood, which only emboldened his resolve and his power. He liberated MacKenzie's key ring from his pocket and found success with the third key, whisking Candy inside. The lights came on automatically and it took him all of five seconds to make his selection.

He grabbed a blue shop rag from the tool bench and stuffed it into her mouth while hog-tying her with two extension cords. Candy's body bucked and she attempted to voice her complaints, but they came out as muffled moans through the gag. Pop Pop took two minutes to secure her to a small Bobcat bulldozer, then stood back to assess his work. Satisfied, he nodded to himself, then turned to her.

"Don't go anywhere, sweetheart," he said, which was met with wild eyes and another muffled scream. He jogged to the door, flipped off the lights and locked the garage behind him.

Phoenix and Cynthia stirred the libations, making sure the tranquilizers had properly dissolved before placing them on their serving trays. "You ready for this?" Thing One asked Thing Two. Cynthia nodded. "Try to keep your head down as best you can, okay, honey? Try to avoid eye contact." Another nod.

Phoenix gave a thumbs-up gesture to her men, who were watching through the patio door. These new twins, Things 2.0, each grabbed a tray, nodded to each other and, with eyes cast to the floor, slowly passed through the doors of hell.

As she made her way further into the room, the level of disgust Phoenix felt was only trumped by her utter rage. Grown men, probably titans of industry and power, were sprawled about on various white leather couches, each of them lounging with at least one young, frightened, and sexually exploited elf-girl on their laps. These innocent creatures' identities had been stripped of them and they were reduced to the numbered placard pinned to their backs.

Phoenix's blood began to boil, as if magma. She could feel the temperature rise within her, and her downcast eyes burned with hatred for these carefree, raucously laughing pigs to whom she was delivering drinks. She studied their shoes as they plucked the flutes from her tray, never making eye contact. As the twins had been gone for a while, these thirsty jackasses were each grabbing two flutes at a time. A sideways glance to Cynthia confirmed she was successfully making the rounds as well.

As Phoenix made her way over to the final couch, she focused on the feet of its occupant. This asshole's bare feet were stuffed into Birkenstock sandals. It was all she could do not to puke on his expensive pedicure.

She felt her tray lighten as the remaining two flutes were lifted from it. Out of the corner of her eye, cascading from the man's lap, Phoenix glimpsed a swatch of white chiffon and a satiny wing. Phoenix watched as the man set down one of his drinks, freeing up his hand to find a very tiny knee. A tsunami of bile rose within her.

She was standing two feet away from her own kidnapped daughter.

From Rose.

Cynthia risked a sideways glance to Phoenix, and she could tell something was wrong. Three of the men rose from their couches, draining their champagne flutes as they did, and were leading their elves in various directions, toward various bedrooms.

Phoenix took a couple of steps away from the couch, her eyes still staring at the plush white shag, as the Birkenstock-clad man got to his feet. He paused to drain his glasses and set them back atop Phoenix's tray without so much as a thank you. He took Rose's little hand in his.

"Let's go, Angel," he said in a too-friendly voice. "I've got another present for you."

At this, Phoenix's head lifted, and she directed a Linda Blair-level of vomit all over Will Masters, former CEO of Brow-zMasters, and unofficial dean of what surely must be the Pathetic Posse of Perverted Pedophiles club (PPPP). With its release, he jumped back in horror and gasped as his bare feet sloshed in the warm goo. Phoenix's fierce kick to his tiny balls was part two.

Cynthia took this as a cue. Phoenix had shown her what to do and she chose this moment in which to do it. She spun around to the sound system and switched the input switch from the offending hip-hop CD to the cassette deck and pushed Play. It was shock-and-awe time and as the tiny reels turned on Phoenix's mix tape, the opening power chords of Judas Priest's "You've Got Another Thing Comin'" began to rock every inch of the Manor.

As Masters doubled over, Phoenix's metal drink tray came crashing down hard onto the back of his head like a gong, its clang loud enough to turn the heads of the others.

Dr. Talbot's heart skipped a beat as he froze in his tracks. His mouth hung open, like he'd just stepped barefoot on a Lego, as he released the tiny elfish hands in each of his.

Patrick Felice, being the spineless worm he was, dropped the two hands he'd been holding, and looked around the room in a state of panic, looking for an exit and finding none.

The good congressman, Martin Connelly, had been mid-staircase with his three minions when Pop Pop ascended upon him and delivered a sharp punch to the kidney. Connelly doubled over, then rolled back down several steps, spilling into the main room.

Phoenix yanked off her blue wig and looked down at her baby girl. As recognition began to flicker in Rose's eyes, Phoenix felt a jolt of electricity coursing through her veins. Rose's eyes began to well with tears, as did her mommy's. "Mommy!!!" she squealed, as she flew into Phoenix's arms. "You came for me!!!"

"Oh, baby...Rose, honey...baby...of course we did!" Phoenix gushed as she lifted her little angel into the air and held on to her for dear life. "We would never stop looking for you, Rosebud..." she managed through a river of tears. "I love you so much forever, my little gingersnap!"

With great force, and little concern for conking heads, Curt threw Felice, Connelly and Talbot together, into the biggest couch where they whimpered like pathetic schoolboys who'd been caught doing something that would get them grounded for a year. Seconds later, Pop Pop added the pathetic host, Sebastian Brewer, née Richard Atkinson—the *Dick*—to the pathetic pile. Will Masters was still groaning in a heap on the floor.

Curt and Pop Pop joined Phoenix and Rose in the family reunion hug, and the tears flowed all around as the foursome's bodies quivered in an earthquake of emotion. As the Judas Priest track faded, Robert Palmer kicked in with "You're Gonna Get What's Comin'."

Cynthia tapped into a vein of maturity she didn't realize she had, as she gathered all the startled girls into the kitchen and did her best to comfort them in the ensuing chaos. She pulled out the folded shuttle manifest she'd been entrusted with and dialed the phone number Phoenix had scribbled on it.

Twelve-hundred miles away, a cellphone rang, nudging the first domino. Ramage picked up on the first ring.

Long-lost smiles had returned to MacKenzie and Rebekah Olson as the they'd watched the events play out on the bank of video monitors. It was better than any TV show they'd ever seen. The unmistakable sound of choppers landing in the clearing outside the Manor's walls got their attention, as did the arrival of a half dozen Suburbans roaring up the drive with their lights blinking.

As agents approached the front of the house, Pop Pop turned away from the big picture window. "The cavalry's arrived!" he called out to Curt, who was holding his daughter close.

Not wanting to miss the opportunity, Phoenix retrieved her phone from Cynthia and approached the long leather sofa. She held up her phone sideways and activated the camera function, making sure she was fitting every one of the pervs in the shot. The motley crew was buzzed and disheveled. The congressman made a particularly lame attempt at hiding his face from the camera but failed.

"Smile!" Phoenix called out in a singsong-y tone. "Everybody, say...*pedophile*!!"

Click! Click! Click! "You're going to be so famous...and not in a good way, assholes!" she promised them as the room began rapidly filling with over a dozen agents, each sporting blue jackets and ball caps, all emblazoned with their easily identifiable **FBI** insignias.

Agent Muro led the charge, with Agent Anderson running interference as they fanned out to their assigned zones. It was glorious chaos as agents cuffed and took custody of these five disgraced and crumbling pillars of the community and led them outside. Congressman Connelly was crying like a panicky stepchild with a full diaper.

"Someone kill the damned music!" Muro yelled and, moments later—aside from a sniveling congressman—all was quiet.

Upon getting a statement from Pop Pop, two other agents were dispatched to the garage to collect the madame. Others were leading an assortment of vulnerable elves outside to safety, while Phoenix, Curt, and Cynthia gave their accounts of what had transpired.

Agent Anderson approached his superior, carrying a notepad and the satchel. "We've got a list of all the children, including two more—twins—who were in an outbuilding on the property," he said to Muro, handing him his notepad.

Muro shook his head slowly as he looked at the list of names, and at their ages. He recognized several names from some cold cases he'd been assigned to. This list, as well as the extensive manifest of others they'd found at the Ecks property, would undoubtedly expose a much larger iceberg.

"Good work, Agent Anderson. Get the medical examiner on the phone. I want all the girls looked at—tonight. Let me know their status once you have it. I'll personally make the calls to families after we have all the information. Not before. Got it?"

"Got it."

"Anything else?"

"Yes, sir. The outbuilding I spoke of. There's a video system. Appears the owner enjoyed making recordings of the goings on here. There are a bunch of hard drives, with evidence going back several years. It's disgusting...."

"Jeezus..." Muro said, shaking his head at the thought of it. This was going to break things wide open, and it remained to be seen how many more arrests would be forthcoming. "Have agents photograph the room and the setup. Hard drives and any associated media get packed and sealed. It all goes with us. These monsters—all of them—are going away for a very long time."

"As we speak, sir," Anderson said, pivoting to leave. He

turned back just as quickly. "Oh, and we also took a couple of other guys into custody. Drivers, maybe, as they were hiding behind the garage building when we rolled up."

Muro nodded. "So, what's with the duffle?" he asked, almost an afterthought.

"Cash. A lot of it. It was with the perp we found tied to the tree."

"Secure it, tag it, lock it in our vehicle."

"Will do," Anderson confirmed as he peeled off.

Muro approached Pop Pop. "Hell of a way to spend your Christmas, Mr. LaFlamme."

"You could say that, yessir."

"The two gentlemen out by the tree line there—"

"Well, I can tell you one of them's no gentleman—that'd be the short guy who's tied to the tree. My work, by the way. You'll find he's responsible for not only several cases of child abduction and human trafficking, but also a few mur—"

"Yes. We've IDed him as one Dieter Ecks. We know all about him."

"You've been in contact with our local Gilbert PD then."

"Yes, we have. Officer Ramage has been very helpful in connecting some dots for us. And the other?"

"Murf. Yeah…he's one of the good guys. We go back a long way…served together. Navy. *Wayne* Murphy. We couldn't have made any of this happen without him, Special Agent," Pop Pop replied, rubbing his bloodshot eyes.

Muro looked back at the man for a long moment. It had been a very long day for everyone. "I'm happy to know you've got your granddaughter back safe, sir," Agent Muro said. "We'll have some more questions later. We'll be in touch."

"Very well. Just…not tomorrow," Pop Pop said with a tired chuckle.

"Tomorrow…." Muro had forgotten all about that. He waved the notebook in the air as a gesture of acknowledgement as he walked away. "Merry Christmas!"

CHAPTER 36

CHRISTMAS DAY
EVERYWHERE

I T'S ARGUABLY THE most magical day of the year and, in addition to Rose's, nine other families were particularly blessed beyond measure this year—and in ways they could never have imagined.

To wit: the Shannons, of Portland, Oregon. Their youngest daughter had "only" been missing a little over two weeks, but in kidnapping cases, that can feel like an eternity, and with the passage of time the outcome is rarely a good one. The late night Christmas Eve phone call from Special Agent Muro had been an absolute answer to prayer, and the return of their precious Cynthia Elise was tangible proof of a loving God. They would learn later that she was also a hero, having mustered bravery beyond her years.

The same could be said of the Olson family of Minnetonka, Minnesota. Having had their nine-year-old twin daughters, MacKenzie and Rebekah, taken from them during an innocent family shopping trip to the mall in Minneapolis the year before, they'd all but abandoned any hope of ever seeing their precious angels again. Their faith, which had been running on fumes, had been tested every minute of every day these past fourteen months, and the early morning call from Muro had been the lightning bolt that restored their faith in an almighty, if not in humanity.

Similarly, a family in Modesto, California received the best gift ever with the return of their twelve-year-old daughter, Alicia. In Henderson, Nevada, it was twelve-year-old Haley. Spokane got back its Miranda, gone two years, and now fourteen. Nampa, Idaho got to celebrate the miraculous return of eleven-year-old Marybeth, while another eleven-year-old, Faith, was reunited with her beyond-grateful parents in Willits, California. A single, down-on-her-luck mother in Surprise, Arizona was more than surprised to learn that her fourteen-year-old had been found safe and would be home for Christmas. As she ended the call with Agent Muro, she made a vow to herself to give up drinking, right there and then. With the safe return of eleven-year-old Cassie to her loving family in Whitefish, Montana, it would be a white Christmas of the most wonderful kind.

These families' lives would be forever changed for the better as a direct result of the miracles bestowed on each of them, and none of them would ever know want again. Collectively, these stories would give some context to the heinous crimes committed by the powerful figures arrested at the Manor. They'd also serve to populate the news cycle with rare stories of hope and positivity and be celebrated around the world.

They would be tidings of comfort. And even real Joy.

CHAPTER 37

POP POP'S HOME
GILBERT, ARIZONA
CHRISTMAS AFTERNOON

SPECIAL AGENT MURO had pulled some strings and scored a redeye flight home for the weary crew. With no checked luggage, there were no baggage claim delays upon arrival at Phoenix Sky Harbor Airport, and the five of them—Murf included—poured themselves into Phoenix's Road Runner for the torturously-long twenty-five-minute drive home.

Murf, having never been to Arizona, decided to take the family up on their kind offer to join them for Christmas. He would grab a flight back to Lee's Summit in a couple of days, and Pop Pop pledged to join him as they'd pick up his Piper and fly her back to Coeur D'Alene together.

Murf took comfort in remembering he'd set out extra kibble and water for the cat before leaving the cabin that day; it would be sufficient until his return. He planned to introduce his former shipmate to some good local beers, and "Flamer" could return his rental Tahoe to Spokane before catching a flight back home.

Upon arrival at Casa LaFlamme, it had been face-plant city. Apart from Phoenix, who didn't relish sleeping in her adventure clothes, everyone crashed in whatever and wherever as quickly as possible. At least she'd changed out of her vomit-covered Thing One outfit before catching the flight. TSA would've had a field day with that.

For Phoenix, Curt, and Pop Pop, sleep was fitful as each replayed the events that made up the insane, nonstop, twenty-four-hour whirlwind of danger. From the crack-of-dawn airport run, to meeting up with Murf and discovering a double-murder scene to rescuing their captive child and a Christmas Eve battle for the ages against the most insidious of monsters, it had been one of *those* kinds of days.

Rose, bless her, slept like the dead, safely bundled in a group embrace between her mommy and daddy, while sharing space with Prick and Luke.

Murf stirred from his roost on the living room sofa. He swung his feet over the side and ran his fingers through his bedhead. It was the sound of a chainsaw that had awoken him, and he quickly realized it was his old shipmate sawing logs down the hall. Pop Pop's snoring was nothing short of legendary, and he had forgone his CPAP machine for the first time since he'd brought it home three years before.

Phoenix shuffled down the hall in her Scooby pajamas and bunny slippers. Her Medusa doo was impressive, but she didn't care one bit. Coffee needed to be made and, more importantly, consumed in great quantity. She was momentarily startled to see Murf on the couch.

"Hey…mornin'," she said groggily.

"Mornin' to you," Murf managed.

"Want coffee?"

"Does the Pope wear a funny hat?"

"Yup," she replied as she went about assembling a fourteen-cup pot.

"Your pop can sure rattle a house, can't he?" Murf asked, his inquiry more statement than question.

"Probably explains why he's still single," Phoenix said as she poured the water into the chamber. "His apnea is something else."

"Mm…my doc told me I should get one of them—what do you call it? See pup?"

"C-*PAP.* I think it stands for…continuous positive airway pressure, something like that. It definitely helps with his apnea, and our sleep," she replied, pushing the brew button.

"I'll bet."

"Only downside, I'd say—in case you're thinking of getting one—is that you'll probably never have sex again! Ever!" she said with a chuckle. "I mean, he says it feels like being John Hurt's character in that *Alien* movie…that thing strapped onto your face. Add a big hose and a machine that sounds like Darth Vader with black lung…it's so sexy. I couldn't do it."

"Food for thought. Not like I need to worry about that anyway." Phoenix didn't have a reply to that, and she was saved by the flurry of paws making a hasty entrance.

Prick scurried into the living room and immediately gave Murf a chihuahua's growl of disapproval as Luke bounded in and saddled up to the stranger like a long-lost friend. Luke was one of those anything-goes German shepherds and would probably happily greet an intruder at the door and even bring them a flashlight.

"Heyyyyyyy, boys!" Phoenix called out. "Be nice to our friend, Murf, you little prick!"

"Name suits him," Murf said with a chuckle.

"Mornin'," Curt mumbled, clearing his throat on his way to the kitchen. "Mornin', baby," he said, giving Phoenix a peck on the forehead. She loved those.

"Morning, sweetie," she replied, punctuated by a hug. "And Merry Christmas."

"Shut *up*...it is not.... Oh, my God..." Curt said, snapping out of his sleep coma. "It is!" He looked out the kitchen window and noticed the sun was getting low in the sky. "What time is it, anyway? We almost slept through it."

"Little after four," Phoenix said, confirming with the coffeemaker's display. "Rose up?"

"Still lights out, poor thing," Curt replied. "Want me to go get her?"

"Nah, let her sleep a little longer. We can shower and stuff, have...*dinner*...then open presents."

"Sounds good," he replied through a cavernous yawn.

"I think I'm gonna switch out her Christmas stocking with the one she used last year. Not sure she needs to have a bad reaction to the snow globe and angel sewn on the new one."

"Good call."

"Mornin'," the unmistakable voice grumbled from down the hallway. Ten seconds later the matching visual shuffled in. Pop Pop was standing there, all Flock of Seagulls bedhead, in his boxers and inside out USN tee-shirt. Everyone was staring at him.

"What???" he asked.

Phoenix was the first to burst out laughing, which got Curt and Murf going as well. "Nothing," she lied. "Merry Christmas, Pop Pop!"

"Wow," he acknowledged with a quick peek to where his wristwatch usually was. "What time is it?"

Thankfully, the neighbor's daughter, April, had set out a few of the frozen casseroles the neighbors had brought over. Phoenix excused herself and carried what was left of a tuna casserole, a traditional lasagna, and a veggie lasagna over to the kitchen counter. The adults had each happily overdone it, as they really hadn't had much in the way of sustenance in a couple of days.

"Mommy, can I have some more Jell-O?"

"*May* you have some more Jell-O?" Phoenix replied, wiping her hands on a towel.

"Yeah! *May* I have some more Jell-O? *Please?*" she asked, her doe eyes channeling Cindy Lou Who from *The Grinch*.

"Yes, honey, but not too much. We're going to open presents in a few minutes, okay?"

"Yay!" A moment later another query: "Mommy, do we have school tomorrow?"

"No, honey," Phoenix replied with a tired chuckle. "There's no school for...gosh...two more weeks! We're on Christmas break, remember?" *Thank God....*

"Yay!"

Curt brought the remaining dishes over and, after scraping off the food remnants, placed the plates in the sink. "Just soak 'em, honey. I'll do 'em after," he said, which earned a peck of appreciation from her. "Love you," she said.

"Love you too," he replied, giving her a longer kiss than

they'd enjoyed in quite some time. There was more emotion behind it, and an appreciation for having survived their ordeal.

"Okay...okay...yeah...thanks. I'll be right there..." Pop Pop said from down the hall. He entered the kitchen, pocketing his phone. "Um, I need to duck out for a few minutes. Be right back," he said, trying to conceal a mischievous smile.

"Now? We're just about—" Phoenix replied.

"Start without me," he said with a glance to his wristwatch. "I'll be quick."

"O-kay..." Phoenix said, shaking her head as she watched him walk out to his truck.

"Mommy! Come on! Let's open presents!"

"I thought you wanted more Jell-O, you little stinker!" Phoenix said, mussing Rose's hair and tickling her.

"That was before...come on!" she said through her giggles.

"Okie dokie, artichokie!" Phoenix said as she lifted her little angel from the chair. "Let's get this party started!" She led Prick and Luke to their respective crates, while Curt squeezed behind the tree and switched on Christmas.

Forty minutes later, Pop Pop's truck pulled up the driveway and he cut the engine. He glanced over at the other seat, then closed the door and went inside.

The living room looked a bit like a war zone, and Rose had managed to rifle through every single gift in the significant pile her parents had meticulously wrapped with six different kinds of paper. Phoenix looked up at him and smiled. "You missed the happy mayhem," she said. She wasn't upset. She was just happy to see the joy on her little girl's face, especially considering everything she—and all of them, really—had just been through.

"Well, there might still be a little happy mayhem to be had," he said, as he went back outside to the truck. A minute later, he returned, holding a good-sized, unwrapped, cardboard packing box. He looked down into it, then back to the group.

Rose looked over to him with an expression of intrigue. "What's that, Pop Pop?"

"What? You mean this box?" he replied teasingly.

"Yes, silly! What's in the box? Is it a present?"

"Maybe...."

Phoenix was just as intrigued as her daughter as she had zero heads-up on whatever this was. *As long as it's not a puppy.*

"Is it...for me?" Rose asked.

"Hm... let's see..." he replied, reaching in with his right hand. "Close your eyes, Peanut."

"I'm not a peanut...I'm a little girl!!" she said with a laugh as she covered her eyes. Pop Pop pulled his hand out and with it something white and fluffy.

Phoenix's eyes went wide, and she exchanged a surprised look with Curt.

Good thing we didn't do the stuffed German Shepherd reveal yet.

"Okay...open!" Pop Pop said with true excitement as he set the living wind-up toy loose on the floor. It was a tiny, off-white terrier pup, about the size of a Costco chicken and, as Rose's eyes opened, the little critter enthusiastically bounded through the mountain of crumpled wrapping paper and made its way into her open arms. "A PUPPY!!!!" Rose screamed out gleefully as the little fluffball jumped up and awarded her with a thousand kisses.

During the several minutes of happy giggles that ensued, Phoenix, Curt and Pop Pop exchanged a series of wry smiles that collectively indicated it was the right decision. Pop Pop mouthed "thanks" to them, and they all returned their attention to the happiest little girl on earth. It was Christmas. Their precious gift of a little girl was home safe. She was experiencing a level of joy they'd never seen before. Their family unit had never felt stronger, nor more rooted in love and appreciation for each other.

Murf quietly took all of this in from his chair in the corner of the room. This was what a happy family was supposed to look like, he decided, and even though he missed his dear Doris, this was, without a doubt, the happiest Christmas he'd ever had.

He turned his attention to the small, hastily wrapped present in his lap and began fiddling with it. The paper fell away, joining the mountain of other discards, and he opened the small box. He pulled back a layer of tissue paper and his heart skipped a beat. There, in his lap, lay six tight bundles of hundred-dollar bills, courtesy of an unwitting Dieter Ecks, along with a note:

Merry Christmas to a very dear friend.
Hopefully this bit of kidnapper cash
might help buy that new truck.
Thanks for everything...
~ Flamer

Murf looked up, his eyes moist with unscheduled tears. Pop Pop had been watching and offered him a nod and a wink. Murf nodded back, got up from his chair, and hobbled over to give his best friend a long bro hug. "Roger that," he whispered.

The doorbell rang. "Are we expecting anybody?" Curt asked the adults as he got up from the couch. "I'll get it; watch the puppy!"

"'Kay," Phoenix said, navigating the papers as she kneeled next to Rose. "Oh, my goodness…look at you!" she squealed, almost as giddy as her daughter. "Hi there, little one… What's your name?"

"Sidney! The foster family named her, and she responds well to it," Pop Pop said.

"Then Sidney it is…" Phoenix said to the pup.

Curt opened the front door, and it was the very, very, *very* last person he expected to see standing on the porch.

"Who is it, honey?" Phoenix called out, her hand grasping the tiny pink collar.

Curt thought he might be hallucinating; he was punch drunk from lack of sleep after all. The man standing there looked very much like a future version of himself.

"Hello, son," the man he hadn't seen in ten years said to him, shifting a gift bag to his other hand. "Sorry to show up unannounced, but I saw you on television the other day. I tried calling several times, but my calls didn't go through," he said, awkwardly. Apologetic, even.

"Dad…" Curt said softly, clearing his throat. He stared at the semi-stranger in disbelief, thinking how ten years' estrangement could've sprung from something as insignificant as the man disapproving of his son's seemingly rudderless move to California from their home in Castle Rock, Colorado.

So much had been left unsaid. So much had happened.

Phoenix walked up alongside Curt and looked at them both. The silence was deafening, the awkwardness palpable.

"Hello," she said, offering a smile to the almost-familiar-looking man on the porch. "I'm Phoenix."

The man looked back at her, and he had a flicker of recognition, having seen her on TV. His eyes softened and his smile traveled to their corners. "Yes, of course. It's very nice to meet you, Phoenix. My name's Len. Len Martinsen."

Phoenix's hand went to her mouth as she let out a gasp. "Oh, my goodness! I thought you looked familiar! Wow... please," she said, stepping onto the porch and initiating a hug. "Please, come in!"

"Thank you, dear," Len said. "You're sure I'm not intruding?"

"Not at all," she answered with a reassuring smile. "May I take your bag?"

"I'm fine, thanks. You might want to grab that plate of cookies though," he said, pointing to them. The festive treat plate was wrapped in a clear foil and sat next to a poinsettia near the doormat.

"You really shouldn't have, Len! Oh, my goodness," she said picking up the cookies. "And...they're in the shape of saguaros! Plus, a poinsettia? You're sweet!"

"Truth be told, those were both sitting there when I arrived. You'll have somebody else to thank for those," he admitted.

Phoenix grabbed both items and stepped aside. She looked over to Curt as the man squeezed past them and entered. Curt looked shellshocked but not entirely displeased. "C'mon... it's your dad. It's Christmas!" she whispered as she smiled and led him in.

Curt closed the door behind them and cleared his throat. A million emotions were buzzing his mind like so many bees.

"Dad—wow, I can't believe I'm even saying that…Dad, I'd like you to meet…the family."

Pop Pop got to his feet and crossed the room with a warm smile and his hand extended. "Dave. Dave LaFlamme, Phoenix's dad. They call me Pop Pop."

"My pleasure, Dave. Len."

"Our good friend, Wayne," Pop Pop said, as the men shook hands.

"Murf, call me Murf."

"Happy to meet you, Murf."

Phoenix set the porch gifts on an end table and waded over to her daughter, who was completely wrapped up in her pet to the exclusion of everything else. Phoenix picked Sidney up and cradled her in the crook of her left arm as she took Rose's hand and led her across the room toward their guest.

"Rose, honey, I'd like you to meet somebody very important. Okay, sweetie?"

Rose looked up at the man. She'd met a lot of new people recently, but this man seemed especially non-threatening. His eyes were kind, like her daddy's. "Hi," she said shyly.

"Hello, Rose, dear," he replied, kneeling to her level. He smiled warmly, as if he already knew her. "I'm…" he started, his voice catching briefly. "I'm your daddy's daddy." Rose took a few moments to process that statement as she looked back and forth between her daddy and this man who looked kind of like her daddy. "So…you're…my *grandfather?*"

"Yes, dear, I'm your grandfather, and I am very happy to meet you," he said, sensitively, not sure how this little person might react to this news. Rose looked up at her parents, to Pop Pop, even to Murf. Their smiles of approval seemed to confirm this fact, which was all she needed. She flew into her grandfather's arms, and they held a hug.

"Merry Christmas, Grandpa!" she said before turning back to her parents with a grin as wide as the Grand Canyon. "This is the best Christmas ever!"

Phoenix crouched down and met her daughter's sparkly eyes. She was feeling it too. They all were. This almost light-headed high wasn't just from exhaustion. It was something unquantifiable, and surreal.

Lots of good, impossible-to-explain magic was happening here—and was playing out in similar fashion in at least nine other households this morning.

"Yes, my little gingersnap," Phoenix said, nodding her complete agreement as she shared a smile with everyone. "This *is* the best Christmas...*ever!*"

AUTHOR'S NOTE

I have a lot of people to thank, so I'll start with you, the reader. Thank you very much for taking a chance on my novel. I truly respect your time and appreciate you coming along for the ride! I'd also be remiss if I didn't give a huge shout out to my wonderful and very supportive wife, Martina. Danke, sweetheart!

To Lisl, my amazing editorial guru, you're the best! Thanks for your awesome sauce!

Additional thanks go to my growing legion of enthusiastic supporters on Facebook. As an indie author, I am deeply indebted to the wonderful admins of my favorite book-related Facebook groups for their incredible and generous support, as well as to their members. There are too many to mention all of them here—and forgive me for not including everyone—but I'd like to give shout-outs to Dawn, Laura, Rhonda, CP Ann, Raven, Linda, Blair, Janet, Dotti, Leidy, Patricia, Mandy, Darla, Susan, Kathleen, Amanda, Lisa, Nancy, Theresa, Daniele, Norma, Francine, Ronnie, David, Jeff, Marty, to name just a few...I couldn't (and wouldn't!) do it without you all. My heartfelt thanks.

And to our rescue animals, Luke, Barney, Sidney, Candy, all of whom endured Dad's long stretches at the computer. They're not big readers of my books, but I did include them as characters, so there's that!

If you enjoyed **X**, and are so inclined, I hope you'll consider leaving a review on Amazon and/or Goodreads. Your feedback not only helps the author but might also help another potential reader find the book as well. So thank you in advance!

The writing process for **X** once again took me down some very troublesome paths. It was a slippery slope dealing with such unsavory characters and exploring the underbelly of a very sick world—that of the dark web and pedophilia. I made every effort not to delve into the specific deeds these animals engage in as that would surely prove too much for this author, and my readers, to endure. Unfortunately, these depraved individuals are really out there, so, while shining a light on every parent's worst nightmare, I hope I handled the story line with sufficient tact and sensitivity as not to offend the reader.

In researching this story, I immersed myself in several troubling accounts of child abductions. I also had to visit the aforementioned dark corners, delve into real-life stories of families torn apart by stranger abductions and, in some cases, horrific incidents of human trafficking. I can't begin to imagine the pain a family must feel. It was hard enough putting my beloved characters through it.

As with my previous novel, *Leaving Phoenix,* the story is largely set in the glorious state of Arizona. I also wanted to explore another region, in its winter season, to present a stark contrast to the desert, thus the choice to extend the geography a little. Amazing Idaho remains one of my all-time favorite states, and I enjoyed exploring it a bit for the story. I hope you enjoyed it as well.

I wanted the topography to be accurate, so I procured a myriad of maps and road atlases of the regions, as I wanted their portrayal to be realistic. I don't pretend to be an expert on aviation, but I tried to get the aircraft right, as well as research routes, airports, and flight times, etc. The same applies to the law enforcement aspects I wrote of. If there's something I didn't get right, it's not for lack of research. The book isn't meant to be a police procedural. I took dramatic license, and if anything is inaccurate, it's on me. As with my previous books, the music references had to be right, and—as usual—I took it to the next level by making sure the cassette playlists timed out properly.

I loved revisiting my favorite heroine, Phoenix. She was so much fun to create and to explore in *Leaving Phoenix*. Trouble found her once again but she continues to rise to the occasion. Curt and Pop Pop remain enjoyable characters to explore as well, and it was fun to reassemble this little adventure team in order to kick a little ass and make things right.

I'm exceedingly happy to have arrived at this bend in the circuitous path to becoming an author. My debut novel, *The Other Cheek*, offers some context as to some of the intense challenges and struggles I had along the way, but I'm grateful for the experiences and the lessons I've learned from them. I'm stronger for them. I remain optimistic. I try to see the positivity. I try to infuse this in my characters as well. Our girl, Phoenix, has truly risen from the ashes on more than one occasion, and so have I. Blessings your way.

~ Jafe Danbury

ABOUT THE AUTHOR

Jafe Danbury hails from the trenches of the Hollywood production scene, where he spent decades as a camera operator, director of photography, and director. He has also worked as a teacher and is a decorated U.S. Navy veteran.

He enjoys noodling on the guitar, long road trips, likes his bacon crispy, and loves a good dive bar—especially if it happens to have a twenty-two-foot shuffleboard table. He prefers a leisurely walk to running, unless being chased by a clown with a chainsaw.

Jafe and his lovely bride currently reside in central California and are working on their exit plan. Their children currently consist of several rescue dogs and a wacky umbrella cockatoo, but their house has a revolving door when it comes to rescue critters and may include the occasional owl, abandoned sparrow, or wayward kitten.

X is his third novel.

ALSO, BY JAFE DANBURY:

Leaving Phoenix
The Other Cheek

Made in United States
North Haven, CT
21 September 2023

41811596R00193